"I am bought and paid for. What happens next?"

"I continue to visit your bed or you mine until you bear me at least one son—though more would be better. Then you can go back to your family if you'd like."

Jocelyn clenched her teeth against his words. Never had she felt so inconsequential before. Yes, she'd asked him for candour, but this brutal assessment was more than she'd expected or deserved.

With pain still tightening around her heart and soul, she lashed out.

"Did you make the same offer to your first wife?"

He reached her in the blink of an eye, his hands on either side of her face and his body against hers. His gaze burned into hers and a fury she'd never seen before blazed within his eyes. But it was his voice, almost a whisper, that struck the deepest fear.

"Do not speak on a subject about which you know nothing." He leaned in closer, his breath hot against her cheek. "Do not say her name to me or anyone else here. Do not even refer to her in your words."

He released her and she stumbled. Her legs would not hold her steady and her knees shook. Jocelyn fell before him.

She had dared the Beast and would not live to tell of it.

TAMING THE HIGHLANDER

Terri Brisbin

™ MILLS & BOON®
Pure reading pleasure™

First published in Great Britain 2009
Harlequin Mills & Boon Limited,
Eton House, 18-24 Paradise Road, Richmond, Surrey TW9 1SR

© Theresa S. Brisbin 2006

ISBN: 978 0 263 86785 5

Set in Times Roman 10½ on 12¾ pt.
04-0609-81009

Printed and bound in Spain
by Litografia Rosés S.A., Barcelona

This book is dedicated to the romance readers' groups who support the genre and romance authors by buying and reading romances every month of every year. And most especially to my 'home' groups—the Romance Readers at Borders in East Brunswick, NJ, the Treasured Hearts at the Barnes & Noble store in Wilmington, DE, and the Romantiques at the Borders store in Marlton, NJ. Thanks to all of you for your warm welcomes and enthusiasm!

Terri Brisbin is wife to one, mother of three, and dental hygienist to hundreds when not living the life of a glamorous romance author. She was born, raised and is still living in the southern New Jersey suburbs. Terri's love of history led her to write time-travel romances and historical romances set in Scotland and England. Readers are invited to visit her website for more information at www.terribrisbin.com, or contact her at PO Box 41, Berlin, NJ 08009-0041, USA.

Recent novels by the same author:

LOVE AT FIRST STEP
 (short story in *The Christmas Visit*)
THE DUMONT BRIDE
THE NORMAN'S BRIDE
THE COUNTESS BRIDE
THE EARL'S SECRET

Prologue

Scotland, 1352

He knew his wife was dead when her body hit the fifth step below him with a sickening thud. Connor MacLerie watched as the awareness and acceptance of her fate was replaced in her eyes by the dull glaze of death. Kenna never screamed as her body fell, and now all he heard was the bone-breaking thump as she landed at the bottom of the tall stairway of stone steps.

She may not have made a sound, but he did—roaring out his fury in a burst that brought family and servants from the great hall. They gathered below him, staring and pointing, already certain of the way things had happened here since undoubtedly some had heard the argument from the beginning. Connor closed his eyes for a moment and then he turned and walked away.

And, in that moment when his wife died, the Beast was born. His reputation spread through the Highlands—his wife's last words pleading for his pardon and his refusal to attend her burial only added to the tales of his cruelty. Mothers feared for their daughters, fathers wondered about the rumors and maidens from all the neighboring clans prayed nightly that they would never be part of any treaty or bargain that placed them at his questionable mercy.

Less than a year after his first wife's death, Connor took over the high chair upon his father's passing, becoming laird of the clan MacLerie. A bride was now a necessity. And so the Beast prowled the Highlands searching for a mate.

Chapter One

Three Years Later

"Is there no other way then?"

She fought not to let the trembling show in her voice. Jocelyn clenched her hands together tightly and pressed her nails into her skin to keep herself from fainting at the news.

"Nay, lass. He specifically asked for you. 'Tis the only way to save yer brother's life."

Her father would not meet her gaze now. 'Twas over. The Beast had made his wishes known and since refusal to agree to his demands was impossible for her clan, she would be sacrificed to save another.

"Mayhap, he will fill ye quickly with a son," her mother whispered from her sickbed. Turning to face her, Jocelyn felt the blood drain from her face as she realized the result of this agreement would give her, body and soul, to a man whose physical desires and cruelty was rumored throughout the Highlands. "If ye give him the son he craves, he may be merciful to ye."

She fought to maintain some sense of calm, but the soft sobs that followed her mother's words made it impossible. The tremors shook her and she feared fainting, something she swore she would not do in front of the MacLerie's emissary. Dragging in a deep breath, she turned back to her father and his councillors.

"You do not need my consent for this, Father, so do as you must."

Nodding to him and the MacLerie's man, she drew herself up as straight as she could and walked slowly from the room. The urge to run and hide almost overwhelmed her as her mother's crying became louder. But, she was the daughter of the MacCallum, and she would not disgrace herself in this, even if he had. A few more steps and she was out of the solar and in the great hall. Looking around, she noticed a few servants at work, cleaning the tables from the noon meal. Jocelyn realized that word of her betrothal would spread quickly once the meeting was ended and she knew that she had to be the one to tell Ewan.

Taking the shorter way through the kitchens, she left the keep and walked to the practice yards. Shading her eyes with her hand, she searched through the various groups of men until she found him.

Ewan MacRae. Her first love.

The man she thought she would marry.

Now, she was faced with the task of telling him they would never be husband and wife. He met her gaze with a smile and a wave as he walked to meet her.

"Good day to you, Jocelyn," he said, his deep voice so familiar to her.

"Ewan, we must speak," she said, motioning to him to follow her.

Ewan climbed over the fence and walked silently at her side until they were away from the training yards. She turned to face him now with the news that would change both of their lives. Her throat and eyes burned with tears that threatened to spill, but she gathered her control and looked at him.

"Jocelyn. What is it? Your face has lost all its color and you are shaking." He took her by the shoulders and pulled her close. Improper as it now was, she stayed in his embrace, savoring the warmth and protection and affection that she knew she would never feel again. After a few moments, she stepped out of his arms and faced him, her face now wet with the tears she'd fought to keep inside.

"My father has betrothed me to someone else, Ewan. We cannot be together as I'd hoped. I'm to marry the… Connor MacLerie."

"The Beast?" he asked in a whispered voice full of dread.

She could only nod as she was filled with even more foreboding. The MacLerie's reputation was known throughout the Highlands and although she wished that it was simply silly women's gossip, that hope could not lessen her fear.

"Your father has agreed to this?" Disbelief was clear in his expression.

If she had not been in the room earlier, she would not have believed it either. There had been no formal agreement between her and Ewan about their future together, but they had grown closer and closer during his time fostering here and Jocelyn knew he planned to offer for her as soon as he visited his parents in the spring.

"He has. I'm to accompany the MacLerie's men back and the wedding will take place when I arrive there." She said the words, but they did not feel real to her.

"You will be married there? Without even your family around you? The man truly is a beast!"

"Of all the titles he carries, the MacLerie has no liking for that particular one."

Jocelyn whirled around to find the MacLerie's emissary standing behind them. How much he had seen and heard, she did not know. She watched as Ewan's expression turned to stone and he stepped in front of her in a protective motion. Crossing his arms over his chest, he faced the stranger.

"Who are you?" he asked in a challenging voice. "What right do you have to speak for the MacLerie?"

"I am Duncan MacLerie," he answered, sliding his hand down to rest on the sword hanging at his side. "I am his man and represent his interests in this matter."

"This matter? You mean his betrothal to Jocelyn?"

"Aye. I carry out his wishes in this matter." Duncan's voice was low and even, but she knew by his stance that he did not take this challenge easily.

"She is not 'a matter'," Ewan said. "Jocelyn is…"

"The MacLerie's betrothed and none of your concern from this time forward."

Jocelyn gasped at the cold announcement and started to step around Ewan when Duncan spoke again, directing his words once more to Ewan.

"Unless there have been promises made between you before witnesses?"

Ewan turned his head and spit in the dirt. Without looking at her, he answered for them.

"Nay."

"Unless she carries your bairn?" Duncan pointed at her as he said the words. The insult to her honor and Ewan's was a shocking one. So much so that she pushed around Ewan and slapped the MacLerie's man on his face as hard as she could.

"How do you dare insult my honor?" She stood before him with her hands on her hips.

"I will not bring back a bride to my laird who carries the seed of another within her."

"Oh, we all ken that your laird wishes to plant the seed himself."

As soon as the words escaped, she wished she had not said them. Duncan's face darkened in rage, his gaze burning into her as he stepped forward.

"Aye, my lady," he said through clenched teeth. "We all ken his feelings on *that*." Looking from one to the other, he continued, "Make your farewells for we leave in two hours, whether you be ready or not."

She watched in surprise as the MacLerie's man turned and strode away, fury evident in his every step. This was not how she wanted to begin her life as the MacLerie's wife. Insulting him to his own retainer was a bad move, one that he would surely be informed of upon their arrival in Lairig Dubh.

"I will speak to your father, Jocelyn. I fear for you in this marriage," Ewan said softly, still standing behind her as they watched Duncan walk away and take up a position near the training yards.

"Nay, you cannot, Ewan." She turned to face him for the last time. Remembering her brother's dangerous status, she knew there was only one path she could take. "There is more to this, I fear, than either of us ken."

"So I am supposed to stand here and simply wish you well as the MacLerie's wife?"

Tears clogged her throat once more as she nodded. "Please?" she asked.

He took her hands in his and drew her closer in spite of the obvious scrutiny of the man across the yard. Gently, he smoothed her loosened hairs out of her face and touched her cheek.

"I wish you a long and happy life, Jocelyn. And if it must be with him, then may God go with you. I pray that he will not crush the spirit in your heart and soul."

Ewan kissed her on the forehead and stepped back. His comment about her spirit was meant to lighten her, for her temper was well-known among her family. Then he walked away without another word. Her tears flowed freely now as she watched the man she thought she would marry walk away forever. She wiped her cheeks and took a deep breath. She did not have the luxury of grieving for what might have been between them. There were many things to be done if, as Duncan had told her, they would leave in two hours. Turning her thoughts to packing and preparing for her journey instead of the misery she felt tearing at her inside, she walked back to the keep.

Although she knew she should apologize to Duncan for her insult to his laird, a spark of pride would not let her do so as she passed him. Instead, she met his gaze and glared at him. All he offered was a nod in return. Puzzled over his meaning, she entered the keep to begin her work.

Duncan fought to keep a smile from his face as Jocelyn walked past him. He felt some measure of sympathy for the lass, one minute believing she would marry one man and the next finding out she would leave home and hearth to marry another. Although it was to be expected of a laird's daughter, he had no doubt that this could have been handled in a better way.

Turning, he leaned against the fence and watched her enter the keep. She had gumption—his face still stung from her well-delivered slap. And other than that blow, even in the face of her mother's pitiful sobbing, she'd kept her control intact before him. And her mother's ranting made him nearly cancel the arrangements. Connor would have his balls if he did that, but the terror in her mother's voice did give him a moment's pause. Jocelyn slammed the door behind her as she entered and Duncan finally gave in to the smile that had threatened.

She would do. Neither fair of face nor a terrified twit were Connor's instructions to him. He shook his head at such an order. The "not fair of face" was easy enough to determine, but how did one ascertain whether a lass was a terrified twit when they all trembled at the mere mention of his laird's name?

Connor MacLerie, the Beast.

Duncan kicked the dirt at his feet in disgust. Even though he knew most did not speak freely before him, he could not believe the extent to which this frightful name and reputation had spread through their allies and enemies. He could have fought the rumors…if he knew the truth of Kenna's death. But he had not been in the keep during that terrible night. All he knew were the tales told afterward, for the laird who was also his friend never again mentioned Kenna's name after her death.

His thoughts were interrupted by the approach of the man who Jocelyn had run to at the news of her betrothal. Ewan MacRae, son of Dougal. The MacCallum told him that no agreements had been made to marry Jocelyn and this man, but their mutual affection and their understanding of a joint future had been clear to him when he watched them. Duncan stepped back from the fence and faced the man.

"Will you tell your laird of what you saw?"

"Do you mean that his betrothed ran to you at the first chance?" Duncan slid his hand down once more to rest on the sword at his side.

Ewan broke free of his gaze and looked off in the distance before answering. "She is loyal to a fault. She wanted me to hear the news from her own mouth and not from another's."

"Loyalty is an admirable trait," Duncan said, not answering Ewan's question.

"Aye, 'tis that," he replied. He turned back to face Duncan and continued, "I would not want to see her punished or mistreated because of that loyalty."

"And, you think the MacLerie would do that?" Duncan moved a step closer to him.

"I have heard the same tales as you. If I cannot be with her, I only want to ken that she is safe."

Duncan nodded and took a step back. "My laird will simply ask if the arrangements have been made. He will not care who she spoke to on her leaving."

He watched the younger man accept his words and nod to him. This Ewan did not have any choice in this and Duncan respected his attempt to protect Jocelyn. Here was another life inexorably changed by the events that caused his laird to become the Beast. He turned and walked to where his men stood waiting for his orders. How many others, he wondered, would be caught up in the fear before the truth was known? Shaking his head at the entire situation, he called out to his men to prepare to leave for home.

Chapter Two

The winds whipped his hair and clothes as he stood waiting on the parapets. Shielding his eyes with his hand, Connor searched off in the distance once more and did not find what he sought. They were late. Duncan's message said they would arrive by midday and 'twas well past that time already.

Striding to a different location on the highest tower of Broch Dubh Keep, the MacLerie peered towards the horizon again as fear nagged at his mind. Duncan would keep her safe on the journey here—his man for years, his cousin knew and carried out his duties with a dedication unmatched by any other in the clan MacLerie. Late or not, she would be safe with Duncan. Startled by the sound of a clearing throat, Connor turned to face another of his men.

"What is it, Eachann?"

"Do you wish me to send out more men to search for them?"

Connor followed the path of the road leading away from the village of Lairig Dubh once more and then shook his head.

"Nay. Duncan has his orders. He would not fail me in this."

Eachann nodded in agreement and stepped away, not bothering him with more words or questions. Standing at his side in silence, the captain of his guard crossed his arms over his chest and awaited further orders. With a nod of his head, Connor positioned himself near the stone wall to watch and wait.

He cursed his own foolishness under his breath. He was always one to take advantage of an opportunity presented, but demanding the young MacCallum's sister in marriage in exchange for sparing his life was not an opportunity. It was a disaster.

After spending so much time and effort cultivating the horrible rumors and stories that kept him safe from marriage's grasp, his father's death now necessitated it. Unfortunately, with the Beast's cruel ways whispered widely, no one, ally or enemy, would offer their daughter to him. In spite of his personal and clan wealth, his title and the wide expanse of the Highlands that the MacLeries claimed as their own, a bride was not in the offing.

Shifting his weight, he leaned over the edge to watch his warriors train in the yard below. He would like nothing more than to continue to train with his men and have them ready for battle at a moment's notice. The MacLeries boasted of well over five hundred warriors of their own and when combined with the numbers of their allies, their fighting force was unmatched in the Highlands. But one of his duties as laird was providing an heir to follow him.

Although he had several cousins and uncles who would lead the clan well, the elders favored more and more following the Sassenach custom of primogeniture. And so, he was under a great deal of pressure to find a suitable wife and get an heir.

A call from one the guards alerted him of someone's approach and he looked at the road leading to the castle. A small group on horseback left the cover of the forest and approached the main gate. Squinting into the setting sun's rays, he tried to make out Duncan's form in the group. Unable to identify him from this distance, he trotted to the steps that would take him to the ground floor of the keep. Never slowing his steps, he made his way through the great hall and out into the yard just as the group was cleared for entry.

Realizing that his hurried pace could be misinterpreted by those watching him, he slowed and walked out to greet his friend…and his betrothed. As they rode closer, boys from the stables stood ready to take their mounts. A crowd gathered around waiting to get a look at their new lady. The interested murmuring turned to snickers and guffaws as a woman was revealed to them.

Duncan reached up and assisted her from her mount and Connor found himself leaning forward to get a better view and to see if his orders had been followed. A plain bride, one who was not a mindless twit, was what he had asked for. Duncan was not to sign the documents on his behalf and with his seal unless she met those conditions.

It was difficult, nay impossible, to determine her appearance since she was covered from head to foot in a thick layer of mud. Not even her hair color could be seen through it. He was tempted to join in the merriment until he remembered that this woman was to be his bride. Then he realized that Duncan was also covered in the same muck. An explanation was required. Now.

"Duncan?" he called out above the noise of the crowd. As he expected, everyone quieted and waited for his reaction to the sight and the woman before him.

"Aye, laird," Duncan answered, guiding the woman to the bottom of the steps before meeting his gaze.

"Do you have the betrothal agreement?"

Duncan reached inside his sodden leather jacket and pulled out a packet of parchment. Holding it out to him in a way not to soil it, Connor was certain he saw a hint of a smile on his friend's face. He took the packet, peeled it open and looked over the words inside. Content that they were exactly as he'd ordered, he nodded to Duncan.

"Welcome…" he looked to the parchments once more for his bride's first name. "Welcome, Jocelyn MacCallum, to the clan MacLerie. Clean yourself up for the priest waits for us in the chapel."

He noticed Duncan's glare and then the one his be-trothed gave him. She knew the arrangements were for an immediate ceremony. Her brother would not be released until her vows were said and consummated, although that act felt much less attractive now as she stood before him dripping odious globs of mud at his feet. His clan stood around them watching every move-ment, hearing every word.

"I would see my brother before we wed, my lord." Her voice was clear and indignant. She did not want to offer herself to him for naught.

"He is well. Now, wash up and make haste." Now that he had made the decision to wed and found the suitable bride, he was tired of waiting. The long day in the freezing wind above the keep did nothing to soothe his mood. And now she questioned him?

She took a step closer, bringing all the odors with her. "I would see him now, my lord."

His people gasped at her insolence. She questioned his word before them. She must have realized her mistake for she seemed startled and blinked several times as she looked at those around her. Her gaze moved back to his and she was bold enough to meet it directly.

"Disrespect seems to run within the clan MacCallum, I see. You would question my word?"

"Aye, my lord. I would see my brother before any vows are taken."

He took in a breath, ready to lash out at her for her challenge to his honor and his orders, but Duncan's expression warned him off. Putting her in her place, as appealing as that might be at this moment, was not the way to begin her life here in the clan. Connor knew there would be plenty of time and opportunity to correct her ways once she was completely his. He motioned to one of his men and whispered an order to him. Stepping back, he crossed his arms over his chest and waited, giving her the full weight of his gaze during the time it took to fetch her brother from the dungeon.

He took advantage of the waiting to make a more thorough examination of his soon-to-be wife. Connor tried to see beneath the layer of mud, but could determine nothing other than the color of her eyes. They were green.

Kenna's had been green.

He felt the bile surge in his stomach as it nearly reached his mouth and fought to control it. Another wave of nausea flowed through him and he almost lost the meal he'd eaten that afternoon. He had not thought of Kenna in a long time and wondered why it was now that she invaded his mind and his memories. Probably the upcoming marriage had stirred things better left alone.

He brought his thoughts back to the woman who stood before him and realized that she was staring at him with the same intensity of his own gaze. Had his discomfort been apparent to all? He shifted his stance and turned towards the door of the keep. Two of his soldiers stood there, each one grasping one arm of Athdar MacCallum. The young man, his left arm in a sling and bruises covering his face, looked dazed and confused as the men held him in place there.

Connor heard Jocelyn's gasp and caught her arm as she tried to run past him to her brother. She struggled against him, but she was no match for his strength or determination in this.

"I must go to him. He is hurt," she said as she tried to pull free.

"You said you wished to see him and you have. Now, you will fulfill your part of the bargain," he whispered through clenched teeth so that only she could hear.

"Fine, my lord. Let us marry now so that I may see to my brother's injuries."

Connor yanked her back to her place before him. "You were told the provisions of the agreement, were you not?" He looked to Duncan for confirmation of that fact. At Duncan's nod, he continued, "Once you are wedded and bedded and the agreement fulfilled, the boy will be released."

He couldn't be certain, but he thought she blushed under the filth. Duncan coughed and choked at his words and the others around stood with their mouths gaping at this news. So much for discretion.

"Then, my lord, let us find the priest and have done with it."

"You should wash and change before…"

"I can take my vows dirty or clean, my lord. I would prefer to do it as quickly as possible."

She was insufferable! Standing before him and his clan, she was the obvious loser in this agreement, and yet, one would not be able to tell it from her stance, her words or the demanding tone of voice she used to him. Well, he was not one to back down from a challenge, especially one from a woman who should learn her place as quickly as possible.

"Duncan, fetch the priest to us."

"But, Connor," Duncan stepped forward, already arguing.

"You heard the lady. She wishes to take her vows now. I would accommodate her in this. Get him now, Duncan."

Duncan had been his friend for too long not to recognize the fury that even he could hear in his own voice. The lady under discussion knew him not, but must have realized her mistake for she took a step back away from him. He held her fast, not allowing her to escape the fate that she had hastened. Turning to his men on the steps, he ordered her brother returned to his place in the dungeon. When she would have contested his orders, he squeezed her arm tightly, drawing her attention.

"Not only his life, but also his comfort depends on your behavior, my lady. Think you well on it before the words spill from your mouth."

He watched as she started to speak and then stopped, clamping her lips shut. She used her free hand to move the long tangled mass of her hair out of her face and over her shoulder. Globs of mud and muck dripped onto her already-sodden cloak.

And they waited in a silence that grew even more uncomfortable as the minutes passed until finally a stirring among the crowd opened a path for Duncan and the priest. The priest walked to him and bowed.

"My lord, this is very unusual."

"Aye, Father, 'tis that."

"Should we not allow the lady to prepare for the ceremony and hold it on the morrow?"

"Nay. My betrothed has requested, nay demanded, that we speak our vows now. If you will be good enough to hear them and say the words?"

He knew Father Micheil was confused by his actions, but he also knew he would do whatever Connor wanted him to. So, a few minutes later, he found himself married once again. And if he felt overwhelmed by it, he could only imagine what his bride felt. The tremors he felt in her arm and her chattering teeth told him that she was not reacting well to the honor of being his wife.

"Ailsa," he called out to one of the women who served him. "Take the lady to her chambers and see to her."

He relinquished his hold and watched as Jocelyn wordlessly followed Ailsa into the keep. Turning to Duncan, he motioned him to his side. Connor waited until the crowd had dispersed and the activities in the yard resumed their natural noises and pace.

"Come inside and explain why you and my bride are covered in the same mud."

It was only by sheer determination that Jocelyn was able to remain standing throughout the wedding and to follow the woman through the keep and up several flights of stairs in the far tower. Every step was a challenge. Every moment brought pain to her. She knew if she faltered or hesitated she would collapse in a heap on the floor. So, she focused on the hem of the woman leading her to her chamber and prayed it would not be long in coming.

After witnessing the extent of the disregard of her newly acquired husband, she was not certain what she should expect at the top of the stairs. Ailsa opened the door to a chamber and waited for her to enter first. Dragging her sopping garments across the threshold, Jocelyn was stopped by the sight of the comforts before her.

The room was a large one, facing east, with several windows of glass. A large hearth filled one part of one wall and an alcove set below the larger of the windows. Cushions made the wooden bench look very appealing. Even more appealing to her was the huge bed in the far corner. Hesitant to dirty the fresh rushes with the filth she carried, she looked to Ailsa for guidance.

"Here now, lady," Ailsa said as she approached. "Let me help ye out of those clothes." Jocelyn had neither the desire nor the strength to resist the woman's efforts. "I have called for hot water for a bath for ye."

Jocelyn fought back the tears that had threatened ever since she discovered her fate was in the hands of the MacLerie. She blamed it on her exhaustion and her fear for her brother's safety and well-being. She stood and allowed Ailsa to peel the soggy layers of gown and chemise and plaid from her shaking body. When the noise outside the chamber signaled the arrival of the promised bath, Ailsa guided her behind a screen and continued to undress her, removing the mud that had found its way inside her garments. After a few more minutes, Jocelyn found herself sinking into the overly large tub of steaming scented water.

She later remembered Ailsa lathering her hair with a pungent soap and rinsing it at least twice and helping her to wash the rest of herself. Then Jocelyn remembered being wrapped in heavy towels and sitting on the bed as a tray of food was delivered. And that was the last thing she knew until the rays of the rising sun flooded her room and roused her from a deep sleep.

Panic filled her as she realized in an instant that she had not fulfilled the second part of the bargain. For unless bedding was an incredibly overrated experience and could be done on someone sound asleep, she doubted her husband had exercised his marital rights during the night.

Climbing from the center of the bed and still wrapped in the towels from her bath, she searched through the trunks lining one wall for anything she could wear. Jocelyn did not know where her own small bundle was and she could find nothing suitable for her. A sense of dread engulfed her as she realized that without the consummation of their vows, Connor could still seek retribution on her brother. Unable to locate anything but bed linens in the chest, she slammed down the lid and shook her head. She was a prisoner until one of the servants came to her. Grabbing a brush from the table next to the bed, she pulled it through her hair and braided it quickly.

Her activities must have alerted the servants that she was awake for soon a knock came on the door of the chamber and a young girl entered with a bucket of steaming water. After curtsying, the girl poured an amount of it into the basin by her bedside and sat the bucket near the hearth. With an efficiency born of experience, the servant had the fire within the hearth burning brightly with just a few adjustments to it. Then the girl turned to leave, but stopped once she'd pulled the door open.

"Milady, the laird asks that ye join him in the hall to break yer fast."

"I fear I cannot do that…what is your name?"

"Cora, milady." The girl curtsied again.

"Cora, please tell the laird that I cannot do as he asks—"

Before she could finish, the girl was gone. Jocelyn did not think a body could move that fast, but in a blink of an eye, she was alone once more. Hoping that someone would seek her out and discover her need for clothes, she decided to wash up. Rearranging the towels around her, she leaned over and dipped her hands into the hot water. Splashing it onto her face, Jocelyn reached for a cloth to wipe the water off. The noise behind her startled her into turning and losing control over the layers of toweling around her until it loosened and slipped down her. Grasping it before it fell to her waist, she looked up expecting Cora.

She found her husband. Connor MacLerie.

And from the dangerous look on his face, she knew why he was called Beast. All the words she thought she would say to him froze in her throat as his gaze moved down her and settled on her breasts. She longed to slap the now lustful stare from his face, but as her husband, she knew she must submit to not only his gazes but also his touch, his possession of her body. She could not control the shudder that moved through her. Finally, he met her glare with one of his own.

"I see that even the night of rest I allowed you has not sweetened your disposition. You would disobey even my smallest request?" He crossed his arms over his chest as he took several steps toward her. Although she would have liked to back away, she had nowhere to move.

"Laird," she said, looking around the room once more. "I did not disobey you."

"I called you to the hall below and you refused me. What else is it, but disobedience, plain and simple?"

This was no way to begin their married life. A simple misunderstanding, but it could become something larger if she did not handle it well enough. Looking at him, she realized that she had not really taken his measure on her arrival. Exhausted, soaked through with icy muck and fearful for her brother's well-being, she had stumbled through their meeting and their vows. Now, in the full light of the sun, she found she had married a wildly attractive man. Taller than her father, taller than even Ewan, Connor towered over her. His black hair was pulled back from his face and tied in small braids at his temples. Shaven clean of any beard, the rugged angles of his face proclaimed his masculinity. Eyes nearly the color of bronze glowed back at her, full of fire at her challenge to his authority, both as her husband and now as her laird.

"My lord, I have no clothes." She lowered herself into as deep a curtsy as she dared before him. With her head bowed, she could not see his reaction, but heard the cough he let loose.

"No clothes?" he asked.

"None, my lord. And there seem to be none in this chamber that I could cover myself with to answer your summons to the hall. Unless you want me to appear naked before your clan?"

She heard his choking cough again and the sound of laughter from outside her chamber. She looked up just enough to see his booted feet move to the doorway. A scuffle ensued and a few moments later a bundle was dropped on the floor next to her. Jocelyn looked up to find him staring down at her, and staring down the loosely held towel at her chest again. When she tried to stand, she lost her balance and toppled backward. His hands around her arms prevented her from hitting the stone floor. She found herself being pulled in close to his chest until she was steady on her feet.

"Get yourself dressed and down to the hall now." She felt his gruff voice as he whispered the words into her ear.

"Aye, my lord," she answered.

He released his grasp of her and walked away. But she could not let him go until she discovered her brother's condition.

"Laird?" she called out. He stopped, but did not turn to face her. "Did my brother suffer for my failure to consummate our vows last night?"

Another strangled cough erupted, this one from the hallway, but Jocelyn could not break her gaze from him as he turned and met hers. Rising even taller and looking as dangerous as a beast could, he stalked over to her, clenching, tightening and opening his fists with every step. Standing as close as possible but without touching her, he looked down at her from his height and spoke through clenched teeth. She could feel the waves of anger pouring from him as he spoke.

"I hold your brother accountable for his own behavior as I hold you accountable for yours. Now, get you dressed and get you down to my hall."

She stood frozen by the cold fury in his voice until he turned and left, slamming the door with enough force to rattle the windows in the room and her head. A muffled argument outside her chamber drew her attention for a few moments, but when it quieted she knew he was gone. She sank to her knees as the tremors of fear shook her to her core.

Jocelyn did not know how long she stayed on her knees, but she soon became aware of whispered voices outside her door. Rubbing her hands over her arms and face, she roused herself and climbed up onto still-shaking legs. Rummaging through the bundle at her feet, she found a clean shift, gown and stockings. With a few minutes of struggling with the laces, she was dressed. Jocelyn decided to use a length of plaid as a shawl and wrapped it around her shoulders tightly, trying to ease the trembling that still filled her.

After a few deep breaths, she felt ready to answer Connor's call. Pulling open the door, she was surprised to find Duncan and Ailsa standing before her. Ailsa curtsied as Duncan bowed to her, a far cry from the disrespect he had showed her every leg of their trip here.

"The laird asked me to escort you to the hall."

"Fine," she answered, waiting for him to lead the way.

"Mayhap shoes would make the walk a bit more comfortable?" He pointed to the floor and her shoes that now lay cleaned and brushed. "I do not think the laird would want his bride appearing in bare feet."

"Fine," she answered once more as she bent down to pull her shoes on.

"Here, my lady. Let me help ye wi' these." Ailsa said.

It took the efficient servant but a few moments to secure her shoes on her feet and then she was ready. Well, she was dressed now, but she doubted she would ever truly be prepared to face what awaited her in the hall below. She had drawn Connor's fury in questioning her brother's safety. Honor required that a hostage be unharmed during their captivity, but there was unharmed and there was alive and she knew that many were mistreated, even beaten or starved while held. The thought of her younger brother being ill-treated while she had been bathed by servants and had slept the night undisturbed in a huge and comfortable bed brought tears to her eyes. And there was only her honoring her part of the agreement to keep him alive.

Duncan held out his arm and she placed her hand on top of it, allowing him to guide and support her as she walked down the stairs. Unable to keep from trembling, she focused her attention on the steps below her, counting each one silently as she passed it. A terrible thought entered her mind as she reached the lower landing—were these the same steps where Connor's first wife met her death?

Her momentary pause drew Duncan to a halt. He must have sensed her curiosity for he shook his head even as he answered her unspoken question.

"Nay. 'Twas not there."

"I…heard…" She did not really know what to say. Duncan had made his displeasure at her use of the name, *the Beast,* quite clear when she'd used it before. How would he react now that she had revealed her knowledge of the rest of the sordid tale?

"He would not put you in her chamber. No one has used that since her death."

"Is it true then? Did she die at his hands?"

Duncan stared at her and the sight of his anger took her breath from her. Lifting her hand from his arm, she stepped back, in truth a bit fearful of his next action. Before another word could be spoken, a different voice broke in.

"I asked you to bring my wife to the hall, Duncan, not to conduct her on a tour of the stairway."

Chapter Three

Connor stood watching them a few paces away. His arms crossed over his chest once more, Jocelyn was certain he was still angry over her words questioning his honor. He held out his arm to her and she walked silently to his side and accepted it. Turning with him and following his lead, she took her first good look at the great hall and the people in it.

'Twas much larger than her father's hall, and in much better condition. The changing fortunes of the clan Mac-Callum could be seen in the deteriorating keep and the lack of decorations and comforts in their hall. That approach to poverty was what had made her father vulnerable to the MacLerie's offer. They entered from the back and she could feel the gazes of those there to break their fast. No one smiled at her, no one called out to her, she recognized no one. Trying to read their expressions was impossible for they turned from her as soon as she came close.

Never had she felt so unwelcome in a place. Was it their fear of their laird that kept them silent? Did they hold her in the same lack of esteem that their laird did? She shivered and clutched at her shawl more tightly as they finally approached the high table. If her husband noticed her discomfort, he gave no sign. He ignored her even as he walked beside her, greeting various men among those present. Once at the table, he waited for her to take her place next to the large carved chair that was obviously his as laird and then dropped his arm to his side. The low murmurings throughout the room quieted as he waited.

"This is the lady Jocelyn MacCallum, now my wife," he called out in a loud voice.

She waited for the rest of her introduction to his people, but there was no more. She turned to look at him and found he was already sitting in his chair. Jocelyn did not know what she had expected in his words, but she knew that this brief statement was disappointing at best. She glanced at those at the table, but none would meet her gaze. Realizing that she drew more attention by her actions, she sat down and pulled her own stool in closer to the edge of the table. At his nod, the servants brought forth trays of bread and cheese and pitchers of water and ale. Next, bowls filled with steaming porridge were delivered to each of them. The aromas wafted through the air and her stomach grumbled in anticipation of eating.

If her husband noticed, he gave no sign for he tore a loaf of bread apart and began eating. Jocelyn waited, her hands clenched on her lap until the others had followed Connor's example. Aware of their indirect scrutiny, she took a small spoonful of the thick porridge and lifted it to her mouth, savoring the taste and consistency of it as she swallowed. Her stomach made even more noises and she held her hand there, trying to cover them.

"You did not eat enough last evening?" Connor asked without pausing from his own meal.

"Nay, my lord."

"Ailsa was told to see to your needs. Did she not bring you food?"

"She followed your orders, my lord, but I fear I was too tired to do anything save bathe and sleep."

He grunted at her words and asked no more questions. Her thoughts were suddenly filled with her brother and her appetite fled. Her spoon clattered on the table as images of him in some filthy cell, injured and hungry, raced through her mind. Her distress must have shown for she gained Connor's attention.

"Are you ill? The blood has just drained from your face." He leaned over and stared at her.

Jocelyn did not know how to respond. She had already challenged his honor about her brother once today and he would without a doubt see any more questions as another attack. Given his reputation for taking offense and defending his name, she feared what would happen to her if she asked the questions that burned within her.

She never knew what revealed the truth to him, but in the next moment, he stood with a speed belying his size and knocked over his chair. As it toppled behind him, he grabbed her wrist and pulled her from her stool. Without a word of explanation, he dragged her from the table, out of the hall and down a corridor toward the back of the keep. Her struggles lasted all of a minute since his advantage in size and strength and intentions overwhelmed her efforts to resist their motion. Yanking open a door in the wall with such force that the door banged against the stone and shook on its frame, Connor lifted a torch from a sconce and led her into a dark tunnel.

The air grew thicker and more humid as he dragged her farther and farther along the passageway. Jocelyn could not see past him and could not gauge how much longer they could travel along this corridor. Connor slowed momentarily and then he began to walk down some steps. Where did he take her? Had her defiance cost her her life? She struggled against his hold trying to slow his pace.

"I do not expect you to challenge my every word and action, lady wife. You are like a dog gnawing on a juicy bone. You will not give it up until you are forced to it."

"My lord…" she began.

"Here now. This is the last time I will be so lenient with you."

Grabbing her by her shoulders, he shoved her forward until she was looking into a small cell. The dungeon. Her brother. Pushing up onto her toes, she peered into the room until she saw her brother lying on a small pallet in the far corner. Even when she called out his name, he did not move.

"You may have five minutes with him, not one more. Duff," he said to a guard she had not noticed before, "Bring the lady back to the hall when her time has passed. And she is to remain out here and not enter the cell."

"Aye, Connor." The tall man, rightly named for his dark hair and eyes, nodded at Connor.

Without another word to her, but with a glare that clearly expressed his aggravation, Connor turned and walked away leaving her where she stood. Jocelyn turned back to the door and called out her brother's name once more.

Connor shook his head in disbelief at both his wife's behavior and his own. When he'd summoned her to the hall, he had no intention of letting her see or speak to her brother. He intended to stand by his words and by their marriage agreement—her brother would be released as soon as Connor had wedded and bedded her. But something in her eyes as she challenged him and his honor made him change his mind.

He was mindful that she had literally given up her life to save her brother's. He knew also that she was terrified of him. However, he realized that she controlled her fear and continued to push him on the matter of young Athdar. She might be more offended if she discovered the truth of how she came to be married to the Beast MacLerie and her brother's part in it.

Reaching the main floor, he strode back to his seat and tore off another piece of bread. It was only a few moments before he noticed the quiet of the room and then saw the shocked faces of those staring at him. They thought he'd imprisoned her? Slamming his fists onto the top of the table, he rose to his feet and let his gaze pass over those in the room.

"You cannot blame them, Connor," Duncan said. The humor in his friend's voice did not please him. "You have cultivated your own reputation and use it when necessary. Do not hold it against them that they now believe the worst about you."

"And you, Duncan?" he asked, taking his seat. "Do you not believe it? Do you think I have imprisoned my wife below, even as I hold her brother?"

"If she continues as she has begun, I think you may wish that you had locked her below."

Connor nodded, understanding Duncan's comment completely. In her first day here, she had already caused him to change his mind several times. When he sent Duncan to her father, he envisioned a marriage that would have her in his bed at night and out of his way during the day. He knew undoubtedly that he could never love another woman the way he had loved Kenna and so he accustomed himself recently to the idea of simply marrying to fulfill the clan's need for an heir. If he did not let himself care for her, if he kept her at a distance, he could guard his heart from ever having to experience the agony of loss again.

Somehow he now knew that this wife was going to be more trouble than he bargained for. As if his thoughts had conjured her up, she entered the hall with Duff at her side. She kept her gaze on the floor as she walked back to the table. Her next action stunned him.

Stopping before him where all could see, she dropped into a deep curtsy with her head bowed and eyes still lowered. Her voice carried throughout the hall, filling the silence with her words.

"Your pardon, my lord. Please forgive my earlier rash behavior in questioning your honor."

Connor felt his throat tighten and he could not swallow the mouthful of ale he had just taken. He did not sense anything but a sincere apology in her words. That this was done for show was obvious to him, but he knew with a feeling of certainty that it was honestly meant. He swallowed forcefully.

"Join me, lady, and break your fast."

She rose smoothly to her feet and slid onto the stool next to his chair. He held out a loaf of bread to her and she took it, her fingers brushing his as she lifted it from his grasp. Connor watched as she moved the bowl of now-cooled porridge away and broke off a chunk of cheese instead.

"Ian? Bring the lady another bowl of porridge. Hers has cooled."

"Nay, Ian. I do not need any more."

She challenged him again, even while the words of her apology still echoed through the hall. He closed his eyes for a moment and then let out his breath. Glaring at her in her defiance, he repeated his order to the servant once again.

"Is this to be the way of it, then? I give an order and you disobey it?"

Part of him wanted to laugh—at the least, she was no empty-headed ninny as he feared he would be forced to marry. Although his well-developed reputation served him, it also caused women, and some weak-nerved men, to lose their wits around him. If he had to be married, he was inwardly pleased that she did not shrink from him and his every word. But, as laird, he could not, would not, have every order he gave undermined by her.

Jocelyn finally met his gaze and he watched her expression change from defiant to something less disobedient. She pursed her lips and looked as if she was fighting to keep her words in. Good. Let her consider her actions before she took them. He knew she understood him when she moved her bowl over to the side where Ian stood waiting for the outcome.

"Please, Ian," she said in a quiet voice.

He nodded, satisfied. This could all work out. He finished his meal and engaged Duncan in a discussion about their duties for the day. Connor also took advantage of the time to make a more thorough study of his wife as she sat next to him eating her meal.

She was plain in appearance; her face, eyes and hair were neither exceptional nor unattractive. After Kenna's extraordinary beauty, Connor did not want another comely wife. She did move with a certain grace as she walked and her form was definitely the better of her attributes. When the sheet she'd held around her had dropped, exposing her bare shoulders and the slopes of her breasts to him, he knew, and his body's reaction told him, that consummating their union would not be difficult for him. Shifting now in his chair as the memory of her creamy flesh stirred him once more.

As if she felt his scrutiny, their eyes met. Mayhap he had been premature in his assessment of her features, for when her eyes flashed as they did now at him, they were quite attractive. Turning back to face Duncan, he tore his gaze from hers. Aye, 'twould not be difficult after all. Thoughts of her naked beneath him, *soon,* filled his mind with images that would be better left until later.

"You should see the seamstress today and have some clothes made."

"I can sew, my lord, and I have clothes…just not with me. Your orders did not allow me time to pack my belongings."

"Then I will replace them with new since I cannot have the Lady MacLerie wandering through keep and village as I found her this morn."

Her mouth opened and shut and a becoming blush crept up her cheeks. So, she could be quieted.

"Ailsa will make arrangements for you. If you will excuse me—" he rose and nodded to Duncan who stood next to him "—we must see to our duties."

They walked quickly from the hall, the heat in his body cooling even as the distance between them grew. Tonight should prove interesting. Tonight she would be his and the marriage would be consummated.

Tonight.

Darkness had fallen some time ago, yet Connor had not shown himself within the keep. Each time she asked one of the servants if this was his habit, she was met with various grunts or nods and she knew no more than before she asked her questions. Realizing that they would not be cooperative with her efforts to learn more about her husband, she finally gave up and sought comfort and privacy in her chamber.

The day had been a frustrating one for her. She visited the seamstresses within the keep and then the cobbler in the village, all under Ailsa's watchful eye. Her excursion was successful for a few garments were available for her and an additional pair of shoes was found that needed only a few minor adjustments to fit her well enough. Returning with her new possessions, Jocelyn was surprised to find that Connor had not arrived back from his duties. Dinner came and passed and his absence from the hall made her too uncomfortable to eat under the scrutiny of his people. She asked for a tray to be delivered to her in her room and that was where she had spent the last few hours.

Waiting.

Jumping at every noise.

Anticipating the coming night…and him.

She knew that the reprieve granted her last night was over and she would be held to the bargain made. Could she do this? Expecting to marry Ewan, Jocelyn had welcomed and even enjoyed his occasional but fervent kisses. She knew what was expected of a wife in the marriage bed, just not the details of the act itself. She just could not imagine now submitting to this stranger and his desires. She shivered as waves of fear and confusion and curiosity pulsed through her.

Cora, the young girl who had precipitated her misunderstanding with Connor, was back, this time straightening the room and tending to the fire in the hearth. Jocelyn stood by the window, gazing out over the yard. She could see the guards moving up on the main wall in their slow progression around the perimeter. No other movements were apparent to her as she tried to calm the emotions within her.

A soft knock at the door brought her around quickly. Cora opened the door, but instead of her husband, Ailsa entered carrying a pile of linens. The older woman whispered something to Cora and the girl was gone from the room in a few moments. After laying her bundle on the bed, the servant approached her.

"Here now, my lady. I've brought ye a fresh gown and a robe. After ye change, I'll brush out yer hair, if ye'd like?"

Moving without thought, Jocelyn did as Ailsa directed and soon found herself wrapped in a heavy robe and sitting before the fire. The long, slow strokes relaxed her frazzled nerves as she awaited her fate. Would he arrive soon? Would he simply take her and give her no choice in the matter? She shifted nervously on her stool as more and more doubts and concerns came to mind.

"My lady, is there anything ye would like to ask me?"

Jocelyn was startled by the offer and turned to look at the servant. "What do you mean, Ailsa?"

"I thought that mayhap yer own mother did not prepare ye for yer wedding night."

"Nay, Ailsa, I have no questions for you."

"Good then. Yer mother told ye what to expect?"

"Well, actually she told me that my husband would tell me what I needed to ken," Jocelyn whispered, not certain now of the wisdom of such a thing. If it had been Ewan, mayhap, but now that Connor was the one, she wished she knew what was to happen between them.

"If ye're certain?" Ailsa asked again.

"You heard the lady, Ailsa. Her husband will answer her questions."

Jocelyn gasped and turned. The sight of Connor, his height and breadth filling the doorway, took her breath from her. She clutched the edges of the robe more tightly and watched as Ailsa nodded at him and moved around him to leave. He stepped farther into the room and closed the door behind him, dropping the bar into place with a noisy thump. She could not move as he approached, her throat tightened and her chest would not take in the air she needed. After no more than three steps, Connor stood before her and she finally raised her gaze to meet his.

"So, lady wife, what is it you wish to ken?"

She fought against the urge to jump up and run across the chamber, seeking some measure of protection and shelter on the far side of the large bed. Jocelyn instead forced her fingers to relax their grip on the handle of her hairbrush. Placing the brush carefully on the table before her, she slid her hands onto her lap and tried to form an answer in her mind.

What did she wish to know? Everything? Nothing? She knew the mechanics of the coming act; that was not what had bothered her since she'd heard the news of her impending marriage. Finally, the question pushed itself forward.

"Why me?"

She did not meet his gaze. Jocelyn was not certain that she wanted to see what would be revealed there. His manner toward her so far had been less than welcoming, even bordering on hostile and contemptuous, but the reason behind their marriage had plagued her.

"I had need of a wife and you were available."

His voice carried no sign of hostility, no sign that this was more or less than the truth. His explanation spoke of a thing common to lives like theirs—marriages were not made with any regard for the tender feelings of those involved. And the tender feelings that she bore for another had even less importance now.

Jocelyn sensed his movement forward for he made no sound as he approached. Only the crackling of the wood in the hearth broke the tense silence. She turned to face him.

"You do not wish to be married?" She thought 'twas clear from his words and from his treatment of her.

"I have no feelings one way or the other on it. I am laird—I need heirs. For that, I must have a wife."

"And any woman would do?" She closed her mouth, but the words had escaped. He blinked at her tone and even she could hear the sarcasm in it. This was truly not the time to anger him. His reaction surprised her. His laughter filled the room. Connor looked almost approachable when he smiled.

"Nay, I am more discriminating than that. I asked for a wife who was plain of face and not an empty-headed ninny."

She gasped in surprise—both that he would think of such requirements and that he would admit them to her. It took only a few moments for her to realize the insult to her appearance in his words and she looked away before he could see the hurt she knew would be there.

"I meant no insult, lady," he said walking closer. His voice dropped to a whisper as he crouched next to her stool. "I did not want a wife who cowered from me or cringed at my every word. I wanted a wife with gumption."

"And a plain face?" She lifted the brush from the table, mostly to distract herself from the pain she felt.

"I confess 'twas more of a jest than a true requirement." Connor reached out and took the brush from her. "Can we move onto something less argumentative?"

The skin on her neck tingled as he lifted some of her hair and pushed it over her shoulder. Would it be now? Was it time?

Chapter Four

"I do not know what to do."

Horrified that she'd let the words escape her mouth, Jocelyn stepped away from him. His size and strength and nearness unnerved her in so many ways and she needed some distance to keep her fears under control. That he allowed her to move from his grasp surprised her. Once a few paces away, she turned back to look at him.

"I would not expect it of you, lady. Someone who had never milked a cow or slaughtered a hog would not know how to do such a task when it was asked of them."

Taken aback that he was comparing what would happen between them to the duties of a butcher or milkmaid, Jocelyn felt her mouth drop open. He held out his hand to stop any reply she would make and took a step toward her.

"I can see the argument building within you. Is this to be the way between us in all matters, then? I say something and you contest it?" His gaze grew dark as he spoke and his expression changed from smiling to intense.

Jocelyn considered his words before speaking. It had been that way since their first meeting, then in the hall at their meal, even now. She closed her mouth and found she had no words to answer him. Oh, there was an argument within her as he'd said, but the warmth of the room and his scent crowded around her and she remembered once more what awaited her. The heat of a blush flooded her cheeks and she touched them as she felt it.

"Ah," he said, walking now to a small table at the bed's side. He lifted the jug of wine there and poured some into two goblets. "I suspect that the true problem here is an innocent's fear and not a wife's challenge to her husband."

He turned and held one out to her, waiting for her to take it. Jocelyn crossed to him and accepted it. Wine might soothe her nerves a bit and make the rest somehow easier to allow. Not that she had a choice. Her brother's life, even the very life of her clan, all depended on her agreement to this bargain. If she were sent home in disgrace… She nodded in acceptance of the cup and then realized that she was inadvertently agreeing with his words.

He held his goblet up and drank it down in one mouthful. Over the rim of his cup, he watched as she tilted hers to her lips and drank it down as well. The wine slid into her stomach and she felt its warmth spread out to her limbs. Mayhap more would help ease the fear she did feel? Jocelyn held out her cup.

As he poured more of the wine into her goblet, Connor looked closely at her face. A deep pink filled her cheeks and a bead of sweat trickled down her brow. Aye, the fears of the innocent. In consideration of those fears, he poured a small amount in and handed it back to her. Wine to soothe her nervousness was one thing; a puking woman in his bed was another.

Connor put his own cup down and took a step toward

her. The sooner started, the sooner finished, he thought as he reached out and lifted her hair in his hands. The woman nearly stopped breathing so he waited for her to swallow the last of the very strong wine before he came closer. Her cup had just settled on the table when he grasped the belt of her robe and, tugging her closer, pulled it loose. The garment fell away revealing a thin linen gown and her lush figure.

Jocelyn stiffened at first as he slid his hands inside the robe and took hold of her hips. In spite of her stance, she was soft in all the right places and he breathed in the scent of the oil she'd used in her bathwater. She was breathing, a good thing, but she stared off into the room above his shoulder.

"Put your hands on my waist," he said.

She startled again but met his gaze. "What?"

"You said you knew not what to do. I am telling you. Put your hands on my waist."

He wore a plain shirt and plaid, but he could feel the heat of her touch through it. And the trembling, which he forced himself to ignore. His body, tempted by the curves so close beneath his hands, readied itself admirably for what was to come. He waited for a moment and then drew her closer, sliding his hands behind her and pressing himself against her.

Her nipples tightened, whether in fear or anticipation he knew not, and he turned her slightly, rubbing his chest over hers. The gasp that escaped left her openmouthed, but he would not touch her there. Instead he leaned in to her and kissed the edge of her chin, and then kissed along the line of her jaw until he reached her neck. When her breathing became ragged and her fingers clutched at his waist, he knew he could proceed.

Connor released her from his grasp and lifted her hair from her shoulders. He kissed her neck and her ear and wrapped her hair around his fist, turning her head for easier access to the sensitive areas he discovered. He took the edges of the robe and slipped them off her shoulders. When she let her hands drop to her side, he pushed the robe to the floor.

Whether instinctual or simply protective, Jocelyn tried to cover her breasts as his gaze moved over her from top to bottom. She most likely had no idea of what the flickering light of the candles set around the room did reveal to him. The dark triangle at the top of her thighs enticed him to reach for it, but he waited. Stepping behind her, he began again at her neck, kissing and touching with his tongue and nipping gently with his teeth.

Waiting for some sign of resistance and receiving none, Connor moved the linen of her shift away from her neck and kissed the heated skin of her shoulder. She trembled now beneath his touch and her breathing became a series of gasps as he slid his hands around her waist and up until they rested just below her breasts. She leaned back against him and he took advantage of that movement to cup her and draw her back tightly. Jocelyn's head fell back against his chest and he suckled there, on the sensitive skin of her neck as he touched her breasts.

She'd been kissed before. Aye, she'd even allowed Ewan to touch her breasts once, but nothing that had happened between them could have prepared her for this. In spite of the lack of love or even familiarity between them, this man was teasing and tempting her body in ways she'd never imagined. Her head had fallen back on its own to rest against the hardness of his chest once he covered her breast with his hands.

The sensations that his mouth created against her skin simply intensified the tightness in her breasts and the heat between her legs. The heat and the aching between her legs. And the wetness there. His fingers now teased the tips of her breasts to a tautness she'd not felt before and he cupped her in his hands and used his thumbs over them, rubbing and rubbing until they were hard.

It made her want…something. Something more. Jocelyn waited and hoped he would reveal the more of what they did before she asked him about it. Not knowing what to do now, she twisted the fabric of her gown and held it in her fists.

His hands were moving again and she held her breath as they slid down her thighs and caught the end of her shift. He tugged it higher and higher until she felt the touch of his fingers on her bare skin. He moved one hand back up until he held her firmly against him, over her stomach and cupping her breast. The other he used to caress the skin of her thighs and she bit her lip when he touched her belly just above.

The roughness of his tunic and plaid against her naked bottom and back and the strength in his arms and chest and legs as he held her in place intrigued her, for they were so different from the touch of his hand and his fingers as they approached the place that ached now. She could almost forget that this man was a stranger to her. That she was forced by obligation and need to marry him and not Ewan.

Ewan!

It should be him touching her so. She should be giving herself in this intimate touching and joining to the man who loved her and cherished her. Not to this stranger.

Everything within her tensed as she realized that by the

end of this night all of her dreams would be gone. All hopes for a marriage made in love with a man whom she chose were gone. All hopes for living a life within a family who cherished her and appreciated her were over. Once this man, her husband, claimed her body, there was no hope.

She realized that he felt the change within her, for his hold on her tightened around her. His hands, which she now clutched in hers, stopped their sensual strokes and, although he kept his mouth near her neck, she could feel only the warmth of his breath and not his lips now. Jocelyn waited for his response.

"Hush now," he whispered. "I mean you no harm."

She allowed him to turn her to face him and met his intense gaze. His eyes flickered gold in the candlelight and the flames in the hearth threw shadows across the hard angles of his face. After feeling the strength of his arms while in his embrace, she knew that everything about this man was hard. Only his voice and his plea came softly to her.

"Come, let me do this the right way for a bride," he urged in a velvety tone as he lifted her hand in his and led her to the side of the bed.

Once there, he leaned over and, with little effort, picked her up and laid her on the bed. As she watched, he loosened his belt and let his plaid fall to the ground. Jocelyn could not help herself as she looked down at the strong thighs now exposed below his tunic. She leaned against those thighs while he…touched her and knew the feel of them. Swallowing nervously, she returned her gaze to his face just as he climbed into the bed with her.

He had not bothered to pull the covers from the bed, so they lay on top and Connor moved over until he could stretch out next to his now-unwilling bride. She had not voiced her objections, but her body had told him with a certainty that they had reached an impasse in their trek toward consummation. Connor now faced the difficult task of stirring her passion anew so they could accomplish this duty and get on with their lives.

"Easy now," he whispered to her as he put his hand on her leg and began to push her shift up inch by inch. He shifted onto his side so that he could lean up on his one hand while he rubbed her thigh with the other. When she did not soften beneath his touch, he changed his approach. She had liked the attention he'd paid to her breasts as much as he had. He would begin there.

Connor leaned over and touched his mouth to the tip of her breast, nuzzling it through the thin shift. He took her fullness in his palm and rubbed his thumb over the damped tip again and again until it formed a perfect bud against his mouth. Then he suckled it until he felt the tension in her begin to seep away.

"Aye, lass. Just think on the pleasure you feel and let me lead you in this," he urged as he moved against her hip with the hardness between his own legs. Although at first she gazed at him with a haunted expression in her eyes, then she closed them and nodded.

Her body slowly responded to his touch now and soon he gauged her ready for more. Connor knew he was certainly ready and at the edge of his own control. This time when he eased her shift up and moved between her legs, she seemed to welcome his presence there. He slid his hands beneath her knees and lifted her legs up, bringing himself to the opening of her body that was now hot and wet and ready.

It was at the moment he entered her that the absurd

thought struck him—this was the first time he'd made love to a woman that mattered in his life since he'd made love to Kenna more than three years before. Pushing past his new wife's maidenhead, he could hear the voice inside of him begging for Kenna's forgiveness for this act. His heart and soul screamed out that he was somehow being unfaithful to the vows they'd exchanged even as he moved to claim his wife's body.

And he needed Kenna's forgiveness for so many things and now it was too late. Too late for all of them.

Clenching his teeth as he filled Jocelyn's body with his, he watched as a tear escaped the corner of her eye and ran down her cheek into her hair. Not daring to slow for a moment or risk humiliating himself by not being able to complete this duty, Connor pushed into her as far as he could and then slowly removed himself. Even knowing she was not enjoying this, he could not stop now. Finally after a few minutes, he felt his seed empty inside of her.

Out of breath from his exertions, he leaned over her for another minute or two until he could withdraw from her body. He wiped himself of the spent seed and her blood with the edge of the tunic he still wore and climbed from between her legs and off the bed. Gathering his plaid, he threw it over his shoulder leaving enough to cover the front and back of him, not taking the time needed to get it completely in place. He was only going to his chambers from here and no one would be in the corridor against his orders.

She lay unmoving in the large bed, her legs still spread apart until he touched her thigh while tugging the shift down over her. Her lips were clenched tightly together and her face was nearly as pale as the shift she still wore. All hints of the previous attractive blush were gone. The unexplainable and impossible urge to gather her close and soothe the hurt he had caused her was building within him, so he strode to the door of the room in three steps. Three very hurried steps.

He tried to speak but found his throat clogged with some emotion he chose not to try to identify. Clearing it, he spoke without looking back at her and with one hand on the latch.

"I will send Ailsa to you."

"Nay," she cried out, as she sat up, shaking her head at him. "Please send no one."

"As you wish, my lady." He nodded, accepting her words without asking any questions. Once in the hallway, he closed the door tightly and leaned his head against it.

Not certain what he was waiting for, Connor turned and left, deciding that he had much of the same strong wine awaiting him in his chambers that sat on the table within. He'd no sooner reached his chambers when the storm hit—bright flashes of lightning followed by loud crashes of thunder and torrents of rain poured from the skies over Lairig Dubh.

Somehow it felt right. He slammed the door behind him and found the jug where he'd ordered it left for him.

The door closed and she fell back on the bed, overwhelmed and exhausted by what had just happened between them. The hurried leave-taking and the grimace on his face told her of her failure without the need for words of recrimination.

Had she spoken Ewan's name aloud? She thought not, but she'd repeated it over and over in her thoughts and in her heart to block out the identity of the man who truly claimed her body as his. When he ordered her to think on the pleasure, his voice and his face became Ewan in her thoughts. She imagined Ewan's lips against hers and on her skin, suckling at her breasts, and his hands on her body, making her ache and throb as never before.

Only the piercing, burning pain had ruined the imaginary scene in her mind and the grim expression in her husband's eyes as he plunged into her confirmed the truth—she belonged to him now and he was not pleased.

The place between her legs both ached and stung now and Jocelyn looked around the room to see what she could use to clean herself. Her robe lay on the floor where he'd dropped it so she picked it up as she made her way to the table near the hearth. As she took another step, wetness gushed down her legs. Without anything to use, she tore off the bottom of her shift and used it to wipe her legs of the blood and seed.

Realizing her shift was beyond saving, Jocelyn pulled it off over her head and dunked it into the jug of cold water on the table. Squeezing out most of the water, she washed herself as best she could, shivering as she did. Once clean, she rolled a piece of the shift up, soaked it in the water and then pressed it between her legs...*there.* Although a shocking feeling, it soothed the area and she repeated it a few times until the burning disappeared.

Finally, she slipped into the robe, wrapped it tightly around her and tied the belt to keep it in place. Jocelyn approached the bed and knew she could simply not climb back onto it. She would have to face it—and him—soon enough, but for now she wanted to avoid both, so she tugged the top blanket off and threw it aside. Then she pulled off three more blankets and two sheets and made her own pallet in front of the hearth. It would be warm enough for her and she would face the rest in the morning.

It was only later, when the storm raged outside and the sound of the winds and rain and thunder grew louder that she let out the emotions she'd been holding within her. The terror of being given to this man, the heartbreak of leaving her family and her one true love behind, and the hopelessness of her future all poured out of her even as the clouds poured their storming rains on the castle and keep.

Rolled in a cocoon of bed linens and exhausted by the physical and emotional price she'd paid for her brother's safe release, Jocelyn drifted off to a sleep unbothered by the reality of her life now. And her dreams were filled with the face and the touch of the man she loved.

The darkness and warmth suited her, Jocelyn decided when she heard someone moving around her chambers. Tempted to lift the layers and layers of bed linens she'd wrapped around herself in the deepest, coldest part of the night, she remained still and kept her eyes shut tightly. She knew from the previous attempts to rise that her head would throb and the room would swirl uncontrollably and she would be forced to vomit again.

No, the dark and warmth and keeping her body still suited her just fine. But, the voice softly calling her name became more insistent.

"Lady? Lady Jocelyn? Are ye well?"

It was the old woman who'd assisted her in so many ways, but still, the aches and pain and unease in her belly tempted her to ignore the woman's call.

"Lady? Should I seek out the laird?"

"Nay!" she called out, pushing the coverings aside.

Spying Ailsa leaning her old, crooked frame over to nearly the floor to speak to her, Jocelyn shook her head and then paid the price she feared. She was fortunate that Ailsa was perceptive enough to recognize what was about to happen and grabbed the pot quickly.

It was some minutes before her stomach eased and she could lay back. Ailsa soothed her with soft words and a cool cloth to her brow.

"Lie back, lady. It will pass."

"'Twas the wine," she whispered, trying to explain to the servant.

"Spoiled?" The maid picked up the jug from next to her on the floor and sniffed at it suspiciously. Her decision was said with a shake of her head. "Smells fine to me, lady." The woman turned the jug bottom up and not even a drop trickled out. "Mayhap the amount was the problem and not the quality?"

Jocelyn did not respond—there was no need. With the cloth back in place, the noise of the awakening keep seemed to recede. Ailsa coughed lightly, gaining her reluctant attention. There would be no way to stay here, cocooned away from everything, and everyone, that she wanted to avoid for the rest of her life.

"Lady, I called for a bath and it will arrive shortly. Mayhap I could help ye to the chair to wait for it?"

"I would rather stay where I am, Ailsa."

The knock at the door told her that would not happen. Sliding the cloth from her face, she met the woman's gaze for the first time. Old though the woman may be, Jocelyn had recognized Ailsa's steel will at their initial encounter. Now, too worn out by the night before to resist, she accepted the hand held out to her and climbed to her knees and then to her feet. Her head complained with each move and her stomach felt as though it might rebel as well. Closing her eyes once more, she allowed the maid to guide her a few steps to the chair and sat down there.

As though she knew the effort it had taken her to manage even those few steps, the maid arranged the robe she wore over her lap and stepped away without saying a word. Jocelyn let her head tilt back and rest on the back of the chair. Ailsa's gasp forced her to look.

The torn and bloodied chemise she'd left in the corner on the floor was now in Ailsa's hands and a look of horror and piety filled her eyes. Jocelyn's stomach twisted.

"Lady…" Ailsa began softly and then she paused, lifting the apron from her skirt and wrapping the bloodied garment and setting it aside. "Have ye need of our healer?"

Jocelyn could not find the words to answer. Other than the effects of too much wine, which had successfully blocked out the other parts of her that had hurt, she thought she simply needed more sleep and that promised bath. She shook her head.

The old woman looked around the chamber and tsked. It had the appearance of being the site of a battle. The bed torn apart. The linens spread on the floor. The jug on the floor. Her own disheveled condition could not help but add to whatever the woman was thinking.

At her gesture, Ailsa nodded and began cleaning and straightening the chamber, apparently ignoring the others who waited outside the room. Another knock and Ailsa crossed to the door, opened it, whispered some instructions and closed the door again, returning to what she'd been doing.

As Jocelyn watched, the bed was stripped and, with the efficiency of many years' practice, made once more in a matter of minutes. There was a hesitation when she'd lifted the blanket stained with her blood, but Ailsa simply put it aside with the other bundle and finished the task. When the room had been brought back to some condition that pleased the maid, she stood back and nodded.

"Rest there, lady, until I return."

"I am fine, Ailsa. Truly," she said, although her tone did not even convince her of the truth of it.

"They will not enter until I give them leave to, so close yer eyes and rest. I will bring something to soothe yer belly from the wine. Then ye will feel stronger and ready for the bath."

With barely a sound, she exited and Jocelyn was left alone in a room with no sign now of what had occurred the night before. Only the pain in her heart which would not be repaired as easily.

Chapter Five

Connor stared out the small window in his chamber and tried to gather his thoughts. He did not often drink the amount of wine he'd consumed after returning to his room last even. After the second jug of wine, he'd ordered the MacCallum boy released. After the third, he'd locked himself in his room and tried to block out what he'd done that sent him running from his new wife. The fourth jug seemed to finally work and he'd passed out in his chair.

The haze of the wine now helped him to block out Duncan's droning on about some small matter about stolen cattle that needed to be found. He'd been ignoring him for several minutes when the door to his room opened with a crash and a small, old madwoman accosted him.

Although she could barely reach that high, Ailsa swatted him hard on the side of his head and then again a second time when he did not get out of her way fast enough.

"Ailsa! What has gotten into you?"

When she came at him again, looking not a bit regretful of her actions, he grabbed her hands and held her fast.

Although Duncan gave a generous smirk, he offered no other help.

"How could ye? I nursed ye at my own breasts and know that no one ever mistreated ye." She tugged one of her hands loose and swung at his head again.

"Tell me what has brought on this fit of madness. In spite of your past care of me, I will not permit this to continue."

The woman backed away and took several deep breaths. Her furor kept her focus on him, so she had still not noticed Duncan standing in the shadows of the room.

"I ken yer feelings on marrying again. We all ken. But she is yer wife now and she was a maiden at that."

He could feel his anger building from deep inside. He had no desire or intention of talking about the situation or occurrences between him and his wife with anyone, not even his old nurse. Before he could put her in her place, she whispered harshly.

"I just left yer ladywife's chambers where I found her huddled on the floor in front of a cold hearth. She'd passed the night there heaving and wrapped in whatever she could pull from the bed."

"What?" he roared. "That canna be true. She was in that bed when I left her."

Now she stepped closer and poked him sharply in his chest with her finger. "She drank whatever was left of yer fine wine and slept on the floor, I tell ye. And this," she shoved a bundle into his hands and shook her head at him with something in her gaze that resembled disgust, "This is what ye left her in."

The sodden fabric fell open and he found himself holding a woman's shift that had been torn and was red with what looked to be dried blood. His thoughts might be muddled by too much wine, but it took only a moment to realize what Ailsa had handed him.

Connor clenched his jaws together. Could it be hers? She had not seemed overly distressed when he left. Indeed, she'd been more upset by what he'd been doing than when he'd finished and moved off the bed. And her refusal when he'd offered to send Ailsa to her showed someone who was well.

"She was well when I left her."

"Weel, she isna now."

They stood toe-to-toe until Duncan made some noise that broke into their private conversation. Ailsa noticed Connor's second-in-command standing near the door and stepped back from the confrontation.

Still unwilling to discuss what he did and did not do, unwilling to even think about it, he crossed his arms over his chest, signaling an end to any more talk.

"Ailsa, see to your duties and I will see to mine."

"Aye, laird. As ye wish," Ailsa said, her voice filled with anger.

"I did not harm her, Ailsa."

The old woman muttered something which Duncan heard for his face bore the look of someone trying not to laugh. The only words he had heard involved not caring for her either.

"I think that someone of your years may not be the right maid for my new wife. Seek out and train one of the girls from the village to serve in your stead."

If she feared the threat, there was no sign of it. If anything changed, her expression hardened and the anger in her eyes flared anew. Ailsa crossed her arms over her own formidable chest and met his glare with a more insolent one. He'd used the threat on many, many occasions but had never rid himself of the woman yet.

Mayhap 'twas time?

"Connor?" Duncan's voice interrupted the two-sided argument.

"Keep your thoughts to yourself, cousin. You have no place in this discussion."

"Then I bid you good day," Duncan replied. With a hard smile and narrowed eyes, a nod to both of them and a few steps, he was gone from the chamber as was any hope that Connor had of keeping the full wrath of Ailsa at bay. He would not let this escalate into something that had him examining his motives or his intentions about this new wife. Not even for Ailsa. He raised his hand in front of her and shook his head.

"Ailsa, go and see to the lady's needs. I will speak to her later."

"And when she asks of her brother?"

Damn! How did the woman discover so much so quickly?

"Say nothing. I will speak to her of it later."

It could have been something he'd said or the tone of his voice, but Ailsa paused, sticking out her chin and meeting his gaze for a moment. Mayhap she'd sensed he had truly reached the limits of what he would accept from her in personal commentary or intrusion? Whatever had worked, he was glad of it. The servant nodded and backed away. When she'd reached the door and was pulling it closed as she left, the words escaped him.

"I did not harm her, Ailsa."

"As ye say, laird," she replied without slowing or looking back.

Pushing aside all thoughts of the woman at the center

of discussion, Connor decided he'd been inside enough this day. He needed to get back to his duties as much as Ailsa did, so he strode down his tower chamber, through the hall of the keep until he left the tall, stone building. Following the path to the stables, he ordered a small troop of men readied to accompany him to the site of the most recent complaints of incursions onto his lands. A few hours later and miles away, only his clan and his lands and their defenses claimed his attentions.

Jocelyn's respect for the old woman grew quickly as each of her offered remedies worked its magic on her—first on her head and stomach, both of which threatened upheaval at any moment, and then on the rest of her body. The hot concoction that Ailsa brought her soothed the swirlings in her belly and eased the pain in her head. A long, very hot bath eased the aches and coldness that seemed to have seeped into her bones during the night. Then, dressed in warm stockings, a clean chemise, a new gown and length of woolen plaid, Jocelyn felt as though everything that came before had been just a nightmare.

Never one to suffer from self-pity or bad humors, Jocelyn faced the rest of the day knowing that the worst was behind her. She'd lived through the arduous journey to this place. She'd lived through meeting and wedding and being bedded by the infamous Beast. It had not been a pleasant experience on the whole of it, though parts of it were. His touch made her feel things that she'd only heard hinted at by other women, things only sampled lightly with Ewan.

If he kept his word, and she had no doubts that he would, her brother would be free to return to their clan along with the aid and protection promised by the clan MacLerie. Jocelyn intended to ask about the arrangements as soon as she could find the laird. Athdar's treatment at the hands of the MacLeries was uneven at best and she only hoped that his temper did not get him into more trouble than he already was. He would learn to control it, she was certain, as he grew closer toward manhood.

Soon though, according to the provisions of the marriage contract, Athdar would arrive home with the resources and men to rebuild their keep and village and feed the entire clan through this next winter. No more a target for the hungrier clans around them, her marriage insured her family's survival. For now, at least as long as her heart ached over Ewan's loss, she could content herself with the knowledge that no one in her family would die due to a lack of food or shelter this year.

The sun had fought its way through the thick clouds that lingered after the storms of the night, and now it beckoned to her. Jocelyn found her cloak and made her way down to the hall. Determined first to see to her brother and confirm the arrangements for his release. Then, mayhap with his company for she was certain he would welcome the chance to be out of the dungeon cell, she would explore the keep and castle. She made her way to the stairs that would take her deep underneath the keep.

Pushing on the strong wooden door, Jocelyn hit its surface when it did not give under her pressure. Stepping back, she turned the knob and still it did not open. Stretching up to peer in the small opening, she tried to remember the name of the man guarding it last night.

Two nights ago, she corrected herself.

So much had happened in the last few days, she

looked around to make sure she was trying to open the correct door.

It had not been locked when the laird had brought her to see her brother, but it was now. Finally remembering, she called inside to the guard.

"Duff? Duff, are you there?"

No one answered. Jocelyn lifted the latch again and pushed. It was locked and by the sound, or lack, of it, no one stood guard below.

"Duff?" she called out louder. "Is anyone there?"

"Does Ailsa know you are creeping around outside your chambers?"

She let out a scream as someone whispered in her ear— from just behind her. Turning quickly, she discovered the laird's cousin Duncan apparently up to more of his mischief. Her bottom twinged as she remembered how his last scare had caused them both to arrive mud-covered from their journey.

The pace on their journey here had turned into a test of wills with her slowing to avoid and him hastening to arrive at the designated time. When Duncan slapped her horse to spur it and her on, she purposely slid from it, grabbing him to cushion her landing, never dreaming the wretch would drag her down, too.

"Duncan," she said, not moving from her place in front of the door.

"Lady," he replied, bowing and smiling that irritating smile he had. The one that said he had all the answers but chose not to share them with her. Why had the laird chosen him to come to her home and escort her here? "So, does Ailsa ken of your escape from your chambers?"

"Am I a prisoner then? As my brother is," she looked at

the door now and then back at him. The expression he wore in that instant spoke of spoiled eels…or too much wine.

"You are a wife, lady. No prisoner. Ailsa mentioned your state of…that is, that you were not feeling well this morn." He would not meet her gaze now and she was glad of it. She did not need to know that others knew of her personal matters. Especially not this one who would use it to cause her discomfort.

"I am well now. And am seeking out my brother," she said turning back to the door and knocking on it. "But Duff does not seem to be at his post." She paused, hesitating to ask anything of him that would put her in his debt. "Can you take me to him?"

His face took on a more miserable pallor and she thought him the ill one, until he shook his head. "You must speak to the laird about your brother." He stepped back and gestured her away from the door. "Come, I will see you back to your chambers."

"I have no wish to return to my chambers. I want to see my brother and arrange for his freedom. You know the agreement—you negotiated on behalf of the MacLerie." Jocelyn pulled the woolen shawl up higher around her shoulders. "If you say I must speak to the laird before I can see Athdar, then fetch the laird here."

"Fetch the laird?" Duncan sputtered and choked on the words. "You speak of him like some animal to do your bidding. You must have had a coddled upbringing if such behavior was permitted of you. 'Tis no wonder that your clan lies in ruins if your father allowed his clan to speak to him or even think of him in that manner."

His sharp words brought her to a stop. Although she thought he was putting too much meaning into her words,

Jocelyn knew that this man had the laird's ear and confidence. If he wished, he could make the difficult situation even worse between her and her new husband. She'd sensed honor within him, but he was, after all, the laird's man.

"You mistake my words, Duncan. I will happily seek out the laird to ask him about Athdar, if you would but reveal his whereabouts to me. I mean no disrespect to him."

He seemed to think on her words and then he nodded at her. "'Twould appear that you have not yet recovered from the journey here or the…events of the last few days. Your concern over your brother is understandable, even admirable, not unnecessary. Connor has said he is safe, and so he is."

Only the Blessed Mother knew how she stayed her hand in that moment. Everything within her wanted nothing so much as to make a fist as Ewan had taught her and to swing it at the side of this fool's head. But then she realized something—he'd never answered her question. He'd evaded and deflected, but never answered.

He knew something he was not supposed to reveal to her.

"Duncan, where is my brother?" Jocelyn stared at his face and watched the momentary search for words as he tried to piece together some explanation or excuse.

"Ah, look, lady. Here comes Ailsa now." Duncan spun on his heels and called out across the hall. "Ailsa, your lady is here. You have arrived not a moment too soon for she needs to rest."

Now that he had made certain that everyone in the hall or passing through it heard his words, she knew she could not allow this to become a confrontation. Fear struck her deep and hard as she worried that something ill had indeed

befallen her brother. She would play his game and allow
him to win this encounter, but she must know of her
brother's fate. As she nodded her acquiescence to him, she
leaned in close so that no one else would hear.

"At least tell me he is alive," she whispered. "At least
that." She clasped her hands together so she would not
grab the plaid he wore over his shoulder. His mouth tightened into a grimace and she could see his jaws clenching
and releasing. The bottom of her stomach dropped and bile
rose hot in her throat.

"He is alive and well, lady," he answered. "You must
speak to the laird about the rest."

Ailsa arrived at her side and glanced from one to the
other. Someone as astute as this woman could not miss the
tension between them. Instead of agreeing that she should
rest, Ailsa took her by the arm and guided her toward the
doors of the keep.

"Come, lady. I think a short walk would aid you more
than keeping to your chambers." The maid began walking,
but Jocelyn paused. This was not done yet.

"Duncan, when can I speak to the laird? Where will
I find him?"

"He's ridden to one of the outlying villages. He will
return late this night or in the morn."

So, she must wait hours and possibly a day to find out
Athdar's fate. There was nothing she could do now,
nothing but insult or provoke Duncan, which would give
her much enjoyment but no favorable results. She did not
doubt his words about the MacLerie's return or that her
brother was well.

"I will speak to him on his return then," she agreed and
followed Ailsa's guiding steps away.

She looked back at Duncan once as she walked away, trying to read his thoughts. His face was filled with as much frustration as she thought hers must be, but for exactly the opposite reasons. However, she knew that Connor MacLerie was at the center of both of their situations.

Speak to the laird?

Oh, aye. She would speak to him.

Jocelyn discovered that Ailsa was in truth a tyrant disguised as a small, old woman. The rest of the day and even after dark fell, the woman nearly forcibly escorted Jocelyn from place to place within the keep and without, until Jocelyn was ready to drop. When the laird had not returned in time for the evening meal, she was tempted to curl into a ball and fall asleep in some secluded corner where Ailsa could not find her.

Her plan was not a success. Ailsa did relent and allow her to retreat to her room and eat her meal there. The lack of appropriate women and men for that matter would make it awkward for her to take her place alone at that table. So, she found herself in her room, with a well-blazing fire in the hearth, a tray of foods giving off the most wonderful of aromas, and, even more wondrous than the appetizing food, a book she'd discovered during her tour of the keep.

Although she tried to slow her pace, Jocelyn gulped down her food and finished one full goblet of ale before stopping. Not aware of how hungry she'd become, she shook her head in surprise over it. Now stretching and leaning back against the tall, cushioned chair that had appeared in her chambers just today, she spied the bed.

She would fall asleep the moment she laid her head down—she could feel the physical exhaustion dragging her down now. But, she wanted to be awake and ready when Connor arrived for she had many questions for him.

Questions that had begun simply about her brother and now included many about herself and her place here in Lairig Dubh and the clan MacLerie. Questions that had increased both in quantity and intensity as the day passed and her lack of position in the eyes of these people was made clear over and over again.

They didn't need her guidance on matters of food nor the preparations for winter. The steward, in his position for decades, was quite competent, even creative, in handling those duties. They did not need her assistance in the duties of overseeing the keep or the woman who lived there, for other than the laundry maids, some of whom now assisted Ailsa, there were no women living in the keep.

So, she found herself in a nearly empty keep, with no sign of her brother or her husband, and exhausted from the miles walked this day. The bed, which she'd purposefully ignored, now beckoned to her. It looked so inviting—piled high with pillows and many layers of linen and blankets—Jocelyn soon found herself standing next to it.

"I just put some hot stones under the blankets, lady. Let me help you in." Ailsa lifted the robe from her shoulders and helped her climb up. Then she adjusted the location of the flannel-wrapped stones until they were close enough to warm Jocelyn's feet.

Sinking into the comfort and warmth undermined her plans to be awake to speak to the laird on his return. Her body allowed the cushiony softness of the thick mattress to pull it toward sleep.

"Ailsa," she whispered, struggling to say the words

before she drifted into the oblivion of sleep. "Tell the laird I wish to speak to him when he returns—whenever that is."

"Aye, lady. I will tell the laird."

She wanted to ask about the tone in the woman's voice, but her body was settling into sleep. Although she could still hear the woman moving around the room, Jocelyn had not the strength to form and speak more words. And once more, her dreams were filled with images of Ewan.

And sometime in the dark of the night when the fires had burned down, he came to her in her dreams and warmed her body and soul.

Chapter Six

'Twas long after midnight when he led the men back into the keep. The guards on the battlements, at his orders, had been prepared to wait for his return and to open the gates for him. This was much later than he'd planned to return, but the light of the fullest moon of the month lit their way and gave him the additional time he needed to continue searching for the vermin who had attacked some of his clan in the small village six hours away. The intruders paid for their arrogant beliefs that they could take what they wanted from the MacLeries and not face retribution. The retribution dealt to them was so severe that others of their ilk would think twice before attempting the same.

Releasing his horse to one of the stableboys, he dismissed the men and walked to the keep where he knew Duncan would await him. A few torches burned in sconces set high up on the walls of the great hall, but the rest of the huge chamber was darkened and the sounds of sleep emanated from the men who slept on pallets there. A few sounds not related to sleep also echoed through the hall as he walked quickly to the steps and high table.

Tempted to determine who was involved in those, he shook his head and continued forward. The only women who slept on, or rather, visited the hall's floor were the village whores when invited by one of his men. He did not need to watch that particular transaction of business—the occasional sounds were proof enough of it.

He found his seat and found Duncan sitting nearby and a servant appeared just as he sat down at the high table with a bowl of hot porridge, some bread and a jug of wine. After suffering the effects of last night's overconsumption of wine, he waved it off and asked for some ale.

"How long have the whores been making their way here?" He had not paid attention to the details of house-keeping or who lived here for some time, since before his father died. Truth be told, he had not taken an interest in those matters since his marriage to Kenna. But he remembered not when the women had left and the whores began their visits.

"Only these last few months," Duncan answered, waving off the servant, giving him leave to go. "When you ignored it, the men took it as permission to continue."

The sarcasm in his voice could be an insult, Connor thought, if he cared to consider it. 'Twas Duncan's way— when he believed that Connor was ignoring or disregard-ing his counsel, his cousin could be simply annoying or downright irritating when he chose. Most times Connor did as he suggested to avoid the surliness that would follow if he did not. He knew that the clan thought he left too much to Duncan's discretion, especially since he was only tanist and not laird, but Connor trusted Duncan with his life and with any decisions he made. Hearing the next words, he was wont to question his own judgment.

"Think you that your new wife will be pleased with them plying their wares on her floor?"

"I had not thought on it," he admitted with a shrug. "She will not be down here at night, so I doubt it matters."

Other than giving him an heir, he'd really tried not to waste much time thinking on what this new wife would do. He'd taken advantage of a situation brought on by the drunken bravado of her brother and he'd ended up in an alliance with a worthless clan he did not need and a wife that he did.

Duncan's glare turned insolent, a warning that his mood was turning sour—not something he really wanted to see tonight. After a long day on his horse, the pursuit and fight that ended it and the return here, he wanted nothing so much as the food before him and the bed above.

"So, the lady gave you more trouble in my absence?"

That was the underlying problem here. Duncan gave no more thought to the lady's delicate sense of propriety than he did. Duncan was mad as hell that he'd been left behind, for fighting with vicious intruders was always preferable if the other choice was a lady's concerns.

"She came searching for her brother."

"Of course she did." He spooned some of the thick porridge in his mouth.

"You bastard! You left me here on purpose." Duncan pounded on the table with his fist and shook his head. "You knew 'twould be her first concern."

"Like a dog with a juicy joint, she is." Connor ate several more spoonfuls of the porridge and tore off a chunk of bread. "And what did you tell her?"

In truth, Connor hoped that Duncan had revealed his actions. Once she accustomed herself to how he had already handled the matter of her brother and the promised aid to her clan, she would then settle down into the role he'd planned for her—in his bed at night and out of his way during the day.

"I told her to speak to the laird about her brother."

Duncan lifted his own cup and drank deeply from it. He was not telling all of it, Connor could feel it.

"And the rest of it?" he prompted.

"She was distraught that Athdar had been harmed in some way or worse…"

"So you told her that I'd sent him off yesterday morn after she spoke to him?"

"Nay," he said, shaking his head. "I left that to you."

He raised an eyebrow at his cousin, letting Duncan know he was on to his attempt to rattle him. "And she stopped asking?"

"I only said that he was well," Duncan finally admitted to giving some details.

"Aha! I knew you could not resist telling her something about her brother."

Duncan emptied his cup and stood, fury etched into his face. "I have known you to be many things, Connor, but to be cruel to her for no reason is not what I would have expected." He slammed his cup down on the table. The loud crack echoed through the hall and the silence that filled the room.

"Mayhap I have my reasons?" he asked, knowing he had none he wanted to acknowledge.

"Then tell me what they are. Tell me your plans for the clan."

"My plans are to make the clan MacLerie the most powerful and secure clan in the west of Scotland, even if that means taking the king's oath as others have. I want my people to prosper and the clan to grow. Those are my plans."

"Your words are those of the old laird. You live under his shadow still and will until you…" Duncan leaned in and whispered in a harsh but quiet voice. "I thought that your decision to finally take a wife meant you were ready to move on from the past…from your past…"

"You dare much, cousin," Connor snapped, rising to his feet.

"Someone must. You were like a stranger after Kenna's death, driving yourself toward some goal and making certain that all feared you. Then your father's death brought out an even sharper edge to you. But now you have a wife…."

"Mind your tongue, Duncan," he said. The anger within him grew hotter and stronger and he clenched his fists against his first impulse to stop his cousin with a punch. "What goads you into saying such things, Duncan? Do you fear losing your position if I have a son?"

Duncan spit on the floor at his feet. Connor guessed that he'd not found the reason behind his cousin's ire. Despite the growing practice of disregarding Highland customs and traditions on inheritance, the MacLeries still followed the old ways, making Duncan, as nearest male relative to the laird his heir. At least they had until now.

"Although I am honored that the elders chose me as tanist, I told you that I wait only for you to have a son of your own to carry that honor. In truth, I do not want the chair on which you sit. I have seen what it does to men and desire only to do that which I do best—fight for clan and laird."

His loyalty was unquestioned, even if his sarcasm and irritating question bespoke of a lack of good sense. Connor sat down and shoveled the last bit of porridge in his mouth. Then he stuffed the crust of bread behind it, washing it all down with the remaining ale. Apparently his plan to apprise Duncan of the day's events was not going forward and eating would be the only thing accomplished by him in the hall this night. Wiping his hand over his mouth, Connor rose and stepped away from the table.

"She wishes to speak to you on your return."

"She?"

"Your wife…Lady MacLerie."

"Surely she sleeps by now. I will speak to her in the morn."

Duncan shook his head and let out a disgruntled huff. "'Tis your choice, laird."

'Twas indeed his choice and he was for bed and to face neither his annoying cousin nor his lying-in-wait wife. Nodding at Duncan, he walked down the steps of the dais and around the perimeter of the hall until he reached the corner tower.

She slept there.

In spite of his words to Duncan, something pushed him up that stairway and into the small chamber that led to hers. Only a few minutes had passed between his declaration to ignore her and his presence before her door.

And he knew not why.

He did not want to face her questions about Athdar. He did not want to repeat the disastrous coupling of the night before. He did not truly want another wife.

Part of him knew that if he began to avoid her, avoid her bed, avoid putting her in her place when she made demands, he would walk away and not return to her. He rubbed his eyes and pushed the hair out of his face. This must be exhaustion, something that had never bothered him when he was younger. Connor turned and almost took the first step away when the door opened.

"Laird," Ailsa whispered, stepping onto the landing and pulling the door closed behind her.

"I have been told that the lady wishes to speak to me." It was a convenient way to explain him standing at her door.

"Aye. The lady asked that ye call on her when ye returned. Should I wait?"

In other words, would he hurt her again? The accusation floated between them for another moment and then he shook his head. Not quite certain what had ensued his leaving her last night, he could not rebut anything to Ailsa. He absolutely refused to discuss the particulars with anyone but the woman involved, so questions were not acceptable. In truth though, he admitted to himself that he did not think discussing such matters could benefit anyone.

"I will call you if you are needed, Ailsa."

Not able to give way gracefully, much as he could not back down, the old woman glared at him and lifted her chin out. A curt nod was all the acknowledgement he would get from her and he took it, watching as she ambled down the stairs.

Now, 'twas him and the door before him. Waiting until he could no longer hear her footfalls on the tower steps, he grasped the latch and lifted it. If he got his wish, she would sleep through his entrance and then he could speak with her in the morn. Connor stepped into the chamber and, after closing the door behind him, he walked to the side of the bed.

She lay asleep in the center of the bed, only her face

peeking out from beneath a thick layer of blankets. The shadows thrown from the dwindling fire in the hearth made it appear as though she laughed at one moment and frowned the next, but as he watched, he realized that she slept so soundly that she moved not at all.

He noticed some small resemblance to her younger brother in the curve of her chin and the shape of her mouth, but they were opposite in coloring—she fair-skinned with auburn hair and green eyes and he olive-toned with black hair and blue eyes. With such differences, he thought that they must each favor one parent or the other.

So now that he was in her chamber, what was his next move? Connor had tried throughout the day to keep her from his thoughts. Each time he remembered the taste of her skin or the lush curves of her breast filling the palms of his hands or his mouth, her image and the sounds of her awakening to passion's call came alive in him. And his body responded, too.

After a full day of struggling with the challenge, he'd nearly convinced himself that he was in control when he arrived back at the keep. A few minutes in her room, breathing in her scent, watching her sleep, and he lost the fight once more.

There must be a way to keep her separate from his world and, more importantly, from his heart. Connor watched as she stirred for a moment, turning her head and murmuring soft words in her sleep, then settling back into a deeper slumber. If he was to keep his clan safe and fulfill his responsibilities, he must discover a way to avoid becoming attached to her. More than three years had passed since Kenna's death and the chaos and torment during that time told him in a way that nothing else could that he could not allow it to happen again.

Nay, a wife in his bed at night and out of his way during his days and while his duties called him to serve the clan MacLerie as laird was what he needed. Love was not. Not only not needed, but a danger if things went as they did in his first marriage. Broken alliances, questions of honor raised and raised again, accusations of murder and suspicions of worse. No, the clan MacLerie would not survive, even as strong and numerous as they were, if the events of his first marriage repeated themselves now when his father was gone and no other heirs remained of his lineage.

Connor nodded, confirming in his mind the decision he'd made and now realizing that, to make it real, he needed to take the next step—he must bed Jocelyn. Though many questions and concerns lay heavy on his mind when consummating their union last night, he had not found it difficult to finish the deed. He must face this matter-of-factly, as often as possible and let it become for him, and for her, nothing more than a duty expected of them both. He would offer her pleasure in return for her compliance in this and he did not doubt that it could turn out to be a duty faced with anticipation and not dread.

With the decision made, he unbuckled his belt and removed his plaid. His boots followed and then tugging his shirt off, Connor lifted the edge of the blankets and climbed into the bed. Easing to her side, he followed her body as she turned. She wore a shift and nothing else, and his cock hardened at her nearness and the heat of her. He paused for a moment and let her body become accustomed to his before reaching one hand around her waist and sliding his palm over her breasts.

The dream felt so real now. Jocelyn could feel the touch of Ewan's hands as he covered her breast and pulled her to him. The hardness of his body, the shape of his chest muscles against her back and his thighs behind hers, heated her when she'd begun to chill in the deepest part of the night. Snuggling back against him now and allowing his heat to warm her, she knew it was a sinful thing to enjoy the thought of another man's touch. But the thinking part of her knew it was only a dream and there was no harm in a few minutes of weakness, was there?

His hand slid down over her belly and grasped the edge of her shift, sliding it up until his hand could reach beneath it on her thighs. His hand was hot there, and his fingers eased between her legs to the place that ached for his touch. One heavy leg lay on hers and pushed hers apart.

"Open for me, lass," he said in a low and tempting voice. "Let me touch you there."

The touch might have been Ewan's, but the voice was not. Jocelyn forced her eyes open and met the gaze of her husband. Jolted from the dream and embarrassed to discover him touching her so intimately, she pressed her legs together and tried to move from him.

"Hush now, Jocelyn. I will not harm you," he said in a heated whisper. Did he realize he'd made the same promise just the night before? Did he consider how he'd failed in it?

"'Tis your right," she answered and then tried to let her body relax once more under his touch. Husband and laird, he owned her body as he did anything she brought with her into the marriage. Surprised that he would want to repeat such a trying experience with her, she waited on his reaction.

He seemed stunned by that response and he leaned away from her. But his hand was still there, gently and slowly sliding his fingers over the already-slick folds. She could not help herself when he touched some sensitive spot and she let out a gasp. Jocelyn reached down to grab his hand and make him stop…or mayhap not.

"I will stop if you wish me to," he offered.

"You did not seemed pleased by this last night. I did not think you would return again so soon."

There. She'd been honest with him. The grim expression on his face at the completion of his duty, his hastened departure from her bed and her chambers, and his lack of interest in her once gone all told her that he did not do this of his own accord. Obviously his need for an heir outweighed any disgust on his part and brought him back to try again.

"There is sometimes little pleasure in a virgin's first bedding."

"I had heard that before."

"And now know it for a fact?" he asked, his fingers never stopping from their dance.

"Aye, laird," she answered. Although some moments had been better than others, and none worth lamenting over now that a whole day had passed, she did not understand why this act was so praised and anticipated.

But, wait. Tiny waves of heat began to course through her core, sending ripples out, to her belly and her breasts and even, she swore as she thought on it, to her own fingertips. Her legs shook as some tension grew in her. His fingers did not simply rub on the outside, every third or fourth stroke he dipped a bit more and then a bit more inside of her. She still held his wrist in her hand, but now her hand moved with his, following the rhythm he set.

The tips of her breasts tightened and she was not certain if she should stop him or urge him on in his endeavors.

This time he wore no shirt and the heat of his body and the thin sheen of sweat now building on his chest spread to hers. Then just when she thought the decision made, he stopped and searched her eyes.

"So, wife. Say you nay or aye? Shall I show you the difference between a first and second joining or should I go?"

He withdrew his fingers then and she did clutch him tighter, keeping him there until she could decide. 'Twas becoming hard to breathe and even harder to put thoughts together or speak the word he wanted. The word she wanted, too. He could have forced her to it, he had the right, but that he stopped and asked her, made her willing to try.

"Aye, husband," she whispered, guiding his fingers back to their target. "Show me."

And he did.

Many minutes later, after using his fingers and then his mouth on her breasts and belly and neck and *there* to stir her passions even more, he pushed his hardness inside her and she knew the difference. No pain this time, only heat and aching and the sensation of being filled. Her body softened under his and he pushed farther in with each thrust, deeper and deeper until she felt as though she would disintegrate from within.

Then as the tension grew stronger in her core, he began to shudder and she felt his seed spill. His hardness pulsed over and over again, each time less and less until he let out a loud sigh and remained still between her legs.

Her husband withdrew from her and rolled to his back, throwing his hand over his eyes and taking in some deep breaths. Although he seemed more pleased by this joining than the last, she was not certain if he was. It had not hurt, but the tension deep inside was still there and she wondered if she'd done something wrong.

After only a moment or two, he sat up and tugged off the covers. The chill of the room raised gooseflesh on her arms and legs and she reached for the blankets. Instead, her husband peered at her legs and moved his hand between them searching for…something!

"No blood this time," he announced as he finally threw the blankets over her. "Do you have the need to heave?"

Completely confused by this change in him, she blinked several times trying to understand. "I feel no need to vomit." Shaking her head, she pushed herself up to sit and pulled the blankets with her. He slipped from the bed and reached for his shirt and plaid that lay on the floor. "Should I?"

"Ailsa told me that you were not well after I left you last night. She told me you slept on the floor. I am trying to make certain you are well so that I can leave."

The hint of embarrassment filled his face as though he only just now realized the words he'd blurted out and how they sounded. Then he gazed at her and she knew he was waiting on her answer…so he could leave.

Mayhap the experience had not been better for him? This second time had been an improvement for her, though still not something she longed to do as so many others seemed to. Her husband did not waste time on it, finishing the task and going to his own chamber or wherever he needed to go.

"I am well," she said, giving him the words he seemed to be waiting for.

He tossed the length of plaid over his shoulder, nodded

to her and turned away. The door was nearly closed when she remembered.

"Laird? I would speak to you about my brother," she called out. Sliding from the bed and tugging her shift down over her legs, Jocelyn reached for the loose blanket at the foot of the mattress and threw it over her shoulders. "I tried to see him today, but no one would let me."

"Lady, can this not wait until the morn?" Filled with frustration, his voice warned her to do as he asked. A tightening in her stomach told of something worrisome coming.

"Nay, laird, it cannot. Where do you keep him? Why did you not allow me to see him today?" She stood in front of him now, for he had stepped back into the room and pushed the door closed again. Then she asked the question, the one burning inside of her all day. "Is he dead?"

"Nay, he is not dead. I thought Duncan assured you of that?"

The plaid hung over his shoulder, covering most of him, but when he placed his fists on his hips, it did not hide the muscles and strong form of his arms or legs. The dark hair on his chest continued down his stomach and farther even, his thighs were sprinkled with it. The bronze shades of his eyes, she realized now, changed with his mood. Just a few minutes ago, Jocelyn caught a glimpse of them and they reminded her of the hues of autumn in the forests around her home—browns and golds and flashes of auburn. Now, they appeared the color of the hardened metal.

"He told me only that he was alive and said you would tell me the rest," Jocelyn explained. Then she wrapped the blanket tighter around her, pulling her own inner strength closer, too. "The simple truth is usually something I can contend with more easily than falsehoods or fiction, laird. Just tell me where Athdar is."

Her husband nodded and crossed his arms over his chest now, less intimidating than his previous stance, but a message to her of his impatience with her. She did not care at this moment. 'Twould be better if he learned how to deal with her now than later.

"I released Athdar yesterday after you spoke to him. He is even now traveling toward your home…rather your family's home."

"You sent him away without letting me see him?"

"You did see him and speak to him and know he was well. Once I knew that you would honor your vows, I sent him home."

Tears began to fill her eyes and her throat tightened. "You have held him for several months with no contact except your offer of a bargain to release him. You knew I wanted to spend time with him," she said.

"This was not a mission of mercy, lady. This was an alliance based on the exchange of goods and aid…"

"And people," she completed.

"Aye, just so. You were here. There was no reason to keep him any longer."

"Nothing else mattered to you." Jocelyn blinked as she made the accusation. This man knew nothing of her, nothing of how her family cared one for the other. He was cold and dark and had no emotions within him but anger and selfishness.

"Lest you think I did not keep my agreement, a troop of fifty MacLerie warriors preceded him to your father. With those soldiers traveled more than thirty carpenters, stonemasons, bricklayers, builders, blacksmiths and other workers needed to repair and rebuild your village and keep. Supplies filled ten wagons with more promised next month." He came closer and menaced her with his nearness. "All of that mattered to me, lady. All of it."

Not allowing him to scare her off, she asked the other questions that would predict her future here. "I am bought and paid for now. What happens next?"

"I continue to visit your bed or you mine until you bear me at least one son, though more would be better."

He paused then as the pain of being needed only as a brood mare hit her and seemed to think on his words. No hint of a family of her own to care for. No hint of being involved in his or his sons' lives.

"Then, you can go back to your family if you'd like."

Jocelyn clenched her teeth against his words. Never had she felt so inconsequential before. Yes, she'd asked him for candor, but this brutal assessment was more than she expected or deserved.

Even though she knew her marriage to Ewan was planned for the alliance it represented, the warm feelings between them gave promise to her role as his wife and the mother of his children. This alliance gave her none of that. With the pain still tightening around her heart and soul, she lashed out.

"Did you make the same offer to your first wife?"

Moving faster than she thought possible for a man to move, he reached her in a blink of an eye, his hands on either side of her face and his body against hers. His gaze burned into hers, a fury she'd never seen blazed within his eyes. But, it was his voice, lower, almost a whisper, that struck the deepest fear.

"Do not speak on a subject about which you know nothing." He leaned in closer, his breath hot against her cheeks. "Do not say her name to me or anyone else here," he whispered through clenched teeth, squeezing her face to make his point clear and his anger known. "Do not even refer to her in your words to anyone."

He released her and she stumbled, her legs would not hold her steady and her knees shook. Jocelyn fell before him and she waited for the blow to come. The stories had been passed from clan to clan throughout the highlands since Kenna MacLerie's death. The stories of her horrible death, or murder as most said, in this very keep. The rumors of the violent arguments that ended with a broken body at the bottom of a staircase. All for the want of a son.

Jocelyn had dared the Beast and would not live to tell of it. Her family would be disgraced by her failure and the treaty broken. Bowing her head, she tried to placate him without words. Mayhap he would accept her acquiescence as an apology? She dared not say anything—his ire spilled out in waves over her and Jocelyn knew she worsened the situation rather than made it better. Her hair fell about her face and tears poured from her eyes.

Everything she'd gone through would be for naught. Her brother and clan's lives forfeit for her willfulness, foolish behavior and childish wishes. She dared not breathe.

Connor could not believe her boldness. Each of their encounters seemed to end badly and this would be added to that tally. He knew she would press about her brother, but he wanted her to realize 'twas over and done—Athdar on his way back and she in her place here. From her brother's words about her, there were no maudlin feelings between them so this constant fretting was for naught that he could figure out. But women, he knew, had such soft ways of thinking about things that men had not the time to consider and they turned most things to something they were not. Apparently, this was a weakness of hers as well.

He stepped back and watched as she huddled on the floor before him. Her body shuddered and he shook his head at how this situation had gotten out of his control so quickly. Thinking that she would appreciate his candid words, he'd gone on about the marriage contract. Not even thinking on the cost of this to his soul, marriage to her had cost him and his clan much—in manpower, goods and protection.

This was not what he wanted between them. Fear and loathing he could get tenfold from many in his own clan and outside of it. Part of him burned inside at the thought that she'd believed the words spread by his enemies. Part of him was not surprised at all. But the disappointment tearing through him was a revelation.

Leaning over he grasped her shoulders and pulled her to her feet, holding her there until he felt her grow more steady. She did not pull away from him, but with her head still bowed, he could not tell if she was crying or something else.

"This is not what I want between us, lady. You asked for honesty between us, and now you have it. Mayhap more than you were prepared for?" He paused and waited to see if she would look at him. When she did not, he continued, "Remember, though, that our marriage contract's terms are no different than most of our standing and position. Accept them as such and we will deal well together."

She looked at him then, a quick glance lasting no more than a second, and then she met his gaze straight-on and not flinching. Tears did track down her cheeks as he'd suspected, but she did not appear to be crying now. Connor released her and watched as she wiped her eyes with the corner of the blanket she held now like a shield around her. A nod, a slight one at that, was her only answer, but he took it as that. These confrontations needed to end.

"I will leave you to rest now," he said, more than ready to make his way out of here. "Unless you have need of Ailsa?"

She did not lower her eyes. Instead, she watched him as he would watch a ill-tempered dog, afraid it would strike at any moment. Her lips pressed tightly together as though she feared opening them. Her gaze assessed him and narrowed and it followed him as he moved toward the door. Finally, the lady shook her head and whispered her answer.

Many words raced through his thoughts, but they seemed too trite or calloused or nonsensical to him now. Better to leave in silence than be thought a fool. The urge within him to offer some better measure of comfort grew from some unrecognizable place and startled him. The many months of contemplation of this step—taking a wife—were supposed to have prepared him for this. And yet, if he was not careful, the same trap would open and catch him in its grasp.

Connor had nearly not survived the last time and would avoid it again with every part of his being, with his last breath and bit of strength. Maintaining a distance was essential to his plan this time.

A few steps and he was out of the room. Pausing in the small chamber, he wrapped his plaid around his waist and belted it in place. Only as he began the trek down the stairs did he realize that his boots were someplace in Jocelyn's room. He would retrieve them or send someone for them in the morn. An escape, once made, should not be compromised.

He met Ailsa at the bottom of the tower where she paced. He shook his head at her antics. He needed nothing to draw attention to his comings-and-goings to his wife's chambers and Ailsa did just that.

"If your old bones can climb the stairs and you wish to, you can check on the lady before you retire for the night. You will find her in good stead, I think."

"That was my intention," she argued back.

"Then I leave you to it," he said, with a bow to her.

He waited for her to make her way up the flight of stairs before deciding that he did not wish to return to his chambers yet. A short while ago he'd been exhausted and ready for sleep. Now, a restless energy burned in him and sleep, he knew, would elude him for some time.

The night was not so cold nor he so old or infirmed that he needed boots to walk outside, so he followed the corridor toward the kitchen and left the keep. Walking toward the guardhouse, he breathed in the crisp air and let it soothe him. He climbed to the battlements and spoke to those on duty for a short time. Then, walking to the corner farthest from the guards, he stared out into the night.

The full moon's rays spilled over the ground and reflected off the surface of the river that meandered down the valley below the castle and past the village. The winds here were stronger and buffeted him as he watched the clouds move across the moon and then off again. The coolness and moisture in the air spoke of a turn in the weather, not unusual with summer coming to an end soon.

His lands spread out before him and he squinted into the distance, knowing he could not see the limits of them even from this high place. The last lairds had consolidated many holdings into this one and he would strengthen and keep it for the clan until his son took the high chair from him. His son.

It had to be. She had to give him a son.

And once she had done that, he could finally enjoy everything that he'd worked toward, everything that had cost so much in toil, wealth, lives and souls. Too many vows were made over this and he could not retreat from those.

He needed a son.

His words about her returning to her family after giving him heirs had not been meant to be cruel. Indeed, if she was still unhappy here, he would allow her to go back to the MacCallums or even retire to a convent. He thought those choices were kinder than forcing her to remain here if she wished to leave. Connor would explain that to her once she settled into her place here.

Chapter Seven

Ailsa woke Jocelyn just after dawn the next morn and Jocelyn decided to break her fast in the hall with the rest of the keep rather than in her chamber. Dressing quickly, she followed Ailsa down the tower's steps and into the hall where many MacLerie soldiers already ate. Peering over their heads, she noticed that the laird and his cousin were already seated at the high table.

Walking between the tables and the wall, she skirted those servants carrying trays to the other tables and made her way to the front of the chamber. Climbing the steps, she crossed behind the table and sat on the stool next to the laird. She thought he may have offered some greeting, but all she heard was something mumbled between spoonfuls of porridge. A servant placed a bowl before her and then reached over and moved the honey and cream closer to her. No sooner had she added them to hers than her husband stood at her side.

"I will return this night," he said, bowing slightly and turning to leave.

Between the surprise and the clamor made when dozens

of soldiers stood as their laird did and prepared to follow him, Jocelyn never got any words out. Caught with the spoon between her bowl and her mouth, she stared at the procession as they moved past her at a quick pace. All she could do was watch as the hall emptied of everyone but a few servants and the steward.

Only Ailsa remained nearby. She did not think the old woman had eaten yet so Jocelyn told her to sit.

"My thanks, lady, but I have already eaten."

"When did you do that?"

"At my daughter's cottage, lady. In the village."

"You have a daughter? Why did you not eat here where you live?" She shook her head—it made no sense that the woman should trudge down to the village to eat before carrying out her duties here.

"I do not live here in the keep, lady. I have not for several…some time now."

Ah, Jocelyn thought, since the last Lady MacLerie was alive. Finishing her bowl, she drank down some ale and nodded to the servant waiting behind her. "So, you come here each day and leave each night?"

"I have only had duties here since yer arrival, lady. The laird asked me to serve ye until an appropriate maid can be found."

Considering the events of these last few days, Jocelyn was glad that no *appropriate* woman had appeared, for this one, with her knowledge and easy manners had helped her in more ways than any young girl could have. Although the wife of the MacLerie should be accustomed to having a servant at her side every waking moment, the daughter of the poor MacCallum laird was not.

Jocelyn had many duties in her father's house and those

had increased as her mother's health declined. So few servants remained as her clan's fortunes diminished that she, along with a few other women, made most of the clothes her family wore. Not unfamiliar with hard work and many tasks to fill her hours, she found not being busy or apparently needed much more difficult.

"I did not know, Ailsa. Does your daughter have bairns?" she asked.

"Aye, lady, she has four now with a wee one just born a fortnight ago."

Jocelyn thought on her words for a moment. Ailsa lived with her daughter who had five children to care for. It would have been Ailsa's place to help her daughter until she could care for the children herself. Instead, the laird had summoned her back to serve his new wife…who could care for herself if given the chance.

"Ailsa, you should return to your daughter. I am certain she needs you more than I do."

"I could not do that, lady. The laird would not look kindly on my neglecting ye." Ailsa shook her head as she spoke.

If she was certain of anything, she knew that this woman did not worry of the laird's displeasure on her own account. She worried that he would be angry at his wife for countermanding his orders and wishes.

"I would like to see the village today, Ailsa," she announced a bit louder now. "Would you show me the way?"

Everyone there knew she'd explored and examined every inch of the keep and castle grounds these last two days. The village was the next logical place for her to go, if she needed some activity to keep her attention. And, if they just happened to go to Ailsa's daughter's cottage and spend some time there with her, then so be it. Who could argue?

"If ye wish, lady." Ailsa looked a bit suspicious, but did not say nay.

"Come then. I am finished here and the weather looks favorable for a tour of the village. And let us get some food from the cook. I am sure we will miss our noon meal and need some sustenance for the day."

The old woman looked at her with disbelief on her face, but did not stop her from making her way to the kitchen and presenting a list of foods she wanted packed in a sack to take with them. The cook's expression reeked of thinly disguised insolence, but he complied with each of her requests. Soon, they were halfway down the path that led first to the river and then crossed a stone bridge into the village.

Pleased that Ailsa had not yet guessed her true intentions, Jocelyn listened as the woman pointed out the various cottages as they passed and introduced them to many others as they walked the paths through the large village. Weavers, seamstresses, tanners, butchers, everyone Jocelyn would have expected to live in or at least work in the keep were here in the village.

Women with children of all ages walked the footpaths, on their way from errand to errand. Ailsa told her their names and their husbands' names and who among them worked the fields surrounding the village and who were warriors in the laird's service. After the emptiness and sullen feel of the keep, the number of people and their prosperity and obvious contentedness surprised her.

Soon, she was able to hasten their arrival at Ailsa's daughter's cottage and Jocelyn was glad for it. The poor woman did not look well and struggled with feeding the bairn. The other little ones scrambled over to Ailsa as they entered and grabbed her happily.

"This is my daughter, Margaret," Ailsa said, nodding at the young woman who held a baby at her breast. Ailsa greeted the other children—touching the head of each of them, smoothing their hair and stroking their cheeks. And smiling.

So much love between them all! It made Jocelyn ache for her mother's touch and soft words now. Had it been a full sennight since she'd spoken to her mother? The journey to Lairig Dubh took her four days and then the day she arrived and was married, the next day and the one yesterday. And she'd never had the chance to give Athdar any words of greeting to send back to her parents.

"...Peggy is the youngest and Brodie is the oldest."

Jocelyn forced herself from the sad thoughts of her own mother and smiled at Ailsa and her daughter. "I ask your pardon for taking your mother from you when you needed her most, Margaret."

Margaret, sitting on a small pallet in the nearest corner, blushed and shook her head. "Nay, lady. 'Tis my failing that takes her from yer side at all. She would hear of no other in her place when we learned that the laird would marry."

"I am honored at such service, Margaret. And not prepared for such attention. I was raised in a much smaller clan and home than the MacLeries here in Lairig Dubh and am accustomed to caring for myself."

Jocelyn realized that Ailsa still stood by the door as though they were stopping for only a minute. She smiled at the children and lifted the sack she'd insisted on carrying. "I brought some food so that we could share our noon meal."

Ailsa looked puzzled and Jocelyn urged her to her daughter's side. "I can feed them while you help Margaret and the bairn." Exposed to bairns in her parents' home, Jocelyn felt quite comfortable gathering them all together and handing out chunks of bread and pieces of cheese and apples. They ate hungrily, as children always do, and soon the cottage quieted as all their mouths were busy with food.

As Jocelyn watched, Ailsa took the bairn, changed its wrappings and held her up against her shoulder. Patting the bairn's back, Ailsa rocked and hummed a soft song. Margaret accepted some of the bread and cheese and began to steer the three younger children to their pallets—rest time for them.

"Brodie? Here now, take this pail and get water for us."

The boy jumped up, clearly relieved that he would not be forced to remain with his younger sisters. "Aye, ma," he said, accepting the bucket that seemed too big for him.

"You ken the right place?" The boy nodded. "And come right back, Brodie," Margaret ordered, her voice too full of love to be as stern as she probably wanted it to be. Too much love in it to be hard.

Overwhelmed by maudlin feelings, Jocelyn opened the door of the cottage for the boy and watched him go, running off down the path.

"He can do that?" she asked, blinking back the tears that threatened.

"Aye, lady. He looks forward to it each day for it gives him the chance to play for a time while the girls rest." Margaret reached for the babe and settled her on her own shoulder now. "My thanks for the food. And for bringing my mother to visit."

"I did not bring her to visit, I brought her to stay."

"But, lady, I canna'," Ailsa argued. "The laird will not be pleased."

"He is busy enough not to notice. And I am quite able to occupy myself. Stay here now," she urged. "If you must, check on me later after Margaret's husband returns."

The old woman looked as though she would argue, but then she gazed around the small room and nodded. She was needed here more than at Jocelyn's side. Margaret looked extremely pleased to know that she would have her mother with her, as she should, for it made it possible for her to get some much-needed rest and still have someone to care for her children.

"I will take my leave now," Jocelyn said, walking to the door.

Jocelyn escaped and walked quickly along the path that led to the center of the village and back to the castle on the hill. The clouds fought the sun for control of the skies now, but it was glorious for a highland afternoon. Dropping her shawl off her shoulders and allowing the breezes to catch her hair, Jocelyn crossed the bridge and watched young Brodie frolic with other boys at its base on the edge of the flowing water. Brodie caught sight of her and waved to her. Waving back, Jocelyn turned to make the trek up the hillside to Broch Dubh.

The tall tower and walls threw dark and foreboding shadows down the valley and she shivered as she came closer to it. 'Twas as though the whole of it carried the same black pall over it as its laird did. Even when the sun burst through the now-thick layers of clouds, its rays did not disperse the somberness of it. Somehow it was appropriate—a dark, forbidding lair for the dark, forbidding beast that prowled it.

As though just thinking of him had the power to conjure him, the MacLerie was there in the path before her. Man and horse blended together, their coloring nearly the same and, from the snorting and stomping of the stallion, their temperaments were as well. He pulled the reins tightly and brought his mount under control.

"Have you lost your way, lady?" he asked.

Arching her neck back to meet his gaze, she shook her head. "Nay, laird. I am on my way back from the village. I know my way."

"Where is Ailsa? She is supposed to be at your side." He looked around her and back on the path.

"She remains at Margaret's cottage."

"She serves you, lady," he said. His horse grew restless and managed to shake its head and roll its eyes as though sensing his master's growing irritation.

"Ailsa serves me by giving me some measure of privacy."

"Privacy? For what do you need privacy?"

"I plan to return to my chambers and rest awhile," she said on a sigh. He would argue every word she said, every point she made, would he not? "I do not need a maid to sit outside my door while I rest, but Margaret can use her help. It seemed the right thing to do."

He did not respond, but seemed to consider her words for a few moments. The sun hid behind the clouds once more and the wind turned chilly. She tugged her shawl back up onto her shoulders and lifted her hair free of it.

"Come, then. Give me your hand and I will take you back to the keep," he finally answered, reaching out for her hand.

She gave him her hand, placed her foot on his and let him pull her up on the horse behind him. The stallion was not used to carrying two and it shifted under them. Her husband held her hand and guided it around his waist while she arranged her skirts. Once she placed her arms around him, he nudged the horse into moving.

Although not intentional, Jocelyn could feel the power and strength in his back and his arms as he controlled the huge horse on the trail. Even through the layers of shirt and woolen plaid, his body gave off heat and she allowed herself to lean against him as they rode. She lowered her head and rested it on his back, too. He was strong, she did not doubt it as she felt his muscles gather and flex against her.

But in spite of his obvious advantages over her physically, he had yet to use it against her. He had not forced his way into her bed or assaulted her in any way. The MacLerie had strength and knew how to control and use it. As did any intelligent man.

Now, he smelled of a masculine mix of leather and wool and some elusive scent that was his own. A potent mix, she breathed it in and remembered the way he felt inside her, moving within and without, touching her there and easing his way deeper and deeper.

Jocelyn shook herself from this reverie to find they'd arrived at the keep and one of the stableboys stood waiting to help her from the horse. Her cheeks filled with heat at her wayward thoughts and she took a moment before accepting the boy's assistance.

Once on the ground, on her own feet, she adjusted her dress and shawl and then looked up at her husband. His eyes blazed now, and she knew that he'd been thinking of the same matter as she. Her mouth suddenly felt filled with sand and she swallowed to easy the dryness there.

"I will not return for the evening meal as planned, lady."

"I will tell the cook," she answered, pleased that her voice gave no sign of the turmoil within.

"Wait for me."

She made no mistake that he referred to holding the meal. His words were more an order than a request, but she sensed once more that he would not force her did she say nay. She caught sight of the way his plaid tented between his thighs, revealing much about his thoughts and plans, and glanced away before answering.

"Aye, laird."

He nodded and pulled the reins, guiding the stallion away toward whatever duty he had then. She watched him ride away and hoped that no one had witnessed their exchange.

Jocelyn spent the rest of the day resting and reading the precious book she'd discovered and waiting for the night. Ailsa did return to the keep to ready her for bed, but Jocelyn managed to order the woman back to her family.

And in the dark of the night, before the moon rose over the horizon, her husband came quietly into her chambers and into her bed. More insistent than their first couplings, this one lasted only a few minutes before he spilled his seed within her. And, as before, the same tension that began during their ride back to the keep, grew inside her at his touch but did not go away at his release. After asking about her condition, he climbed from the bed, threw his plaid over his shoulder and left her.

It was the next day, after a restless night without much sleep, that she realized something peculiar about their joinings—not once during their encounters did he kiss her mouth. As she walked through the keep and yard, down the path into the village to Margaret's cottage, it seemed that everyone else did. Husbands leaving to their duties, young men stealing kisses from maidens, even mothers and fathers kissed their children.

But her husband did not kiss her.

Chapter Eight

"Brodie!" she said sharply. "You should not carry such tales."

"But lady, 'tis true. Robbie told me his sister is carrying."

Her warning aside, she absorbed every word he spoke of the personal and intimate lives of those living here. The boy's face shone with the enthusiasm of one who has knowledge that no one else has…and wants to share it. Jocelyn now spent her mornings in Margaret's cottage or visiting one of the other women in the village and her afternoons, when the weather permitted it, walking with the boy to collect water for Margaret. In truth, it allowed her to learn so much about the people who belonged to her husband's clan. Brodie wasted no time each day as they left his cottage in gifting her with the latest bits of gossip and news from the village.

Her most difficult task was not laughing or scowling when she met the objects of his news. He dragged her along a different trail to the river's edge every day, so she met many of the inhabitants over the course of this last sennight. Mostly the women, for the men were off on their duties, be it in the keep or in the training yards or in the fields. Many of the women tended the fields, too, except those with infants or needed to tend the sick or old.

As the harvest approached, more and more would be called to help and she could feel the anticipation growing as the days shortened. Storehouses would be filled to bulging and the butchers and pigstickers would begin their plans to separate the herds of cattle, goats and swine, and then kill and preserve what they would need for the winter. Feathers, lard, grain and more would be used or stored for the clan's needs.

Even boys like Brodie, and his closest friends Robbie and Jamie, would be given jobs soon. Mayhap that was why they ran and played and swam and chattered like magpies every moment that they could?

"And they're no' married, Robbie says," he whispered, telling her the choicest part of the gossip now, "for he is married to Elspeth already!"

"You should not repeat such things! Surely the laird would not be pleased."

"The laird doesna come here often, lady. If I am quiet, he will no' hear me."

Jocelyn laughed then, remembering thinking those same thoughts when she and Athdar ran wild as children. If they spoke quietly, if they did not do something in their father's sight, if they were careful, they would not end up in trouble. With the wonderful innocence of children, they ran and played and gossiped just as Brodie did.

Now, looking at this as an adult, Jocelyn was struck by other facets of the story. Who would care for the bairn? Who would care for the girl involved? Her father would have stepped in and made provisions or forced the man responsible, married or not, to provide.

She'd not seen her husband act as laird, other than training his men or riding out to seek out those who attacked his village in the south. Her clan's elders met frequently and had played a part in the arrangements that brought her here. 'Twas said that his elders brought their pressure to bear and forced the MacLerie to wed again, though after living with him for even this short time, she doubted anyone could force that man to do anything he did not wish to do.

Truthfully, from the time when she'd found her way here to the village and both Margaret and Ailsa had taken her into their care, she hardly saw her husband do anything at all. Well, except for *that*. And *that* did not matter since she kept her eyes closed through most of it.

Brodie continued to chatter away as they found his favorite spot on the riverbank and found his friends, too. The three boys differed from each other in all things— Brodie, tall and thin, dark-haired and quick-witted, Robert, of medium build with pale hair and a loose tongue, except near her, and Jamie, shorter and heavier than the other two and with bright red hair and freckles that matched. Jamie never seemed to talk much, but it did not stop them from being friends and spending every minute possible together.

They took turns dipping their pails in the now-cooling water of the river and splashing it over each other. She laughed watching them and tugged off the covering she wore over her hair. The married women in the village wore the same handkerchief over theirs and since she was trying to fit in, she followed the custom. The few finer veils she owned did not hold up well when walking or working there.

Jocelyn leaned over and dipped into the water with her hands, drinking it and going back for more. Then she splashed some of it on her cheeks and throat and neck to cool her skin. Soon, she thought a good time had passed for Margaret to rest, and Ailsa as well, and she directed Brodie to fill the bucket.

The sounds of an approaching party on horseback startled her and she stumbled as the group broke through the trees at the edge of the forest across the river. More than thirty by her count, mostly older and gray, but a few young warriors, too. They gave her little notice as they rode on toward Broch Dubh. A short time had passed when the voice behind her surprised her.

"Lass?"

A man about the laird's age but much taller stood there, just watching her. His stare was intense and his strength obvious. He'd shaved his head so there was no way to tell what color his hair would be, but his green eyes were clear as they met hers. He crossed his huge, bared arms over his muscular chest and his legs, encased in tight trews, rippled as he walked.

When he took a step toward her, she felt as though she was being hunted. His male grace and lethal power made her breathless. At the moment when fear began to tickle her nerves, he smiled and nodded and he held out his hand. As anyone would when faced with a predator, Jocelyn took a step back.

"Here now, lass. I only wish to meet ye," he said. His deep voice sent shivers down her spine. No man should be this attractive and so dangerous at the same time. "Ye must be new here for I dinna recognize ye."

It was a dance between them—he stepped closer, she

moved back. Unfortunately, with the river at her back, she had not far to move. Part of her was tempted to cry out to Brodie to get help, but before she could a more familiar voice broke in.

"She *is* new to the village, Rurik. You are addressing Connor's new wife," Duncan called out from on the bridge.

He sat on his horse and apparently was enjoying her discomfort, for his smile beamed at her. Somehow though, she knew she was safe, for he had pledged to protect her as his laird's wife. The man called Rurik examined her closely then burst out laughing, his loud amusement echoed over the river and even up the hill to the castle.

"Great Odin's ballocks!" he cried out. "She is a beauty!"

Jocelyn knew her appearance would never cause men to write poetry about her, but she did not appreciate being humiliated over it. Shocked by his words, she stumbled now and would have fallen into the water if he'd not reached out and grabbed her first. Once her legs steadied and landing in the water was no longer a threat, she tried to loosen his hold on her. As though giving her the message that he would decide when to free her, his arms flexed and tightened and she noted the old-style markings that encircled each of his upper arms.

"You must be thinking of the laird's first wife. I've been told that she was a great beauty," she blurted out, finally pulling free. Then she remembered Duncan sitting not far away. Mentioning *her* was against the laird's commands.

He threw his head back and laughed again. "Ah, lass, I knew Kenna and she was magnificent, but not like you." Before she could scamper to a safe distance, he reached over and grabbed her by the hips, pulling her to him. "You have a womanly beauty that promises heaven between your thighs and many bairns at your breasts."

Before she could think of words to say, Rurik disappeared. Shaking her head, she watched as Duncan, now off his horse, grabbed the man from behind and threw him to one side. Threw him! Then Duncan grabbed Rurik's tunic, whispered furiously to him and shoved him away.

Duncan remained a shield between them, until Rurik gained his feet, gifted her with a wicked smile and dusted himself off. Whistling to his horse that stood in the road, he turned and strode off up the hill, never looking back. Breathless from the encounter, Jocelyn straightened her gown and shawl and waited for the usual biting words from Duncan. 'Twas then that she noticed the onlookers from the village.

The boys immediately imitated Duncan's hold-and-throw on each other and both Robbie and Jamie ended up in the water. A few women stared at Duncan and a few watched as Rurik disappeared up the path to Broch Dubh. How were there more women in the clearing now than before? As she looked from the river's edge to the crofts lining the path, there were quite a few villagers observing them.

"Did he frighten you?" Duncan asked, looking over her from top to toes. "Rurik generally means no harm."

"Who is he? Who were those people?" Jocelyn nodded toward the road.

"They are more of the clan, come to advise the laird as is their custom." Duncan held out a hand and guided her from the water and the raucous boys. "Rurik is the personal guard of one of the elders."

"His name does not sound Gaelic or Lowland."

"He comes from Orkney, where the Vikings still hold power. 'Tis rumored his mother was a Scots woman kidnapped on a raid and kept as the jarl's slave. Rurik appeared at Dougal's keep and pledged to serve him."

"Dougal? One of the elders?"

"Aye, the husband to Connor's aunt."

She shook her head, not quite believing that the incident had occurred at all. "A Viking…" she murmured.

His words and actions had been surprising. His earthy words about her appearance and some mysterious appeal that he could see when no other did unnerved her. Duncan watched her as she thought on this stranger's arrival.

"I must find Connor and tell him that the elders are here," he said, mounting his horse and taking it under control. "And more importantly that Rurik is with them." He turned the horse and nodded to her. "And they will want to meet you, lady."

"I doubt that, Duncan. Surely they will only want to know that your laird has taken a wife as they ordered."

This time the surprise was clear in Duncan's expression. She had learned much in this last week from Brodie and the villagers who were much more forthcoming in speaking of the laird and his first wife than either the laird or his man was. Only Ailsa held her silence and did not speak, even when prodded by her daughter to answer some question.

"I think they want to meet you, lady. I would suggest that you come back to the keep and prepare yourself for the evening meal while I find your husband."

She loathed admitting he was correct, so instead of words, she simply nodded. He tugged the reins and rode off, not sparing any more time or explanations for her.

Well, she'd wanted to gain a place here and this may be her chance to do it. Looking at the soiled gown she wore and knowing that her face and hands carried nearly as much dirt as Brodie's did, she knew she must get back and clean up before meeting the elders who held so much influence over her husband.

She would not summon Ailsa, she decided as she climbed the hill, but would seek out Cora, the girl who served her during her first few days here. Although the girl had caused some problems, she had proven herself dependable over this last week in Ailsa's absence. Part of it was that Cora feared the laird and his men. But, when the girl kept her company in her chambers, she was pleasant enough and seemed eager to learn Jocelyn's ways.

The clamor in the yard as she passed through the portcullis told her that the elders had not yet gone inside. Skirting the group as stableboys ran to them and as the steward and others called out greetings to them, Jocelyn was almost to the keep when the cheering and yelling grabbed her attention.

Following the noise, she stood stunned as Rurik came running around the corner, into the yard with her husband in pursuit. Onlookers jumped away from them, but then turned and ran behind them, as though this was some sport. Much like hunting a wild boar, the crowd chased after the two men, and Jocelyn found herself caught up in the frenzy.

Rurik stepped over the fence as though climbing a stairway and the laird did not hesitate in his pursuit. Soon the MacLerie came within his sword's length and attacked with a frightening ferocity. Having never seen a true battle, Jocelyn wondered if this was one. She shook her head. Too many stood by observing and not running to their laird's side. This was something else.

The clanging of swords echoed through the yard and Jocelyn swore she felt the shock of each blow. How they could even lift such blades, let alone thrust and pummel with such force, she did not know. Minutes passed and still they fought. Sweat poured down them as the swordplay continued with only a momentary pause for them to remove their tunics. Then Rurik turned and pivoted and went on a brutal attack.

The sun came out from its cloudy cover and its light glinted off their skin as they moved to and fro, back and forth. Although taller by at least a hand, Rurik did not put the laird's form to shame. Indeed, they appeared both to be wholly male, wholly in warriorlike form, wholly and wildly attractive to the women, the now large group of women, watching this combat. To a one, they shielded their eyes to see better and licked their lips as the men bent and twisted and feinted around the yard before them.

Those men and boys watching seemed to be divided over which of the men they supported. Convinced they cheered at each swing and hit of the sword, she shook her head and stayed away from the growing crowd. Turning back, she closed her eyes as Rurik struck a blow that drew blood on the laird's chest. Instead of stopping as reasonable men would if this was not true battle, the daft creatures continued.

That was when she noticed him.

Her husband.

This was no longer the serious, sullen man who greeted her with a blank stare at her morning meal or the brooding man who came to her bed. This was the Beast of the Highlands, meeting the challenge of an equal, and possibly his better, without fear or favor. He laughed. He cursed. He smiled both grim and determined and even glared at his opponent.

Filled with a vitality and drive she'd not seen before, he met Rurik blow for blow and drove him back until the challenger stood forced up against the outside wall of the stables with a sword at his throat. Jocelyn held her breath, not knowing the outcome of such a display. Would Rurik accept defeat? Would the laird be vanquished instead? The crowd's response grew in intensity until she winced and wanted to cover her ears.

'Twas then that Duncan appeared at her side.

"I was too late to warn him."

She nearly turned to face him, but did not want to miss the outcome. "Warn him? The laird or Rurik?"

"Your husband," he answered. Jocelyn did glance at him now, for his voice carried a trace of impatience as he spoke.

"Ah," she nodded now. This was an old practice between these two men. From the reaction of those watching, it had happened many, many times. From the hale and hardy appearance of both adversaries and the quickly formed crowd, it was an anticipated event when Rurik arrived at Lairig Dubh. "This is a common occurrence then?"

"Not of late."

"Why would you warn him? 'Tis obvious that he relishes this challenge."

The crowd erupted then in applause and cheers as the laird and Rurik tossed their swords to younger men and clasped arms as comrades once more. Although the onlookers began to disperse, many soldiers entered the yard and celebrated his victory with the laird. Rurik had his own admirers, though a number of them were of the female persuasion. Jocelyn shook her head in dismay.

"Rurik tends to forget himself for the challenge. He goes on the attack whenever and wherever he finds Connor. There have been a few injuries and some damage…" His words drifted off and Jocelyn was left to imagine the worst in such a situation.

"So, this is just entertainment then? Has the laird never heard of having a bard tell a good story or a harper play a fine tune? 'Twould be much less dangerous than this." She held her hand out to indicate the swordplay they'd watched and shook her head, not understanding the appeal of such a thing.

"More than entertainment alone, lady. This is training so that I may defend all in my care if need be."

His voice came from behind her and she jumped. Damn Duncan for distracting her and allowing the laird to sneak up. Facing him, she found traces of the warrior she'd just witnessed in his gaze. The excitement there was dissipating with each step he took toward her. What was it about her that displeased him so?

"Damn ye, Connor. Tell the truth to yer wee wife," Rurik said, coming up behind the laird. "Ye relish the chance to best me in a fight. Though, of late, ye have no' been able to do so."

The smile that filled the Viking's face gave no indication that he had just lost this fight. Indeed, if she'd not been watching, she would have thought the MacLerie the defeated one from the attitude of this man. The only sign of the impending attack was when Duncan scrunched his eyes closed. Rurik reached out, wrapped his arms around the laird and they both landed in the dirt at her feet. Grappling and wrestling for dominance, several minutes passed before they both collapsed, dust-covered and exhausted from their play.

This time, when he met her gaze, her husband looked much younger than he usually did. He seemed to not only enjoy the fighting and rolling in the dirt, but also it appeared to take away some of the tension in him. Did she need to keep Rurik near to beat the breath out of the MacLerie so that she would get a glimpse of this other part of him?

The meeting of their eyes, although certain it was only momentary, stretched out between them. Jocelyn felt this power and strength of his, controlled as he kept it, every night when he climbed into her bed and between her thighs.

What would it be like to touch his skin and feel it ripple beneath her fingers? What would it feel like to have him tussle with her, rolling over and under, pressing against her, into her, joining with her with the same passion and drive for life that he'd displayed here for everyone to see? Her mouth watered as though she'd been presented with her most favorite food, but her throat dried and tightened. Where did these thoughts come from?

Duncan coughed and the sensations beginning to pulse through her disappeared. Feeling the blush rise in her cheeks, she worried that everyone, especially her husband, could read her thoughts. The men stood and brushed the worst of the dirt from themselves. Several others approached and the laird nodded at them.

"Dougal, this is Jocelyn," he said, pointing at her. His

voice even and his expression shuttered now, all sign of interest in her gone…as was the usual situation between them. "She will meet the rest of the elders at the meal."

The grizzly older man, barrel-chested with spindly legs and his graying red hair splayed out like he'd been caught in a storm, simply looked her over from her head to her toes, pausing briefly she noticed on her breasts and hips, and snorted.

"She'll do," he said in a voice that matched his gruff appearance.

Then, with a shrug but without another word, he and the laird and the others walked away, leaving her alone. Peering around her, she noticed that the women followed along, chatting and laughing, but none looked back to see if she trailed behind. Only Duncan remained, and after glancing at her with a questioning gaze, he ran off.

Turning around and around, Jocelyn felt a twinge within her. Something that felt much like her old temper sparking to life again. As the only daughter of the Mac-Callum, she expected better treatment than this. As the wife of the MacLerie, she was due it. 'Twas time now to have it.

She brushed her hands over the soiled gown she wore and decided that, for a successful plan, she needed to know more about the enemy. What better a time and place to learn than at the meal where the clan elders would be? With a purpose in mind, she walked quickly to the keep and up the tower steps to her chambers.

Someone must have noticed her arrival for Cora followed a few minutes later. Jocelyn had convinced Ailsa to remain with her daughter and apparently the laird had agreed to assigning Cora to her instead. Quiet and shy, the girl did not chatter as she helped Jocelyn wash and change the soiled gown for a fresh one.

During the last week, she had spent her mornings with the other women in the village and had used the time wisely, she thought. She'd helped with the mending that needed be done and cut and sewn three gowns for herself from fabric found in the storeroom at the keep.

The gossip and knowledge shared among them happened at as quick a pace as their hands passed the needle and thread through cloth. The only subject or person not touched upon was the laird's first wife. A few awkward moments occurred when someone by chance mentioned Kenna's name or referred to something from when she was lady of the clan, but Ailsa always seemed to guide their conversation into some different direction and past anything that made her ill at ease.

Now, Jocelyn chose the one she'd made in a pleasing green color and exchanged the plaid shawl she'd grown accustomed to wearing in the village for a simple belt. Her usual habit of sweating when nervous would keep her from being chilled.

After deciding to leave her hair uncovered and pulling the unruly locks into a leather tie and out of her face, she took a deep breath. This would be the first meal with the people who mattered most to her husband and, although he did not like her, she hoped they would accept her.

Cora walked close at her heels and moved even closer when the sounds of the hall reached them. Strangers made the girl uncomfortable and kept her within an arm's length when they were anywhere in the keep or yard. Jocelyn paused when she reached the entrance to the hall for a group of newcomers sat with the laird at a few tables and were in the midst of a heated discussion over the recent attacks on the other MacLerie village. Attacks that she knew not of and a discussion she was hesitant to interrupt or enter.

"I have ordered more men to the edges of MacLerie lands, but I will not engage in a war over a few head of cattle," her husband said. "I will discover their true aim by watching their methods and then we will intervene," he explained to those gathered there.

The MacLerie drank deeply from the cup before him and then answered each question put to him in a logical fashion. Without the facts of the matter she could not judge, but his defense of his actions and explanation of what he planned was concise and drew only praise from those listening. It reminded her of days long past when her father held his council. He had kept them safe then. The MacCallums had needed no other clan then for they had their own warriors and land and wealth.

A longing for home filled her heart in that moment. A need to see her family and to be part of it crushed her. The weight on her soul nearly forced her to her knees. Jocelyn clutched the edge of the doorway to regain her strength.

"I would say that they thought the MacLerie was too long a-bed with his new wife and had no fear of retribution." Rurik yelled out so that his voice carried through the hall and everyone there turned to look at her. Rurik, damn the man! stood and held up his cup to her. "To the lady Jocelyn!"

Those just arrived stood and raised their cups, but the MacLeries who lived here in the keep looked to the laird for direction. Unsure of whether or not to join in the cheer, a noticeable lapse occurred until the laird rose to his feet.

From across the hall, she could not see his face clearly, but his voice when he rose from his seat and called out her name spoke of his irritation.

"Here now, Connor. Let me bring the lady to you," Rurik offered and was halfway to her before Connor swallowed more from his cup. Any attempts to dissuade him from his intent were too late.

Jocelyn tried not to back away, but the man's very size still unnerved her. His manners did not help either. He boldly gawked at her, raising his brows and waggling them at her knowing that the others behind him could not see him. Poor Cora grabbed at her arm and trembled violently at his approach.

"Come, lady," he whispered suggestively as he held out his hand. Then he spied Cora behind her and stepped to the side to get a better view. "Who is this? A new lass in the keep?" Now he reached out to take Cora's hand.

"Rurik!" The roar shook the roof of the keep and made her wince. The laird stood and strode to where they were, calling out as he strode across the hall. "Leave the maid be!"

Rurik affected a pose of innocence, but the curve of his wicked lips destroyed any attempt to portray himself as that. He did stop reaching for Cora which was a good thing. The girl was white with terror and Jocelyn feared that she would faint.

"Cora, return to the lady's chambers now," the laird ordered as he took Jocelyn's hand from Rurik in his own. The girl might have been scared, but she was quick-footed, disappearing back into the corridor in moments. "The girl is not to be one of your targets, Rurik. Or you will find the vast hospitality of Lairig Dubh closed to you."

Jocelyn could tell from the emphasis he placed on the

word, that food and drink was not the hospitality Rurik sought in Lairig Dubh. And not what he would be denied if he disobeyed the now-angry laird.

"As you wish, Connor. The elders await."

Rurik smirked as he stood aside and let the laird escort her. She knew there would be something more and it did not take long for Rurik to begin extracting his retribution on her husband. Unfortunately, she heard every word.

"I dinna blame ye for no' wanting any other man to touch her loveliness or come too close to her. It must be," he paused, inhaled noisily and sighed loudly, "close to heaven in her arms."

Jocelyn stumbled and her husband clasped her hand to steady her. She could see, nay hear, his jaws grinding against each other. Rurik ignored the warning and continued his baiting.

"Those breasts," he whispered. "Those thighs. How many times, Connor, have ye died of pleasure between those thighs?"

Just when she thought him finished, he spoke. "See how her hips sway gently as she walks? Lovely curves."

She faltered then, trying to walk very stiffly and not let her hips move as they were accustomed to. In spite of knowing that this had little to do with her, the embarrassment grew and she felt her cheeks and face grow hot with it. A trickle of sweat gathered on her chest and slid down between the very breasts Rurik had just mentioned.

"And that mouth. Does she—?"

The question begun was never finished for the laird did take action then. The glare on his face made her glad that she was not, for this time, the object of his anger. She'd barely taken a step from his side, when he swung and knocked Rurik senseless with one blow. The big man crashed to the floor and the laird turned and, taking her by the arm, led her to the seat he indicated as though he'd not just knocked a man unconscious beside her.

If anyone there thought it unusual, no one said so. They left the man where he landed and soon they were all seated and the discussion continued. In spite of her attempts otherwise, her gaze strayed back to the unconscious man.

"Laird?" she asked. He talked on to the man across from her as though he'd not heard her. "Laird?" she repeated.

"Connor, I think your wife is speaking to you," Dougal instructed. "I thought she was calling out to your father, lad, but 'tis you she speaks to."

"Should someone not see to him?" she asked.

Rurik had not moved and, regardless of the embarrassment he'd caused her, she wished him no harm. There was, she suspected, a great heart under his outrageous and blatantly sexual misbehaviors. For though his size intimidated her each time they met, she knew she feared more the feelings he made her aware of than any fear of bodily harm.

The laird nodded to one of the men standing nearest to where Rurik fell. Rousing him from his stupor, the soldier shook him a few times until Rurik climbed to his feet on his own. Not sure what would happen now, Jocelyn watched as Rurik found his way back to his seat and joined back in the discussion, as though the episode never happened.

Turning her attention to the conversation, she listened and learned about her husband's, and her, clan. Jocelyn tried not to interrupt, but found that she had a few comments about the harvest and the placement of troops near the edge of her family's properties. The elders seemed to accept them, even encouraged her with questions. Soon 'twas time for the evening meal which passed much more quickly and pleasantly with guests there to talk to.

Even if they were all men.

Even if one made her feel that everything she did was appealing to him and if the one next to her did not.

Soon, the laird asked if she was ready to retire and she took her leave of those at the table. Cora met her in her chambers and after a busy day, she could feel the exhaustion closing in her. Climbing into the bed, prepared as Ailsa had instructed with hot, wrapped stones to warm her feet, Jocelyn discovered an unpleasant fact—her courses were upon her.

How did she handle this? Cora would die before carrying such a message to the laird. Did she go herself? Or did she wait for him to come to her bed and tell him then? Deciding on that, Jocelyn asked Cora to bring her the necessary supplies and then watched as the girl finished her duties and left.

She pushed back the covers, slid off the bed and wrapped a blanket around her shoulders. Tugging the cushioned chair over nearer the window, she sat in it, drew her legs up under her and tucked the blanket around her. If she leaned her head back, she could see outside and even glimpse the stars in the sky above Lairig Dubh.

The next moment, and it seemed to happen that quickly, her husband stood before her. She shook herself awake, not remembering when she'd fallen asleep, and tried to untangle the blanket, her legs and her shift. Unsuccessful at that, she met his gaze and shrugged.

"Why are you not in your bed?" he asked, nodding at the piece of furniture that held so much promise and so much disappointment for her.

"I am unsure how to say this. I am…" she began. Searching her thoughts, she could only think to say the words. But, before she got them out, he spoke for her.

"Breeding?" he finished.

His eyes filled with anticipation and a slight smile lifted the corners of his mouth as she'd not seen it before. Ah. She would disappoint him yet again when she gave him the truth.

"Nay, my courses have started."

As she expected, in a moment the look of expectation was gone, replaced with his usual brooding countenance. He nodded and looked away and she saw his jaws clenching. Jocelyn waited, not knowing what would come. The laird turned back to her after a short time.

"How long do they last?"

This was not a subject that she openly spoke about, let alone with a man. Thinking on the normal pattern of her last year, she answered. "Five days."

Her husband nodded and turned away. Covering the space to the door in three paces, he tugged it open and stood there, staring at her as though there was something he wanted to say. His actions spoke the words he did not—he left her chambers, pulling the door closed as quickly and quietly as when he'd arrived there.

So much for her plan for a place in his life. So much for hoping that a positive reaction from the elders would influence him in his feelings toward her.

When she did not hear any noise in the room outside her chambers, she slid her feet to the floor, untangled everything and climbed into the bed.

So much for her hopes of a real marriage. If she could not fulfill the one need he had, what good was she to him or his clan?

Chapter Nine

She should have been on her way by this time in the morning, but Connor had not yet seen her walk past the yard as she usually did on her way into the village each morning. The other exception happened yesterday—she left her chambers only for the evening meal and only, he suspected, due to Dougal's call for her. He stood by the fence that surrounded the yard next to the keep and glanced toward the door from the kitchen. The morning was half gone and she was still inside.

Connor called out instructions to several men in the yard and watched as they made corrections in their use of the long staff. Murdoch came searching for him about the amount of goods and supplies he'd ordered to be sent to the MacCallums, again, and Duncan found him there later. If they thought it curious or strange, well, they would not dare say so.

His mood since Dougal and the others arrived was not the best, even Rurik cut a wide path around him. After their initial combat and his lewd comments about Jocelyn, the rogue was seen only at meals and not often otherwise. He did not worry for he knew that Rurik would always find a place to rest his head or, more importantly to Rurik, his cock. A noise drew his attention and he turned and looked once more, but it was not her.

Damn! His plan was not going as he wanted it to.

Standing here, turning at every sound, waiting to watch her walk by without her even being aware of his observation, even that he knew her ways and the way she spent her days told him of his defeat. Connor was not ready to capitulate yet—too much and too many depended on his leadership and he could not have that clouded by the emotions that had controlled him in his previous marriage.

This approach was causing trouble, too.

Dougal had commented on it several times already and Rurik, damn his soul, had noticed it right away. Dougal, who always enjoyed the pleasantries and pleasures that women offered, whether those were a clean hall or a soft mattress beneath his old bones at night, mentioned the lack of those during this visit.

Rurik pointed out during their last brawl that Connor was the only one not speaking to his wife when she was present. And that was after Rurik insisted that she be present when the clan matters were discussed. The elders, Dougal, Black Ian, Old Lachlan and Lachlan the younger, Callum and Farlen of the Glen, did not object so neither could Connor. Mayhap this was their way of learning about her and her abilities?

"Ye glare doesna scare me off, boy."

Connor turned now to find Rurik at his side. He shook his head and waved Rurik off. "Leave me be."

"If ye are not having enough, just go and find her and bed her," Rurik advised. "'Tis the problem, no?"

"Not everything is caused by tupping a woman."

"True, but most things can be solved by it. If no' her, then one of the whores will take care of yer needs."

Connor groaned. "You have nothing else on your mind but who will you tup next and that is any woman who opens her thighs to you—for coin or not. Do you not care for anything more than that?"

Rurik laughed at his words. "I hunger for battle, but if I cannot get that, then the other is just as good. Since we canna plan the time of our death, I intend to enjoy as much of both before it happens."

"Go then, and be about Dougal's business. I care not for the subject or for your company."

"And ye be about the clan's," Rurik offered. "And that includes yer wife."

Pushed to the very edge of his control, Connor was tempted to teach Rurik the dangers of intruding on his personal life when the man pointed in the direction of the keep.

The woman under discussion left the shadow thrown by the keep and followed the well-worn path to the gate. Her head was down and she seemed to look only at the ground beneath her feet.

"What is wrong wi' her?"

"Wrong? I see nothing wrong." Indeed, he did not. Her pace was a bit slower, not as fluid, not as much of the sway as Rurik had mentioned before.

"She is no' as perky as when I met her a few days ago. Look, her face nearly meets the ground. Is she ailing?"

Connor could explain about Jocelyn's condition, but it was not a matter he wanted to discuss with her, or anyone else. Though, now looking more closely as she walked through the yard, he thought Rurik might be correct. She was different. Her shoulders slumped and her complexion was pale. With her head covered and wearing the worn gown she'd chosen this day, she looked more servant than lady wife.

Why did she not dress better? He'd provided ample gowns and the necessary bits and pieces to go with them since she'd arrived, but she insisted on wearing the ones sent by her family. Barely more than rags, they were.

Since she gave no sign of seeing them, he was willing to let her pass without saying anything. Rurik had other ideas.

"Jocelyn. A good day to ye," Rurik said, waving at his wife. "Are ye well, lass?"

Her steps faltered and then she stopped completely. Raising her eyes from the path, she nodded at both of them and waited.

"Say something to her, Conn," Rurik whispered so only he could hear it. "Greet yer lady wife." Rurik shoved an elbow into his side, urging him on.

Through clenched teeth, he whispered back, "I have nothing to say to her." Instead, he nodded at her and watched as she turned back to the footpath and approached the gate.

Rurik watched her as well, shaking his head and groaning as though in pain. Once she was through the gate, Connor found himself grabbed by the shoulders and shoved against the fence.

"And that is the other part of the problem. There is always something to say to a woman, especially yer wife." A strong shake accompanied each phrase now. "Ye look well, lady." Shake. "I did not care for the stew today." Shake. "Open yer legs and let me f—"

Connor threw off Rurik's hold and pushed him back. But Rurik's superior size and strength soon overcame him and he found himself in a vicelike stranglehold, with his feet dangling above the ground. As though to prove his point, Rurik shook him once more and breathing became difficult.

"There is always something to say to a woman," he growled into Connor's ear. A small crowd gathered and this was not their concern.

"Let me go, Rurik. Now." Connor tried to peel the warrior's fingers from around his neck, but could not loosen even one.

"Yer clan is suffering because ye are. Ye must let go of the past."

"Stay out of this," he whispered back. With the tight chokehold, it was difficult to force out the words.

"She could be the wife ye need," his fingers tightened. "She could be the wife the clan needs. And ye must be the leader ye were born and raised to be."

Then, as quickly as he'd gained control, Rurik let him go and dropped him to the ground. Taking several strides away, the Viking bastard spit on the ground and issued one more warning.

"I pledged to serve ye and yer clan because ye are a man worthy of my faith. Dinna make me change my mind. Ye dinna want me for an enemy."

Gasping to pull air into his lungs, Connor rubbed at his neck and throat. He leaned against the fence and waited for the burning to cease. As he did, he offered up every curse he could think of against Rurik under his breath.

Right now he was willing to kill the bastard for saying such things and for meddling in his life. He was laird and would make his own decisions about his life and his wife. No matter what Rurik said. No matter what the elders declared.

He was laird.

He'd had enough of all of them and decided to ride out to see how the preparations for the harvest were proceeding. That would take several hours and might delay him long enough to miss the evening meal.

"Back to your duties," he called out to those who still gawked at him.

They scattered at his orders and he made his way to the stables, saddled his own horse and rode off. The guards who eventually followed him, more likely than not at Duncan's orders, wisely stayed back a distance from him.

It did take hours to survey the fields, review the plans with Hamish and inspect the new mill upstream from the village. With the half moon sharing what little light it had, he rode up to the gates well after dark. He peered through the night and noticed Dougal standing on the battlements. His uncle waved to him, beckoning him to the heights of the castle wall, and Connor nodded to him.

His hours in the saddle after being throttled by Rurik caused him to think about how he handled many of the responsibilities of being laird. Rurik forced him to face the weaknesses of his leadership and it was not a pleasant task. For two years, he'd allowed conditions here in Lairig Dubh to slide until he barely recognized the home in which he'd grown to manhood.

In truth, once Kenna died, he wanted nothing to do with the place and only returned at his father's death. When it became the home to mostly those soldiers who fought for him, it worried him not. It suited him somehow to have Broch Dubh lose the softness of a woman's presence and become a bastion of male control. So long as his bed linens were clean and his food cooked, he was content.

Connor handed his horse over to one of the soldiers who guarded him and climbed to the top of the wall. Walking the perimeter, he met Dougal where he still stood. Only sure that he did not want to have the conversation about to happen, he knew he could not walk away.

"So, she is not carrying?" his uncle asked.

"Nay," Connor said, taking in a deep breath of the cool night air. "How did you know?"

"Yer aunt had the same look of misery aboot her when her monthly was on her. 'Tis usually a good time to go hunting." Dougal laughed and Connor chuckled.

Dougal turned and walked a few more paces away from the nearest guards. He nodded his head and Connor followed. No one should overhear the words about to be exchanged.

"She seems a good lass, Connor."

"Aye."

"Is that all ye can say aboot her? Many say ye have nothing to do with her." Dougal probed wounds that went soul-deep and Connor would not allow it without some resistance. Despite thinking on the very same questions on his ride, uncertainty still controlled whether or not he should discuss this with anyone. The tightening in his gut told him 'twas not time yet.

"I would say that you all meddled in my affairs and now I have the wife you ordered me to wed. Do not think to tell me how to treat her or what to do now."

"'Tis the clan's affairs we meddle in and we will continue so long as we think need be," Dougal threw the words at him. Then the old man let out his breath and shook his head. "Connor, ye know it can take some time to have a son."

"I think I learned that the first time. And I learned there is no guarantee of success." The bitterness spewed forth. He clutched the rough crenellation in the wall in front of them and stared up at the circular tower nearest to them. Had it just been fate that had guided their footsteps to that very tower? "And there is no guarantee that this wife will not end up as my first did—dead at my hands."

"Ye admit that her blood is on yer hands, then?" Dougal's voice grew softer. "I didna think it possible in spite of the rumors."

"You know the story, Uncle. She gave me no sons, no living bairns at all, we argued, I shoved her down the stairs, she died."

Dougal drew a breath in sharply at his words. They'd been easier to say than he expected. Mayhap the months and months of thinking on how to reveal it eased the way of them?

"I hear yer words, Connor, but canna believe them. Ye are not a cruel man. Ye loved K—"

"She died at my hands," he interrupted his uncle with his admission.

Dougal paced a short distance away, watching him even as he moved, and then returned to his side, searching his face as though trying to read the truth there. Connor hardened his face, not wanting to reveal too much.

"I willna believe it of ye. The elders did not make a mistake in choosing ye as laird. I did not make a mistake in urging them to."

"And if you did?"

"Tell me you dinna wish for the high chair? Tell me ye

are no' suited for it? Tell me ye could walk away from all of it—yer responsibilities, yer power…her," the old man challenged. "Say the word."

"I will not. I admit that I want it all. I was born to it and I want what my father wanted—I want to be the laird for the rest of my natural life. And there is no one in the clan or even the Highlands who would challenge me on this."

"'Tis true—ye are the most feared man in the Highlands." Dougal laid a hand on his shoulder and shook him. "Things must change here, Conn. The king will be ransomed back and take his place on the throne. The regents are anxious to consolidate control of the clans now. They will not grant the charter to a man who wanders his lands like an itinerant soldier, with a reputation for killing his wife. They will no' let ye pledge to him unless they believe ye are worthy."

"The MacLeries supported the Bruce and his father before him. He owes…"

"'Tis not wise to tell a king he owes a debt to anyone, especially one who doesna control the purse strings in his own country. Many good men have ended with their heads on the block for doing such a thing."

Connor did not wish to acknowledge this, but it was true. He knew the regents, on behalf of the imprisoned king, were dangling the same prize before him that they'd held out to others. The Highland way of life was changing and, with Scotland united under one king, even if that king was being held in England as a prisoner, the clans were accepting more of the practices of the Bruce's court.

Although his clan's claim to these lands went back for generations, possibly before even the Bruce's family entered England with William the Conqueror, now the king was issuing "charters" as though he owned the very land on which they lived. To remain a power in the west, the MacLeries must be part of it.

"Even if I do understand the necessity for submitting to the king, it does not mean I have to like it."

"Nay, nor do I. But this is what the clan needs."

Connor nodded but did not meet his uncle's gaze. This same discussion had raged from his father's time, nothing new to either of them. What was new was the presence of the woman in the far tower's highest chamber. His gaze moved to that place and he wondered if she was sleeping.

"I thought that ye accepting a bride was a sign that ye were ready for this. Was I mistaken in that, too?" Dougal knew how to aim and hit the most tender places with the precision of a master archer.

Connor was tempted to touch his chest to see if it bled. He rubbed the back of his neck and rolled his shoulders to release the tightness there. He supposed that in some way, his relenting in his opposition to the elders' demands over a wife gave that message. Mayhap he'd done it just for that reason, a way to say it without speaking the words. But, was he ready?

"Nay. 'Tis just that…." He could not find the words even now to explain the pain that lived so deep in him that he doubted it would ever be gone. His terrible reputation had kept all at bay and given him a way to store up his anger and grief, but now he needed to deal with his people differently. And without appearing weak.

"'Tis been a hard day for ye? I heard Rurik thrashed ye this morn."

Connor did laugh now. The battles between the Viking and him were the source of many stories and much interest. At the bottom of it was Connor's eagerness to test himself and his skills against a clearly superior adversary, only winning some of the time. Rurik, as he'd said this morn, did it because he loved the fight.

"Have a care, old man! You and he prick my pride too often these days. You may find yourself outside the gates if you continue on that path."

"Pah! Ye may try, but I think I could give ye a good fight even at my age." His uncle reached out and clasped their arms, hand in hand, forearm to forearm, and shook them. "I am for my bed now. Think on my words."

"I always consider your counsel, uncle. As I do that of the elders and clan."

They parted, Dougal leaving the battlements and Connor walking them most of the way around the perimeter of the castle. As he approached the stairwell, he realized that Dougal had truly not offered him many words to consider. Nay, his uncle had merely mirrored or repeated the thoughts that had plagued him for many, many months now. More importantly than any words, Dougal offered a reaffirmation of his faith, for his uncle did not believe him responsible for Kenna's death.

If it were only true.

His boots echoed in the dark corridors of the keep as he entered and then climbed the stairs to his chambers. He paused halfway up the steps and considered checking on Jocelyn. She still bled so they could not couple, but he wondered if the effects of her courses sickened her.

Connor shook his head. Not ready to consider a different approach than the one he'd adopted, he finished the walk to his room and sought sleep. He had much to think about, about the clan, their future, his future.

Chapter Ten

How could she ever look Rurik in the face again?

The bairn seemed to feel her agitation and whimpered softly. Jocelyn soothed the babe and adjusted her higher on her shoulder. Patting her bottom, she rocked a bit from side to side as she'd seen Ailsa do. Wee Peggy quieted and snuggled her face into Jocelyn's neck sending all sorts of strange chills through her.

The music of pipe and harp and drum blended together and moved out over the clearing as those gathered to celebrate the wedding of Robbie's sister listened and then clapped in time as the pace of the song picked up. She took a few paces away to a place that was quieter so that the bairn would not wake, giving Margaret and Hamish a bit of time to enjoy on their own.

Some couples, including Rurik and the widow Nara, danced to the music. Some ate food from the tables near Margaret's cottage. Some sat in small groups and chatted, soft or lively, as the children chased each other or played. In spite of the abruptness of the wedding and in spite of it happening just as the most time-consuming part of the harvest began, the villagers and even a few of the elders, joined in the celebration.

Rurik's wink as he caught her eye startled her, and she jostled the babe who began fussing. Turning away and moving farther into the shadows, Jocelyn hoped to hide the revealing blush she was certain stained her cheeks now. 'Twas Rurik's way of letting her know he'd seen her earlier in the woods.

The man was…a rogue. Her efforts to remove the image emblazoned in her mind of the last time she'd seen the couple earlier this day were a failure. Even now, hours and many attempts to forget later, she could hear the sounds that drew her gaze to that place—a small thinned-out copse of trees in the meadow off the path leading from Margaret's cottage to the mill road. She'd walked the same babe as she now held.

At first glance, all she saw was the back of a very powerfully built man, naked and gleaming with sweat in the rays of the sun that dappled the ground there beneath the canopy of trees. He crouched on hands and knees and it was only after he moved that she realized that a woman was beneath him. The shaved head and unique markings that circled his arms revealed his identity and Jocelyn watched as those arms flexed, keeping his weight off the woman. Nothing touched between them except that he devoured her with his mouth.

Jocelyn's own breathing grew shallow and an odd ache grew in her as she watched Rurik dip down and kiss the woman over and over, each one different from the last or next. He laughed once, a husky, passion-filled laugh, that the woman returned. Jocelyn could not hear the words, but the tone between them spoke of a challenge made and resisted. He taunted, she resisted. They played at love.

How did that feel? Her own mouth tingled as she watched him continue the obviously wanted assault on the woman's mouth. There were moments when she could see him tasting the woman, sliding his tongue over her lips and then thrusting it inside her mouth. He moved his tongue the same way her husband moved his...well, moved during their own coupling.

Since her husband never kissed her mouth, she could only imagine what the woman beneath Rurik felt as he kissed her deeply again and again. 'Twas then that she noticed the woman's fingers and toes.

With each kiss, the woman's hand clutched at the ground under her and her toes curled tightly. Her legs moved restlessly and then she let out a groan and Rurik just laughed. He must be winning whatever the challenge was. In the barest of moments, the woman grabbed his face, pulled it down to hers and kissed him with the same hunger he'd shown. Rurik responded by sliding a hand under the woman's skirts, lifting her legs and plunging inside her. Now, the woman's hands grabbed at Rurik's naked back and slid down to his buttocks. Her toes still curled and she cried out at his possession.

Swallowing deeply, Jocelyn realized she was gawking at something best left private. As she stepped back to turn away, the couple moved, rolling until the woman, Nara she now recognized, sat over Rurik's legs. Although her skirts now covered more of them both, Jocelyn could tell by their sliding and grinding movements that they were still coupling. Nara threw her head back and Rurik feasted on her neck and shoulders and naked breasts.

The place between her own legs grew wet and the nipples of her breasts tightened as though her body recognized the very feel of what was happening between Rurik and Nara. Desire flowed through her as she thought of her husband and herself in place of these lovers. Her husband, naked and sweating, kissing her…everywhere.

Jocelyn knew she must leave but hesitated to move away, not wanting to be seen. The bairn stirred then and her only choices were leave or be seen watching. When Rurik leaned back on his elbows and guided Nara over him, she took advantage of their movements to cover her own. Clutching Peggy to her shoulder and ducking behind some low-hanging branches, she hurried back to the path. The echoing cries of passion fulfilled followed her back to the cottage and her own heart beat rapidly at the sound of it.

Rurik's wink just now spoke of her failure to make it away unseen. He knew she'd been there and what she'd seen. Damn the man! She watched as he now walked with Nara, hands entwined over to the food tables. His behavior surprised her, for she had heard the whispered tales of his prowess and popularity among the unmarried women of the village. Rurik stayed at Nara's side through the evening, speaking to others, but remained always with her.

'Twas as though he did not notice the beauty that the other, younger women offered. Nor their fair figures. When one girl, with much laughing and teasing, asked him to join the dance, he looked to Nara with a soft gaze for leave to do so and then returned to her side as soon as it was done. Strange. She thought he availed himself of any willing woman and yet his behavior today would say otherwise.

"Here, lady," Margaret pulled her from her thoughts and reached out for Peggy. "I will take her now."

"Are you certain?" she asked. Without some task holding her here, she should return to the keep and her chambers. Her empty chambers.

"Aye." Jocelyn turned the infant and Margaret lifted her with a mother's gentle touch into her own arms. "'Tis time for her and the other wee ones to go to bed." Hamish reached them and nodded. "My thanks, lady, for all of your help."

Jocelyn walked to the table and poured a cup of ale for herself. Hoping it would temper that restlessness that seemed to fill her, she drank it down quickly and filled the cup once more. Turning around, she saw an empty place among the married women and decided to join them before returning to the keep. No sooner had she walked to that circle when Brodie and his friends circled her, tugging on her gown to gain her attention, telling her of some new secret and seeking her approval of their adventurous plans for the next day. Even Jamie squeaked out a few words, a sign of her acceptance into their lives.

The clearing quieted and Jocelyn looked up to find her husband standing at the edge of it, glaring as was his usual custom when she was involved. The music ceased and everyone stood and acknowledged his presence. As the men walked to greet him directly, the women held back, some with fear in their eyes and others with pity as they looked from him to where she stood.

Farlen's man Angus approached him first and leaned in to say something that no one else could hear. She knew not why he had agreed to this marriage, but his behavior toward the girl involved and during the proceedings showed no hesitation or resistance to the decision or the outcome of it. The laird answered also in a low voice and then Angus motioned to his new wife to come over to where they stood. The MacLerie crossed his arms over his chest and waited, which she had no doubt contributed to the girl's lack of enthusiasm in heeding his call.

Angus held out his hand now and Siusan hastened to his side. The laird spoke to both of them now and, though his features could not be called warm or welcoming, Siusan's fright left her face as she listened. Tempted to move closer, Jocelyn decided that would not be wise. She'd not spoken to her husband in three days and only saw him when she passed him in the yard or hall. Then he shook Angus' hand and nodded to Siusan before walking purposefully toward her. The boys, so lately her friends, now took off at a run in the other direction.

"Lady," he said, nodding and stopping in front of her. He stood so close that he blocked the sight of the others who undoubtedly stared at the two of them.

"Laird," she replied, wiping her palms on the front of her gown. He made her nervous. Though she had lost most of her fear that he inflict some form of bodily harm to her, his words could still wound her.

"You were not in your chambers."

"There was no reason to be in my chambers, laird. And when I was invited to join the people in marking the occasion of Siusan's marriage, I saw no reason to refuse."

His eyes darkened, but not in the fearsome way he did most times that made the color there change to that hard, metallic shade and appearance. Nay, something else lay there deep in his gaze, something she could not identify.

"I was in your chambers, lady. Looking for you. "

Ah, her courses were done and it was time for him to return to her bed and his duty of procuring an heir. "You never come to my chambers until the middle of the night." She placed the goblet that she did not realize till then that she was clutching in her hand on the table. "I did not realize I was expected to sit and wait there for your arrival. Did you think I had gone home?"

Connor looked around and knew that everyone within the clearing was listening or trying to listen to their words. Not certain what reaction he'd expected from his wife, he only knew that this was not it. Her lips took on a firm set and her shoulders straightened giving her the appearance of one preparing for battle.

"This is your home now, lady. There is no other place for you to go," he whispered. "This is not a discussion I wish to have here."

He was the one who should be angry. Returning to the keep for his meal, he found it deserted, but for a few servants to see to his needs and those readying for sleep on the floor of the hall. When he went looking for Duncan, the elders, even Rurik, he discovered that they were all in the village for the wedding celebration. Climbing to her chambers, he found an empty room when he'd expected his wife to be waiting. Early or not, she should be there.

The idea that she had left him had played on his thoughts for a time, a very brief time, but enough to concern him nonetheless. First, she'd given him no sign of anything but her acquiescence to anything he ordered or asked of her.

Right then. He allowed the moment of concern to pass and realized that she spent so much time lately in the village, her presence at the wedding would be expected. Still, although he'd had a hand in finding a suitable groom for the girl involved, he never considered attending the ceremony or the celebration in the village. He fulfilled his duty as laird by simply making it happen.

Connor stood up straighter and cleared his throat. He heard a few gasps escape from those watching, mostly female noises, and shook his head. Other than bellowing out his commands and not taking anyone's counsel well, what had he done to deserve this fear from them?

Well, other than killing his first wife for not pleasing him.

Anyone present in the keep that night, especially the women and he saw a number of them here now, still thought him a danger. Their expressions filled with pity when aimed at his new wife as though they expected him to raise his fist and strike her dead at any moment. No matter that he spent his days and weeks and months seeing to their needs, their protection. They feared him. He turned to meet their stares and some even backed away. Connor'd brought it on himself, he knew, but it still rankled him.

Turning back to his wife, he held out his hand to her. In spite of anything else she was feeling or what her posture said or the message given by her absence from her chambers, she did not hesitate in giving hers to him. He led her past those still gaping and stopped before the new couple.

"The lady and I give you our best wishes for happiness, Angus." He paused and nodded at Farlen's man and the man's new wife before placing his hand over the lady's and walking back to his horse. Reaching it, he looked around for hers and saw none. "Why do you always walk here when a mount is available to you?"

He slid his foot into the stirrup and mounted his horse. He leaned down and held out his hand so she could climb up. Although she watched his every move, her attention

Take a look at what's on offer at
www.millsandboon.co.uk

MILLS & BOON®
Pure reading pleasure

My Account / Offer of the Month / Our Authors / Book Club / Contact us

All of the latest books are there **PLUS**

- **Free** Online reads
- **Exclusive** offers and competitions
- At least **15% discount** on our huge back list
- Sign up to our **free** monthly eNewsletter

- More info on your **favourite authors**
- **Browse the Book** to try before you buy
- **eBooks** available for most titles
- Join the M&B community and **discuss your favourite books** with other readers

was elsewhere. Then he also noticed the voices that carried through the trees to them.

"Angus is not the only man here who will end up in a wife's bed this night," called out one man.

"But Angus will stay there longer than…." The words ended and Connor suspected that there was a gesture made because laughter erupted after a pause. "He finishes in his wife's bed faster than he does with a whore."

If not for her stricken face, he would have run back and throttled the ones who spoke such insulting words. "Come, lady, the night grows colder and you have no cloak." He pulled her forward and sat her across his thighs instead of letting her sit behind him. Connor loosened the plaid he wore and, after settling her in place, wrapped the end of it around her. He guided the horse back to the path and chose a safer subject to speak about with her during their ride to the keep.

"So, why is it that you do not ride here?"

"I am accustomed to walking, laird." She shifted in his lap, sliding on his thighs. "My father did not have horses to spare for my use in going from keep to village. Only his soldiers had horses."

"He has them now as do I. It is not fitting for my wife to walk these roads like a servant." He felt her stiffen in his arms and knew he'd now added insults to those already received. "I only mean that I will order a horse for your use whenever you need it. Speak to Guthrie and he will choose a mount for you."

She did not reply, but only nodded. They rode up the hill quietly for a few minutes and through the gate into the yard.

"Your maid should accompany you to the village," he said, thinking of how the wife of a powerful laird should act. "'Tis her duty to be at your side."

She sighed first, almost a dreamy sound, except he could hear the frustration in it. Then, as though speaking to a child, in the same tone he'd heard Ailsa use on her daughter's children, she spoke. "I dismissed Cora when I needed her services no longer, laird. She is at my beck and call every waking moment and I gave her leave to enjoy the festivities in the village this evening."

He rode up to the steps leading to the keep and stopped. She'd been leaning against him, molding to him, as they rode and he did not want to let her go. And that was exactly why he did.

She let go of the plaid and took his hand to guide her to the ground. Once there, he let the wool fall over his lap. He was not disturbed that his body was beginning to crave hers or reacted to her nearness. After not having a woman on a regular basis for three years, it was only right that his should become accustomed to having one again. These last five nights without access to hers simply demonstrated his need for the normal relations of a wife.

"I will take the horse to the stables."

She nodded but did not move away.

"Await me in your chambers."

This time she did, turning and walking to the entrance into the keep quietly. The guard stationed there opened and closed the door for her without a word or glance at her. Connor loosened the reins and guided the horse to the stables.

What kind of strange feelings bedeviled him this night? He thought on it as he gave his mount to the boy on duty at the stables and walked back to the keep. Looking up, he noticed the light coming from her chambers.

They would begin again this night in their attempts to

create a babe. Perchance once this duty was fulfilled and he had a son or two to insure that his clan would have a heir to follow him as laird and to carry his name and the titles that the king would be granting him soon, they could find some middle ground between them. Once his position and name were secured, he could soften and allow her closer.

Whether by fate's hand or just chance, a noise drew his attention to the other tower in the keep—the one between where his wife's chambers were and the other one where his were. The one in which Kenna had met her end. Shaking his head, Connor accepted the peculiar reminder that to soften in this would be his downfall again. He simply could not allow that again.

He did plan, however, to implement some changes here at Broch Dubh. Dougal's threat to send for his wife Aunt Jean if he did not bring the keep back under his control and make it a place worthy of the soon-to-be Earl of Douran gave him pause. Murdoch could handle what he needed done so there would be no need for his aunt to visit.

"Connor?" Duncan walked up behind him. "Where is Jocelyn?"

Connor nodded in the direction of the keep. "She is inside. Why?" Duncan frowned.

"So is Leana," Duncan said in a low voice. "With Eachann."

One of the village whores was plying her trade in exactly the same place that he'd just sent his wife. When he had time, he would knock the smug expression from Duncan's face for saying that this would turn into a problem for him. For now, he needed to at least warn his wife or guide her away from the situation.

Tugging open the door, he ran down the corridor and entered the great hall. Peering into the darkened chamber, he caught sight of Eachann and Leana, lying together, spent, on the floor in the corner. No other noises disturbed the quiet save those that one would expect from a large number of sleeping men.

Moving onto the tower steps, he climbed to her room and found the door closed. Taking a breath, he knocked and lifted the latch. Unsure of what faced him, he entered her chambers.

Chapter Eleven

She stood in only her shift near the window. With the shutters inside thrown back against the wall, it was opened wide enough to allow the strong breezes from outside to flow in. If she knew of his presence, she gave no sign, standing silently and letting the wind blow over her, whipping her hair, now loosened from the braid she usually kept it in, over her shoulders. It fell in ripples down her back, each new breeze causing waves to pulse down its length. Connor closed the door and waited for her to say something, anything, that would give him a clue as to her condition.

Had she seen Eachann in the hall? Was she shocked by it if she had?

He approached her and called to her softly. "Lady? Are you not chilled from the wind?"

She shook her head, eyes still closed. "The winds soothe me."

"I fear you might take ill from such a chill. Come away," he instructed.

When she did not heed him, he took another step closer

and reached around her to close the panes of glass. This chamber had been his mother's when she lived and these precious glass panes, a gift from his father to her to mark the occasion of their marriage.

He moved away and she followed him, step for step, as he walked to the side of the bed. The shock of finding her so close caused him to stumble and sit on the bed. When he would have spoken, she reached out and placed her fingers on his lips stopping him. Then, she leaned over and put her mouth to his.

Untrained though she was at this, her innocent touch caused heat to pulse through him. He sat unmoving, knowing that this intimacy was precisely what he wanted to avoid with her. When he did not respond as she must have wanted, she pressed on, slanting her mouth over his and touching, with so gentle a caress that he might have imagined it, her tongue to his lips. Her hair fell around them and he could feel it teasing his face.

He hardened and wanted nothing more than to fill her right then, but he knew that control once lost would be impossible to regain. He reached up to move her hair from his face, but its softness tantalized him. When her kiss became more aggressive, he knew his battle was over. Wrapping her hair around his fists, he pulled her in, let his hunger free and tasted her mouth fully. If it frightened her, she gave no sign, indeed, he felt her soften and accept it.

Loosening his hands, he reached down and lifted her shift up, sliding it over her voluptuous hips, over her flat stomach and across her breasts. She did shiver now, but he knew it was not cold but heat that made her tremble. Her nipples became hard and tight and he could not resist rubbing the linen over them and making her gasp…into his mouth. A second's separation and she stood naked before him.

Was this truly the first time they'd kissed? Her lips were soft and her mouth hot as she slid her fingers now into his hair and held him still. He teased and touched with his tongue, sucking on hers when she moved into his mouth's reach. With his hands free, he tore his own clothes free and threw them aside. Once undressed, he opened his legs and pulled her forward and over him until he could wrap his arms around her.

As they met skin to skin, chest to breasts, she pulled back and gazed at him with passion-filled, yet confused eyes. At once hoping and fearful that she would see the folly in this intimate play, he lifted and turned her so that they lay side-by-side on the bed. Now he could touch her. The wetness between her legs said her body was ready for him. Her shallow breaths and little moans as he slid his hand down her body said 'twas so. But, the sounds that came from deep in her throat as she pulled his head down to hers spoke clearly of her readiness.

Connor spread her legs and knelt between them, leaning over so that she could continue the kiss she seemed to like so much. He mimicked it first with his hand, sliding it down into her cleft, then out again, slowly then faster and faster. She panted now into his mouth, unable to keep their mouths together completely, as he brought her to the edge of her own completion.

She reached up now and placed her hands on his hips. Again, her innocent touch sent him reeling. Thrusting into her, he filled her to her core and was gifted with the tightening of her impending release. He gazed into her eyes and knew she did not recognize what was going to happen.

"Shh," he whispered. "Let it happen."

'Twas not his custom to do things halfway, so he paced his movements within her, watching as she moved restlessly beneath him, eyes now closed and gasping with each thrust he made. His own release approached, but he waited for her this time. Reaching between their bodies, he searched for the tiny bud that would send her body to its own fulfillment.

It took only a touch before he felt the waves within her. Her body arched and bucked under his, and as he drove deep inside her, the tightness and the movements within brought him to release. She cried out once and then again as the spasms took over and his seed spilled out, filling her. Still she arched against him, her legs trembling and shaking, her hands now on his thighs holding him inside. With a groan, he felt the last gush of seed and he collapsed on her.

Taking in a deep breath and then another, he lifted his weight from her so she could take a breath. She lay unmoving now, but as he moved to lie beside her, his hand grazed her belly and it rippled and contracted under his fingers. Realizing that her body wanted more, he pressed the palm of his hand against her mons and watched as she arched one, then twice more. Truly spent, she turned to her side and collapsed next to him.

Stunned by what had just happened, Jocelyn could not even open her eyes. No muscle within her would obey her mind's command to move. Nothing had prepared her for such overwhelming sensations and results. The kisses, his mouth on hers and the touching of their tongues and lips, were beyond anything she'd thought possible to feel. The explosion of pulsing and vibrations and waves of pleasure could not be explained.

Waiting until she could breathe again before facing her husband, she tried to sort out her emotions over what she had provoked him to do. And the reason why she had to provoke him to share this pleasure with her.

He thought so little of her, cared so little, that their couplings before this had led only to his release. Now what the women of the village whispered about and spoke of with awe in their voices made sense to her. And he had such little regard for his unwanted wife that he had not shared it with her until now. Until she had pushed him into it.

Jocelyn reached up and pushed her hair out of her face and sat up. Spying her shift on the floor, she slid from the bed and tugged it back in place. Then she looked at her husband who still lay unmoving on her bed. She did not know of her tears until he asked.

"Have I injured you in some way, lady?" he asked when he finally met her gaze.

"I wish you would not ask that," she replied, wiping roughly at the proof that he could indeed hurt her. "Would it truly matter if you did?" A pause first then he answered.

"Aye. I do not seek to mistreat you."

"Yes," she said, "you have hurt me. Grievously, although I hate admitting it to you now."

His face tightened into an anxious mask and she stared at him directly now. The time for dissembling and timidity was over. How dare he treat her as though she had no consequence? How dare he allow his indifference to withhold something so…so…incredible. As her husband, it was his duty to instruct her in the marital duties, and knowing she came to him a virgin, was even more a reason to introduce her to the passion that could be had in such intimate endeavors.

Instead, he'd given her only what was necessary to gain his pleasure and to fulfill his need for a son. The barest of attentions to ease his way, and granted hers too, but nothing more. His men said he spent more time when he coupled with the village whore than he did in her bed. She'd heard also that he'd spent the whole night with Leana and with several other women in the village when he desired physical relations.

Now, he entered her chambers in the darkest part of the night, climbed into her bed, spilled his seed in her body and left. Like the phantom of a husband he was. Granting her a half measure of what she could have, what *they* could have.

"How, tell me, how have I hurt you? Your actions invited me to this," he said waving a hand at the bed. "Was I mistaken in believing that you sought something more than our usual joining?" He sat up now and reached for his own garb. He stared at her and then nodded. "What is this about? What is the cause for your agitation?" He ran his hands through his hair as she knew he did when confused and then narrowed his gaze at her. "You saw Eachann with his whore and sought to taste of that ardor yourself?"

Heat filled her cheeks as the image of the soldier and the whore flashed through her thoughts. Their bare limbs entwined, skirts up and trews down, his muscular buttocks thrusting and pushing himself in deeper with each plunge, and the throaty moans that erupted as the man pushed between the harlot's legs and filled her woman's core.

Even knowing that they were not alone did not stop Eachann from drawing out sounds of pleasure until the woman's whimper built into a husky keening. Jocelyn could not turn her eyes away and the couple moved faster and faster, together and apart, over and over, until the sounds of his completion, *and the woman's,* spilled out, echoing through the great hall.

For the second time in only a day, she'd witnessed another passion and been reminded of her failings as a woman and wife. Nothing like that had ever happened to her. She'd complied every time that he came to her bed and he'd never offered her that kind of pleasure. Or perchance she was incapable of pleasing him in that way?

"Aye, I saw them." She would give him the truth although he was not honest with her, in bed or out of it. "And I wondered why my husband withheld such a thing from me."

"Withheld? Is that what you think?" He strode over to her and grabbed her by the shoulders, pulling her closer until she could feel his breath. "You would have me treat you like a whore?"

She raised her hand to slap the insult from his mouth, but his iron grip was faster and Jocelyn found herself staring into his angry face. Pulling from his grasp, she searched his face for his reaction. Doubt tore through her. Her body wanted more, that which he demonstrated he could give. But, her heart and soul hungered for something else. Tonight though, as her body still thrummed with the satisfaction of a passion and a release unknown to her before, she knew that she did want it all. Not the disregard, but the enthusiasm and hunger that she'd felt beneath him and that which he chose not to give.

"I would have you treat me as your wife."

"You are my wife, lady." She thought it a disastrous attempt until she noticed that his hands shook. Taking a deep breath, she dared him.

"Then why, husband, have you never shown me this pleasure in our marriage bed?"

He started to speak several times and stopped each time. "But you like it not." He frowned and dropped his hands from her. "I try to finish as quickly as possible to spare you the unease of it." He turned from her and ran his hands through his hair. Facing her, his expression turned to one of complete confusion now.

"If hesitant, 'tis only because I did not know what was possible between a man and woman," she explained. "I have heard about it. And I have heard it. I have seen…"

"What have you seen? What have you been told?" he asked.

"It is difficult not to witness it when you see men and women together. Kissing. Touching. Loving." She shrugged. "'Tis a topic of great interest in the village. The women discuss it at length. I saw Rurik and…" His darkening gaze stopped her.

"Rurik? You saw Rurik doing what?"

"'Twas by accident and only for a moment," she explained, purposely diminishing the incident as it had happened. "In the woods near the village. He and…a widow from the village were…tupping. I stumbled on them and left."

Could he tell her body remembered all it had seen of the encounter? Even now, her nipples tightened under her shift, *again,* as she saw in her mind the Viking pleasuring the woman.

"Did he know you were there? Damn him, of course he knew." Her husband closed his eyes, clenched his fists and offered a mean curse. Then he focused on her. "Did you say they speak of these matters in your presence? You are a lady. You are the laird's wife. They should not be talking of such things to you."

He was directing her attention away now, bringing up a different aspect so he could avoid what he did not wish to discuss…from what he did not want to do. Obviously his actions tonight had been a lapse in judgment or control, one she could read in his expression and his manner he would not allow again.

Even sharing something as basic and primitive as lust would be something between them. Many marriages began with less and led to more and there had been that chance for them. But, no more. She stepped out of his path and pulled the door open herself.

"Good night, laird," she said, all the time turning her gaze from his and waiting for him to leave. She'd humiliated herself already by being so forward, but she would not beg him for something he wished not to give…to her.

"Lady, you do not know what you ask of me," he said. A hint of desperation crept into his voice. "'Tis not that I do not want to…" He stopped now, clenching his jaws together as though trying not to let an explanation out.

"Cannot or will not, the result is the same, laird." She did glance at him now and saw a pain so deep that it nearly drove her to her knees. "You have made it clear to everyone here that you have a wife you do not want. My folly in believing it could be different between us was out of ignorance and innocence, but I will learn." Jocelyn motioned her hand toward the door, hoping he would leave now.

He walked to it and turned to face her. "Jocelyn," he began and stopped, startling both of them with his use of her name. Now that she thought on it, he'd used it only once, when introducing her to his clan on their wedding day. Although many others called her by it, he did not. Another sign of his disregard.

"Good night, laird."

She realized then that she never used his given name for other reasons—discomfort, not knowing his mind on it, unfamiliarity. He barely stepped through the doorway when she slammed the door closed, the sound of it somehow soothing her.

Once alone, Jocelyn felt better in some strange way. She'd stood up to her husband. She'd expressed her anger at his treatment of her. She'd learned what a powerful and awesome thing pleasure could be.

Jocelyn blew out the remaining candles in her room and climbed into the bed. Assailed by the memories of the day and overcome by the raw new emotions she'd felt, she closed her eyes and prayed for sleep.

If he'd been one step closer, the door would have crashed into his face. Shaking his head as he walked down the stairs, Connor recognized his failings at once. Somehow in but a few short weeks, he'd broken three of the rules he'd set up when agreeing to this marriage.

First, he allowed her to initiate a familiarity and intimacy that he swore would not happen between them.

Next, he tried to explain his actions to her.

Then, he wanted to explain his actions to her.

And all of it, each step toward a destruction as certain as that which happened in the Garden of Eden, began with a kiss. He knew how Adam felt and offered up a prayer for both of their souls.

The path down the stairway of one tower, through the

corridor and up the stairway of another, seemed to take longer this time. His body, spent in a release more satisfying than any recent ones, moved with a lethargy unfamiliar to him. Reaching his chambers, he opened the window and stood before it to test if it would soothe him as it had his wife.

Jocelyn.

Her name was Jocelyn.

Truly, it had slipped out in that moment of weakness. Unprepared for what happened between them and ill-equipped to deal with her anger and her hurt, he'd let his guard down and spoken it.

And it felt good to say it. Soft like she was in his arms. Strong like the side of her she showed him tonight with her righteous ire. She was correct—he was giving her less than her due as wife. To protect himself, he did what was necessary and no more.

Now, though, after experiencing what could be between them, he wanted it. Oh, not the emotions, but the passion. Feeling her tense and tighten and then throb and melt under his touch was a wondrous thing and he knew he would enjoy it, what man would not? Still, he needed to keep this under his control.

And he needed to make other measured changes in the keep and in the village. Peering out into the darkness, the sounds of the continuing revelry could be heard in the distance. Fear could be useful, even beneficial against an enemy, but it was not the way he wished to control the clan. Generations of faithful bond and service held them together, for their common good.

Stepping back and closing the shutters, he thought on the first changes to be made. He would meet with Murdoch and Duncan to plan for moving most of the men out of the keep and into a barracks hall. That would solve a number of problems and begin the transformation of the keep into a fitting home for the Earl of Douran.

Connor poured a cupful of ale from the pitcher on his table and drank it while he considered the path he would take. The first change would lead to another and another and alter his life forever and break from his past in an ir-revocable way.

A deep, ripping pain shot through him and he realized that the one person who should be at his side through all of this, the one person who had planned and dreamed with him of all the possibilities ahead of them, would not know.

Kenna.

Taking another mouthful, Connor understood that he must also leave her behind in order to attain his goals. No one would dare speak of her to him, so that should ease his way a bit in this. His pledge at her death to never reveal the truth would stand. And though it was likely that Jocelyn would give him heirs and hold a place of regard and respect in his life, she would never have his love. Kenna's death at his hands destroyed his ability to ever trust in someone that much.

Nay, his heart would remain untouched by this new wife, even as his life and the clan's changed. He tipped the cup back and finished it. The next day held such promise for him and now he needed some rest to be prepared to face it. In spite of his intentions, he tossed and turned through the night.

Each time he closed his eyes, she was there. He saw her, felt her beneath him, heard her cries as she lost control and fell into passion's release. Her very presence in his dreams shocked him for he expected Kenna there as she was most nights.

This night it was Jocelyn.

And that signified how she was becoming part of his life even as he knew she must not.

Chapter Twelve

"Good morrow, Jocelyn."

Never expecting him to be lurking at the bottom of the tower stairway, she jumped when Rurik greeted her. Cora began trembling at the sight of his huge frame, but Jocelyn pulled the girl behind her at his approach. This morn, he wore a long, deep scratch and the hint of a bruise on his cheek. Another battle with the laird?

"Good morrow, Rurik," she said, tugging Cora's hand and trying to step around him. Unfortunately, he did not move from her path, indeed, he placed himself even more in the middle of it preventing her from going into the hall.

"May I speak to you for a moment?" he asked. 'Twas then that she noticed the somewhat sheepish expression on his face. "Alone, if possible?" He glanced at the girl and Jocelyn nodded, letting go of Cora. She ran off leaving Jocelyn to face Rurik.

"What is this about?"

Jocelyn looked at him and then could not help herself—she found her gaze drifting down his body. When she realized what she did, she forced it back up, but not before the heat began to fill her face. He wore a sleeveless tunic and his muscular arms with their tattoos were shown to their best advantage. Then, Jocelyn remembered what the rest of him looked like under his garments.

The rest of him.

He cleared his throat, drawing her attention and her gaze back to his face. "Nara is vexed with me," he said in a low voice. Leaning in closer to keep the words between only them, he continued, "It slipped out that ye had been in the woods yesterday and had seen…"

He paused and smiled at her. She thought he might be enjoying her somewhat obvious discomfort and he confirmed it by glancing down at himself and smiling again when her eyes drifted there, too. "Weel, I think ye ken what ye saw there."

Now it was her turn to try to clear her throat. She lifted her hand and fanned her face. "And Nara is angry?" She tried to concentrate on what could be the purpose of this discussion, other than completely embarrassing her.

"Oh, aye. She said I canna see her until I apologized to ye. She said I should have warned ye off when I saw ye there."

Jocelyn could not believe what she saw before her. This warrior, afraid of no one and nothing, feared a woman's anger! "And that is important to you?" she asked.

"Aye, Jocelyn. Nara is important to me, though I would ask that ye no' share that wi' too many others." Now it was his turn to blush—and he did—a deep telltale red filling his cheeks.

"When did you know I was there?"

"I saw ye just before ye left."

"I did not mean to disturb your privacy, Rurik. I was walking the babe and found you."

"Does that mean that ye accept my apology? Can I tell Nara that ye said so?"

"You may tell her I accept. And that all is forgotten."

"Aye, all is forgotten." He smiled. Rurik turned and took a step away before turning back and confirming that, under it all, he loved to flirt with women. "I hope ye dinna forget everything ye saw." He offered a seductive wink that she knew would melt many a woman's resistance to him.

She laughed then, both with embarrassment and relief. Now unwilling to let him escape unscathed, she motioned him back to her. He leaned down and she whispered, "What is the marking on your...?" She pointed to his backside where she remembered seeing a strange marking.

He clutched at his buttocks and first looked startled, then leaned his head back and laughed so loudly that everyone in the room now stared at them. Even her husband who chose this of all days to dawdle over a meal, for he still sat at the head table eating.

He reached out and smacked her on the back, one that nearly sent her stumbling from the force of it. "Ye'll do, Jocelyn. Ye'll do."

His words warmed her heart for they spoke of acceptance and welcome. Not only by him but also by the women in the village, for he would never have done this without being prodded by Nara. That she was worthy of consideration made her smile. At least someone here believed she mattered.

A new confidence lifted her steps and filled her heart. She walked to the front of the hall and to her seat at the table. Jocelyn was about to sit when her husband stood at his chair.

Would he ask about Rurik? Would he berate her for her anger of last night? Would he simply leave as he always did, never taking notice of her? In a way, she hoped for the latter for she did not want his disregard to spoil the warm feelings in her heart. He gained the attention of everyone at the head table and motioned to them to stand.

Well, alone again she would be. Nothing new then.

Instead of leaving, he watched her sit and then motioned again to those around the table to sit. Trying to understand, she looked from man to man and they each nodded a greeting to her. But her husband did more than that—he spoke to her directly and without hesitation.

"Good morrow, lady."

"Good morrow," she stammered out. Accepting the cup of ale from a servant, she sipped it and tried to glance out of the corner of her eyes to see his mood. No glare aimed at her in his eyes. No frown on his face. No anger in his stance or bearing.

Although he continued in whatever discussion he was having as she arrived, he seemed to be aware of her needs. When her cup was empty, he signaled the servant to fill it. When she finished her bowl of porridge, he asked if she needed more.

Strange. It was all strange.

They discussed some new arrangements for the men who lived and slept here in the keep. She watched as it moved from man to man, each offering his suggestions and opinion about this change. Dougal was there, but said very little, only watching with eyes that missed nothing. Soon, they came to an agreement and she knew they would leave on their duties now. The laird dismissed them first with a wave and a nod and they all stood and took their leave of her before walking away.

Then he turned to face her. "What did Rurik want of you?" he asked. "Was he bothering you?"

"Nay, laird," she said with a shake of her head. "He offered an apology for…" She hesitated, not certain of how to explain it to him. "For not warning me off in the woods yesterday."

"And did you accept it?" His even tone of voice was unnerving to her. Where was his anger?

"Aye. 'Tis important to Nara that he speak to me and she seems important to him. I saw no reason to refuse."

"I have spoken to Murdoch and there will be no repeat of last evening."

Confused now, she shook her head. So many things had happened last evening that she could not isolate the one he had in his mind. Did he mean her behavior? Surely, he could object to her forwardness and anger. "Last evening? Murdoch?" Why would he involve his steward in their private matters?

"Leana and the others will not ply their trade here in the keep. Or on the castle grounds for that matter."

"Oh." The heat that had finally left her face from her encounter with Rurik now returned.

"'Tis not fitting for the home of… Well, 'tis not fitting to find them underfoot here."

"My thanks, laird. 'Tis not something I wish to encounter again…here."

Her mother would be scandalized if she heard of it. Whores were a fact of life, but no decent married woman would allow them entrance in their home. If this was to be hers, and she had no plans to leave, then she was pleased that her husband had taken that step.

He stood now and she watched as he nodded and then started to say something and stopped. The frown was back on his brow and she suspected she was the cause of it. He leaned down closer.

"I would speak to you this evening, in private, but I think I may not be welcome in your bedchamber."

Blinking several times and trying to think of a response, Jocelyn sat stunned by this topic. "Ah…" No words would form.

"After your farewell gesture, I hesitate to arrive unannounced."

"You have the right, laird," was all she could think of to say.

"I know that, Jocelyn, but my rights are not in question now. Your welcome of me is." He lowered his voice so that none could hear his words.

He used her name again. The sound of it on his lips was so strange that she stared at his mouth. That made her think of what he did with his mouth and what they did and then the hall was suddenly much hotter than it had been just a few minutes before.

What did she say? She'd not refused him when she feared for her life. Did she refuse him now that he could offer her nothing but pleasure? The decision to stay, not that it was ever truly a choice, had been made much earlier. Her ire over his treatment and disregard still burned and hurt, but she decided that she would find her own place here with or without his favor.

So, did she allow him into her bed knowing there would be nothing else for her?

"You would be welcome."

The words were out before she finished thinking. Jocelyn looked to see what his reaction was and was met by the first glimmer of a true smile she'd seen on his face.

"Very well, Jocelyn," he repeated it as though trying to see how it felt to say it. "Expect me."

Then he did leave, and she was glad of it, for the thoughts now filling her mind, the memories of how he'd touched her, kissed her, made her feel, must surely show on her face. Calling for Cora, she returned to her chambers and planned her day.

Although the clouds opened and the rain continued throughout the entire day, Jocelyn found a thread of anticipation growing inside of her. What would the night bring between them? Did she misinterpret her husband's words or intentions? Was she seeing more there, in the hint of a smile, than he meant? The night would tell.

And it did.

And so did the next and the next and the next.

He took her reminder of his responsibility to teach her seriously, and though the nights were filled with much laughter and pleasure, each night she learned a new ability in the matter of the marriage bed.

The first night, he taught her how anticipation could be drawn out until her body ached and until she was breathless from his touch.

The second night he instructed her on the power of her own touch and the effects it caused to both of them.

The third night he demonstrated the importance of riding skills and how to control the pace and gait of the ride and the pleasure involved.

The fourth night he showed her how to use her mouth for things other than talking or eating. She would never look at fruit sauce the cook prepared for dinner that night in the same manner again.

But, it was the fifth day that taught her the lesson she must not forget.

In spite of his behavior toward her in her chambers and

the passion they shared in the dark of the night, the daylight revealed the truth in their marriage. Any closeness in their marriage bed evaporated when the sun rose. They each went their own way and, other than an occasional meal together or a chance meeting, he never softened toward her at all unless it was in her bedchamber.

She did not understand his need for distance. She tried to ask him about it one night, but he silenced her with well-placed kisses and the pleasure she now craved. Always hopeful that a change would happen between them, she ignored the signs that passion was the only thing they shared.

Until that fifth day when a MacCallum messenger arrived with the news of her mother's death.

"Duncan, I am here," she called out to him as she entered the hall. A servant sent to the village told her that Duncan needed her at the keep.

Duncan stood near the door with another man. As she walked closer she recognized the man as one of her father's retainers. William was his name and he bowed at her approach. Both men looked as though they'd eaten a bad plate of snails and neither would meet her gaze directly.

"Jocelyn, the laird is not here, but I have sent a rider to bring him back."

"Duncan, what is wrong? William, what word do you bring from home…my parents?" She hoped that Duncan did not pick up her slip of the tongue and take offense at it.

"I should wait for the MacLerie's arrival, lady." William crossed his arms over his burly chest and took a stance that announced he'd said his last word until her husband arrived.

"Has he had food and drink?" she asked Duncan.

"He was offered them both and refused."

Jocelyn could not imagine what news could come that needed to wait for the laird's attention. "Then I suppose we will wait for the laird."

Several minutes passed and no one said anything or moved from their place. Tempted to find a chair and see to her embroidery while waiting, she thought both Duncan and William might be insulted by such actions. Crossing her own arms over her chest, she sighed and looked at the roof of the keep.

Never one for patiently waiting for anything, she found that tapping her foot felt good. Duncan cleared his throat and frowned, letting her know that it was not to be continued. The noisy arrival outside signified her husband's return and finally she would discover the news. The door opened and Rurik came in running.

"The laird is delayed, Duncan. He said that ye should see to whatever matter the MacCallum sends word of for him."

"What keeps him, Rurik?" she asked.

"One of his men was wounded. In a training match."

Duncan dismissed him, but Rurik did not leave, he tarried only a few feet away making no attempt to hide his curiosity.

"Well, William. Duncan will hear the message for the MacLerie. You can speak it now," she ordered.

"The MacCallum sends greetings to the MacLerie and to the lady Jocelyn," William said, nodding at her. "And he regrets to send word that Lilidh MacGregor died last week."

Knowing she misheard the words, she shook her head.

"William, what did you say?" She clasped her hands together. It could not be. It had to be a mistake.

"She...the lady passed away." William looked to Duncan, but Duncan only shook his head.

"I am sorry, Jocelyn," he said softly, sending William away with a flick of his hand.

"Wait," she called out to him. "She is dead?"

It did not make sense to her. Yes, her mother had been ill, but it appeared as nothing so serious that it could cause her death. Surely not...

"Who is Lilidh MacGregor?" Rurik whispered loudly though he did not come closer.

"Lady MacCallum," Duncan answered abruptly.

Jocelyn stared at Duncan and then at Rurik. She knew the news had to be wrong. Mayhap her mother had simply worsened and was not dead? Mayhap the messenger left prematurely? Mayhap...

"Oh, Jocelyn. I am sorry that yer mother has passed," Rurik began, in a tone that brought tears to her eyes. So much sympathy and softness from such a hard man...and a stranger at that.

"I saw her buried before carrying the news here, lady."

Her thoughts swirled and raced in her head and she thought the walls around her moved, too. "My father? Athdar?" The walls were indeed closer now than before.

"Are as well, lady, as can be expected."

Pity now filled every face she saw around her. Some of the servants whispered to each other. Duncan looked at Rurik who let out a breath and shook his head.

Her mother was dead.

The walls of the keep began to topple over then, falling toward her. The floor, it seemed, rushed up to meet her as well. And somewhere in the distance a woman had the sense to scream out a warning to all. But the scream went on and on until darkness covered them all.

Chapter Thirteen

It still rained.

Six days since the messenger arrived with the news and still it rained. He told himself the first two days that it was a good thing—Jocelyn felt no compulsion to go to the village in such poor weather and could rest. But after four more, and her refusal or inability to leave her bedchamber, Connor knew it was not.

'Twas as though the very clouds were in mourning. Their gray and surly appearance and behavior, pouring down endlessly on Lairig Dubh, matched those of the people there. They accomplished what they could to prepare for the harvests in between cloudbursts, but they never lost the anger in their gazes when they looked at him.

Damn them all! They knew not what was at stake for him, for them all. It seemed not to matter to all of them. They heard the story—word came of the death of his wife's mother, she collapsed in the hall from the grief, he stayed with his men instead of going to her side—and they believed it. When the priest returned from another

village and said a mass for Lady MacCallum's soul and
its eternal rest, the laird did not attend.

As in the past, they chose to believe the worst.

In this situation, the stories were true.

Turning the corner, he sought refuge this morning in the
passing torrents, on the battlements. His attempt was successful in keeping all but the worst of his assailants away.

"The lady will not leave her bed, my lord."

Ailsa breached his seclusion first. Not long after a dawn
that seemed to happen without the sun rising, when the
horizon remained dark as night and only lightning lit the
sky, she intruded on his privacy. Torrents of rain and now
crashing thunder did not stop her when she felt she was
on the righteous path. And, apparently, anything involving his wife was included in that.

"'Tis early yet, Ailsa. Let her rest." He heard the
epithet she spoke under her breath as he was certain she
wanted him to.

"Have ye spoken to her yet, my lord?" Her voice
dripped with the accusation. But, not liking the question
did not make it false.

"I did not wish to disturb her rest." Another curse
muttered loud enough that she did try to hide.

"She is in pain, my lord," Ailsa said.

"A pain I cannot help, Ailsa. Only time can." It sounded
reasonable.

This time she only stared at him, with her chin set and
her arms crossed over her chest, as the rain poured over
both of them, not saying a word. Not needing to for, in situations like this, her expressions could be worse than her
words and he felt guilt stirring in his heart.

He'd seen to her condition. Rurik told him that Ailsa

had been called to the keep to see to her. So, there was no need to return as though he was besotted and needed to be at her side. Nay, she would simply need time to sort through this and he did not want to take a step he could not back away from later.

Going to her, comforting her, holding her and doing those other soft things that caring husbands did for their wives were not in his plans. That was a distance he would not cover between them.

"Ye could do more," she said. "If ye cannot give her what she needs, mayhap someone else could."

He'd been avoiding meeting her gaze, but now looked at her. "What do you mean? She is my wife."

"Then treat her like one. And not only in the bedchamber. If this is her home, make it so."

"How does one who was never a man's wife know so much?"

He knew he'd crossed a line as soon as the words escaped.

"Ye nourish yer anger, even revel in it, and until ye release it, there will be no healing, no wholeness in ye, my lord."

"Ailsa, do not…" He held his hand up to stop her. She had no right to speak of the past to him.

"The lady is not the cause of what happened with Kenna. She should not be the target of yer anger."

"Now you go too far, old woman." She took a step closer now, the rain rushing over her small frame.

"Whatever happened between ye and Kenna, whatever did not, does not matter now, Connor. This woman is like a gift to ye, one that can help ye forget—"

"I will not forget Kenna."

"Then mayhap ye could forgive her and forgive

yerself? Let go of yer anger, my lord, before it destroys an innocent woman."

"Be gone now!" he shouted at her. She had such nerve speaking of the past as though she had a right to. No one did. No one.

"As ye wish, my lord."

Ailsa bowed to him and backed away, but her intent had been accomplished. He felt the blows as if she'd used a cudgel on his head. Connor waited until she left before turning his face into the storm and letting the rain pour over him. Was there a way to let it go? So many questions, so much anger, could he simply walk from his past and begin anew?

Minutes passed and then he heard the steps behind him, a man from the sound of them. He did not turn, but kept his gaze on the rain as it fell into the yard below him.

"Connor, I need to speak to you." Duncan found him next.

"I think not," he answered. He was still in no mood to talk, but his wishes counted for naught for Duncan continued.

"I heard that Jocelyn is still grief-struck this morning."

"Duncan, you do not need to worry over my wife."

Duncan shifted on his feet and shrugged. "I have something to suggest and I want you to think on it."

"I think I will not like what you are about to say."

"Probably not, but think on it for the good of all involved."

Duncan usually came to him with sound ideas and plans and, although he might not want to hear this particular one, Connor owed him to hear him out.

"Jocelyn has much time on her hands and, other than those in the village, no one to share it with."

"I have duties, Duncan…" he began to argue. But Duncan shook his head.

"I was not thinking of you, Connor. She needs other women around her. And if your plans succeed, she needs appropriate women here, both for company and for guidance."

Other women? Connor thought on his words. She did spend much of her time in the village, and while that was not a bad thing, it would not be appropriate for the wife of an earl. If the title was granted as he hoped in the next few months, visitors from the royal court, the king's emissaries and others would come here to transact business and curry favor with him.

He nodded to Duncan. "And do you have anyone in mind?"

"Your aunt would certainly be a guiding force to ready the keep."

Connor laughed now. Dougal's wife would be more than a guiding hand to Jocelyn. He knew she was chafing to be here and meet Jocelyn and he'd dragged out extending an invitation, or rather, permission, for her to come. "The keep may be all that remains if I loose Aunt Jean on Jocelyn. I have seen the hint of a temper in my wife and Jean would bring that out quickly."

"I was thinking that you could ask your aunt to bring Rhona with her."

"Rhona? I have not seen her…" His words drifted off.

"In three years," Duncan completed it for him. "I thought you always said she was a help to Kenna and to you."

Connor thought on his kinswoman Rhona. She'd come when her own husband died of the bloody flux and had been a calming influence on Kenna during that difficult time. When each month brought disappointment and each happy time of expectation ended in frustration and distress,

Rhona always had a kind word and became a source of comfort to his wife during her stay at Broch Dubh. She'd left soon after Kenna's death and he had not spoken of or to her since.

"She was. I have not thought on her in some time. Is she still unmarried?" He ran his hand over the wet stone, tracing the outline of the blocks. Duncan's idea might have some merit.

"My mother says she is. Rhona has refused any attempt to find a new husband for her."

Connor thought about her—she was certainly of an age close to Jocelyn and would be a great help, not as overwhelming as his aunt could be at times…at most times.

However, would her presence be a constant reminder of the past? Aye, she would, but with her attending his wife, he could be free of worry about her and could avoid them most of the time. This might be a workable solution to many problems and hindrances. So long as she avoided speaking of Kenna to Jocelyn.

Thus far, his strictures had been obeyed and he knew Rhona enough to know that she would obey his word, more than that, she would respect his wishes.

"Send word through Dougal that I would welcome Aunt Jean and Rhona here at Broch Dubh and would like them to meet my wife." Connor smiled. This could work.

"Do you think you should ask your wife before you make the invitation?"

"Jocelyn is in no state to make such decisions now, Duncan." Connor turned and faced his cousin. "She will be pleased when she knows I have done this out of concern for her." He clapped Duncan on the shoulder and began walking to the door. His appetite sprang to life and he needed some food. "It will give her a chance to meet more of the clan and to move past this grief that is overwhelming her."

He could swear Duncan groaned under his breath, but the man's expression was clear when he faced him. "Come, let us break our fast."

It would take about a week for the word to be sent and his aunt and Rhona to arrive. Murdoch should be warned to open some of the chambers for their use. And there would be need for more servants to see to the needs of the women. And on and on. Murdoch would moan and complain, but Connor suspected that he would be grateful for the increase in activity and work here in the keep. They returned to the hall and ate before seeing to their duties. Connor thought about Jocelyn then.

He'd become accustomed to her joining him for the morning meal and had missed her these last mornings. Thinking on the passion they shared, mutually since their argument and his return the next evening to her bed, he realized he enjoyed the moment each morning when she sat next to him and blushed. He knew, they both knew, that she was thinking on what had happened the night before between them. His wife was still an innocent when it came to bedplay and he was taking pleasure in his role as husband and mentor.

Now, with her seat empty and the hall quiet, he did miss her. Since he'd not yet spoken to her, he decided to visit her before leaving the keep. Perchance he would share the news about his aunt visiting and his kinswoman as a companion for her.

He arranged to meet Murdoch later and sent Duncan off with instructions for inviting and retrieving the women and then climbed to Jocelyn's chambers. Cora stood outside the closed door, leaning close and trying to hear what was going on inside.

"Should you not be tending to your lady instead of eavesdropping here?" he asked. The girl startled and swayed on her feet at his question. "I mean you no harm, lass. You must get over this fear you have." She pushed her hair from her face and stood up straighter. Surprised but pleased that she did not faint, he nodded. "Is the lady awake yet?"

Cora's head bobbed quickly and she swallowed several times before being able to speak. "Aye, my lord. Ailsa forced her from the bed."

"Forced her?" Connor lifted the latch of the door, but Cora tugged on his arm.

"Ailsa said she needed some time with the lady alone, my lord. Said the lady's been in the bed for too long."

He would have pushed on but for the concerned expression on the girl's face and the fact that she'd stopped him. Apparently she was growing protective of Jocelyn.

"Then I suppose I should wait for Ailsa," he said.

He walked to the top of the staircase and pushed open the shutters of the small window there. The rain still continued, but the keep and castle grounds were beginning to move to the business of the day. Something was different though. A band of women, about twenty of them, entered through the gate and walked toward the keep. Some carried babes, some walked alone. He recognized Margaret and Siusan and a few of the older women.

His foot was moving toward the step when the bedchamber door opened and Ailsa beckoned him in. Murdoch was still below or even Duncan if there was some need, so Connor walked into his wife's room. Ailsa whispered that she would return shortly and left him there.

The heat hit him first. The hearth blazed with a vigorous fire and the room was sweltering. His first impulse was to open the door, but Ailsa had shut it firmly behind him. Even though he'd spent a long time out in the cool rain this morn, the warmth became uncomfortable in a short time.

Looking around, he saw that Jocelyn sat in the chair closest to the fire and facing away from the door. He approached after saying her name which came out on a shaking voice.

"Jocelyn? How do you fare?" he asked. She did not reply so he moved to stand in front of her. "Are you well, lady?"

"I am cold, laird. I cannot seem to get warm enough," she answered finally in a whisper.

If her voice surprised him in its weakness, her appearance shocked him. He'd seen her only in the middle of the night when he came to look in on her. By the light of a candle or two and asleep, she looked nothing out of the ordinary. Now, awake and in the light of this stormy day, Jocelyn's face was gaunt, her complexion ghostly and she wore the expression of someone lost. He crouched down and touched her hand. It was icy.

"Here now." He drew the blankets up tighter around her shoulders and tucked her hands under the edges, making certain she was covered by them. "How can you be so cold?" Jocelyn did not answer; she simply accepted his attentions without moving.

Connor glanced at the tray sitting on a small table at her side. It had not been touched. Steam rose from the mug there and he picked it up and sniffed. Wine mulled with some spices and still warm.

"Would you like a taste? It is hot and could warm you a bit."

He thought she might refuse, but a slight nod of her head gave her assent. With no one else there and her just now completely ensconced with a cocoon of blankets, he lifted the cup to her mouth. Adjusting it and holding her head steady, he tilted it and let her drink a small amount. After one mouthful, she drew back and shook her head.

"That was not much, Jocelyn. Do you want more?"

"I had enough, laird." She looked around the room as though just realizing they were alone. "Has Ailsa gone?"

"She went to the hall for a moment," he said. "She should return shortly." She stared at the flames and he felt as though she'd dismissed him.

The discomfort that filled him and the lack of knowing what to say made him uneasy. Surely there was something to say, something to talk about? He walked to her window, the place farthest from the blazing fire and stood there. She did not move, did not look to see where he went. Every possible phrase of sympathy or concern or condolence that entered his mind would lead to much more than he could give, so he waited in silence for Ailsa's return.

"My aunt, Dougal's wife, would like to come."

No response.

"My kinswoman, Rhona, will accompany her."

"I fear…" she began and then paused as though collecting her strength before speaking. "I fear I would do no justice to visitors, laird."

It was at that moment that he realized that she never called him by his name. She always referred to him by his title or *my lord* or even an occasional *husband.* Most in the clan called him Connor or Conn. Was she trying to remain apart as he did? Was she not reconciled to the marriage? An uncomfortable twinge moved up his spine, twisting and tugging, as he considered her position in their arrangement. Most likely, she wanted this marriage even less than he had.

Had there been someone else? He thought he remembered Duncan mentioning the possible existence of a prior betrothal when they'd discussed her before his trip there to negotiate with her father. Discomfort aside, none of this mattered. She was his wife now and no one else's.

"They come not to visit, Jocelyn. They are family and will stay for some time." He watched for some interest from her in the news. A slight flicker in her gaze and then it was gone.

"If you wish, laird."

Sharing this news with her had not succeeded as he'd hoped. Worse than he'd imagined she would be, he wondered how long it would take before she recovered from this loss. His own mother died when he was only a child, so he had nurses and maids and then teachers and instructors in his life. He'd not been here when his father passed away, so he had no words of advice to offer.

Now though, looking at the empty shell of the woman who so recently had gifted him with smiles and laughter and soft feelings, he wished he had. He fought the urge to take her in his arms and hold her for days. Connor took a step toward her and stopped at the sound of Ailsa outside the room.

"Lady, some women from the village are here to see you," Ailsa said as she entered the room. "They wait below."

"Ailsa, Jocelyn is…" His words stopped when he beheld the old woman's expression.

"Margaret brought the bairn and Siusan has some questions on the stitches you taught her."

Ailsa moved closer and lifted the blanket from Jocelyn's shoulders. With a few deft motions, she folded it into a shawl and held it out for her. Surprised to find that she wore a dress beneath her covers, he knew that Ailsa had most likely had a hand in planning the arrival of the women of the village. Realizing Ailsa's aim, he went to the door and gave Cora a message to take to Murdoch.

"Come, Jocelyn. Surely you can give them a few minutes of your time after they made the long walk in the rain to see you."

He saw her glance toward the window and caught Ailsa's faint smile. She was not the only one who could play guilt as an instrument. He'd learned it from many masters.

"I am not ready…" Her protests were as weak as she was, and Connor decided that she would not have the strength needed to walk down the stairway to the hall.

"Here now, let me carry you." He did not give her time to voice any more objections. "Stay a few minutes only and I will bring you back when you are ready."

Ailsa moved around him, guiding him as he lifted Jocelyn into his arms. She felt fragile and breakable somehow and she held herself stiffly as he carried her to the door and out of her chambers. No one was in the stairway or on the landing below or along the path to the hall when they reached it. As he'd ordered.

She was not comfortable in her appearance, he knew that from the way she dressed and carried herself. Once well, she would be horrified to know that others saw her in this condition. Now, with the men cleared out and only the women waiting, he walked to the corner of the great hall and into a room that was once his mother's, then his wife's, solar.

Hastily cleared of the furniture stored there, it had a faint musty odor from disuse. Murdoch had pushed everything to one side and lit a fire that even now sparked to life. Ailsa carried a few cushions with her and now set them in a high-backed chair next the stone fireplace that dominated one wall of the chamber. When the old woman was satisfied of their position, she nodded and he lowered Jocelyn into it. Once she was settled, Ailsa went to the door and called the group into the room.

Margaret entered first, shifting her newest babe to her shoulder. Siusan led the others in and helped the older ones to stools that Murdoch left around the room. Connor felt the tension in the room and knew part of it sprang from his presence. Watching his half sister move across the room, he noticed her resemblance to their father again. She'd gotten the MacLerie coloring as well as his father's eyes. He'd gotten his temper and his name.

"Margaret, you look well," he said, taking the first step.

"As you do, Connor," she answered, nodding at him. "Am I welcome here?"

He knew all the women watched their exchange and knew as well that Margaret had not set foot in the keep since she was a child. His mother refused hers permission to enter once Ailsa's relationship with his father became known. Banishment from the keep was within his mother's purview to do, but the village was not, and so Ailsa lived there, visited as often as desired by his father for as long as his mother was alive.

"Laird, she is welcome, is she not?" Jocelyn's weak voice broke into their discussion.

So, no one had enlightened her as to Margaret's parentage. Ailsa's expression revealed that she had not. He turned to Jocelyn and nodded. "All MacLeries are welcome here, lady. Even if they were not previously."

Jocelyn nodded and Margaret approached her, leaning close and saying something that made his wife smile. It was a feeble one, but the first she'd probably had since the news of her mother. The others came close, touching her hand and murmuring words he could not hear and Connor knew it was time to leave.

"Murdoch will see to your needs. Ailsa, summon me when the lady is ready to return to her chambers."

He backed away, but his presence was already ignored. Their womanly rituals, apparently practiced over the last few weeks when his wife spent her time there, began—Ailsa pulled a stool over to Jocelyn's side, Margaret on the other—and various garments and sewing projects were shared between them. Threading the needle, Ailsa passed it to Jocelyn who picked up the shirt on her lap and pushed the thread in and out, repairing a hole or torn seam. His escape was nearly a success; he had stepped into the hall, when he heard Ailsa ask the question.

"Lady, tell us of yer mother."

Was she daft? Why would she ask the very thing that would pain Jocelyn the most? In such a weakened state, he thought that she might collapse. About to step back in the room, he paused when he heard Jocelyn begin to speak.

"My mother loved to dance," she said. "She loved to hear the music and could not resist…" Her voice thickened and she paused as though trying to push out the words. "She could not resist the call of the pipe and…"

Tears poured from her eyes and he knew she could say no more. Connor grabbed the edge of the doorway, fighting himself and the urge to go to her. No one spoke while Jocelyn cried, but he watched as Ailsa and Margaret both reached out and took one of her hands in theirs while she sobbed. Then Margaret urged her on.

"Lady, what was her favorite tune? Can ye sing a bit or hum it for us?"

Jocelyn wiped the tears away with the edge of the blanket around her shoulders and nodded. Too low for him to hear at first, she hummed some of the tune and then whispered the words. Soon, a couple of the other women nodded as they recognized it and joined her until the sound of the song echoed in a hushed chorus across the chamber.

He turned away then, his heart pounding and his throat tight with sorrow for her. Her tears affected him more than he wanted to admit, as did the concern shown by the women. What he thought was a cruel thing to do was in truth a way for her to vent her grief. The song ended and he peered around the doorway and back at the gathering.

"Where was she from?" Siusan asked now.

Before she answered, Jocelyn held open her arms and reached for Margaret's child, Peggy. Margaret stood and placed the babe without hesitation in Jocelyn's embrace. He watched as she closed her eyes and seemed to breathe in the infant's scent.

"She grew up nearer to the shores of Loch Lomond than to here," Jocelyn answered. Now she rubbed the bairn's head and rocked slightly as she held her.

Now that she was involved in the discussion, Connor thought he would leave. But one question led to another and another and he found himself entranced by the way his wife spoke of her mother, her family, her childhood and more. Standing outside the solar, he learned more about her in that short time than he had before.

And he also discovered that his half sister and her

mother knew much about how to handle grief and how to provide support for someone they cared about. He was glad they were there for her in her time of need.

The next days moved slowly, but she did not linger in her bedchamber any more. Ailsa said she ate more, but he thought she still appeared frail. The women came each morning and ate the noon meal with her and then left to tend to their own chores.

She asked him to visit her one night and Connor knew his surprise showed. Jocelyn insisted and he went to her that night. She clung to him with an air of desperation and, if he stayed longer than usual in her arms and her bed after they had finished, she said nothing. This time he waited for her to sleep before leaving her alone.

She improved with each task she did, so he decided he would ask Murdoch to involve her in the preparations for his aunt's arrival. He did it only to help her adjust to her old schedule and not for the warm feeling it gave him to see her smile occasionally. He did not do it because he wanted her to be a bigger part of his life.

And he especially did not do it because he cared.

Chapter Fourteen

The rapping on the door grew louder until she finally acknowledged it. "I hear you!" she called out as she walked to open it. "What do you want this time, Murdoch?"

The steward stood before her, his hand in the air as though he did not believe she would answer his call. Cora was behind him, making some gesture that she did not understand.

"Your pardon, Murdoch. I did not mean to be sharp with you."

"No matter, my lady. I thought to ask you about the rooms for the laird's aunt and cousin."

"Surely, your judgment in this will be fine," she offered.

"Mayhap you would come and see?" Murdoch stepped away and motioned for her to follow him. He stopped when she did not.

"The laird does not wish for me to usurp your duties in the keep. He made that clear to me and to you, Murdoch."

There. The truth of it was out now. Although her husband had been kinder these last days, he had not changed his orders about her place here. Murdoch ran the keep. She stayed out of the way.

"If I ask for your assistance, my lady, then it is not usurping, is it?"

She feared that if she helped him too much, it would gain the laird's attention and his scorn once more. She loathed the thought of that for there was a peace between them these last few days that she was coming to enjoy.

Jocelyn sighed, giving up the fight for now. The steward could be an irritating man if one did not obey him or agree to his methods. In spite of her returning strength, she hesitated to cause a problem for him. "Very well. Show me the chambers you have chosen for Aunt Jean and Rhona."

Following him down the floor below, he opened a door and showed her a largish room he said would be for Jean and Dougal.

"Dougal will move here today and the chamber he uses will be prepared for Rhona."

"Dougal and Jean will share a room?" she asked. Then, she stopped and stared at Murdoch.

"Aye, they usually do," he answered as he led her down to the main floor and to the tower where the laird's chambers were. At the first landing, he opened the door to one of two chambers for her. "This will be for the laird's kinswoman."

As he spoke about other arrangements, changing the mattress on the bed, assigning a maid if the women did not bring their own, and other minor issues, she dared to lean back and peek up the stairs. She'd not been in the laird's chambers. She wondered if his rooms were like hers or larger. Did a servant sleep outside his door? What was his bed like?

"Have a care, Jocelyn, or you will tumble on your arse," Rurik said as he stepped behind her and kept her from doing just that.

"My thanks, Rurik." She smiled at his rough ways as she regained her feet.

"What are ye doing here? If you seek Connor, he is in the stables." Rurik nodded his head in the direction of the room above. "He is no' here."

"We are checking the rooms that Aunt Jean and Rhona will use during their visit…stay here." The laird assured her that, despite their absence from Lairig Dubh for nigh onto three years, they were not to be considered visitors. They were family, he insisted.

"This is a bit small for Dougal and Jean," he said, leaning over her to look in the chamber. "Aye, too small if ye ask me."

"This is for Rhona. Dougal and Jean will be in the chamber below mine. That should be large enough," she explained.

Even though her own parents shared their chambers and so did the elders who lived here in Broch Dubh and Dougal and his wife, she did not share hers with the laird. Truth be told, she'd yet to even see his. She turned back to the men.

If she had not looked at just that moment, she would have missed the strange expression exchanged between the two men. A raised eyebrow. A slight frown. Another raised eyebrow. Then gone and they both met her gaze.

"Is there something wrong with the room then?" she asked.

"This is where she stayed before," Murdoch offered.

"Before? When was she here last?"

"Before," they answered together, making it seem somehow guilty.

Ah. *Before.* Before the laird's first wife died.

"And is it a problem if she stays here this time?"

Murdoch had assured her that the middle tower was the location of the incident. All of the rooms there were now used as storerooms or workrooms.

"Nay, I think not, my lady," Murdoch stammered.

"Is there anything else you wanted to ask me then? Or am I free now to return to my own chambers?"

"'Tis a fine day, Jocelyn. Would ye like to walk?" Rurik asked. "I could tell ye about Jean if ye'd like to hear."

There was a conspiracy afoot to keep her from her chambers. It had been going on since yesterday and many were involved in it. Rurik was but the latest. She suspected that the laird was behind it.

"I am tired, Rurik, though I thank you for your kind invitation. I would like to rest a bit." She waited for their reaction.

"Ye can rest when yer dead, Jocelyn," Rurik muttered. "With winter coming, this fair weather will not last long." Once he'd said it, he seemed pleased with his words. He nodded to Murdoch, who nodded back. A fine team they were.

"When I am dead?" she asked, trying to put a stern look on her face.

"Odin's ballocks…I mean…" His face paled as she watched. "I did no' mean to make ye think of yer mam, Jocelyn." He shook his head vigorously. "Connor will have my balls if he finds I have distressed ye." He rubbed one hand over his bald head and down onto his neck.

"Rurik!" Murdoch warned. "Haud yer wheesht!"

So, her husband was at the middle of this plot. As she thought.

"I can escort you to your chambers, if you are weary."

The laird, not Rurik, made the offer and smiled as he reached her side. Rurik and Murdoch, appearing mightily relieved by his arrival, took their leave of her and rushed away.

"Was it something I said?" she asked. "Or is there something peculiar going on here?"

"Ailsa tells me that you have been eating and sleeping better since you have been helping Murdoch in his preparations for Aunt Jean. I but thought to help by encouraging you to tasks around the keep."

What a kind thing to do, she thought. And unexpected. And especially unexpected coming from him.

"Why?" she blurted out.

"'Tis the right thing to do. To help someone when they need it," he said.

"My thanks for your consideration, laird." She'd hoped for a different answer, but should have known by now that he thought of her in the same way he thought of any other member of his clan—worthy of the concern of the laird.

"I need to get a book of records from my chambers to review with Hamish. Would you like to wait here and I will escort you back to your chambers?"

"You need not take me back. I am capable of getting there myself. May I come up with you?"

He was startled by her request, but nodded his permission. Then he held out his hand and took hers in it. She knew he slowed his pace, for usually his long legs took but one step for every two she did. Even though she was feeling stronger, she was out of breath when they reached the top of the stairway.

He pushed open the door and led her inside and to a large cushioned chair near a window like the one she had in her rooms. His, though, did not have the same costly glass in it that hers did. He had a writing table in one corner and a washbasin on another small table near his bed. His bed.

It was like him, tall, or rather high off the floor, long enough for his entire frame to fit on it in comfort, and without ornamentation. Entirely useful without being too showy. 'Twas no wonder he left hers for this one each time he visited her. She did not realize she'd spoken the words until he gazed at her and laughed.

"It is more comfortable than yours, Jocelyn. Try it and see."

Before she recognized his intent, he lifted her and placed her in the middle of the huge bed. Then he walked to one of three wooden chests and searched within it for the book he mentioned as his goal. Mayhap she could ask him about something that had bothered her for days now.

"Why did you not tell me of Margaret?" she asked.

He shuffled parchments and documents around inside the storage box before answering her. "'Tis not that I did not tell you. I just did not think to tell you. That we shared a father is no secret here in Lairig Dubh or with the clan."

"No one told me."

"Again, Jocelyn, 'twas no secret being kept from you." He stood now and faced her. "What would you ask of me now that you know? Did my mother ken of her? Aye. Did my father take responsibility for her? Aye, he provided for Ailsa and his daughter as he should have—even offering a dowry and finding a suitable husband for Margaret when it was time." He gathered a few items from the chest and closed it.

"You make my curiosity sound unnatural, laird," she began.

"Connor. My name is Connor and I wish you would use it." Irritation entered his voice giving it a sharpness that was not there before. He dropped the book and parchments on the writing table. "Can you say it?" he asked, staring at her.

Uncomfortable with his attitude, she slid to the edge of the bed, ready to leave without her questions answered. "I meant no disrespect, laird." She moved her gaze from his and looked at the floor.

He pushed the pile of documents away and walked to where she sat perched on the edge. "Say my name and I will answer whatever you ask of me."

Why did it mean so much to him? It had invaded his thoughts once he realized that she did not, and apparently would not, use his given name when talking to him. As far as he knew, she did not use it when speaking to others and referring to him either.

He wanted to hear his name on her lips when he pleasured her. He wanted to hear it when she acquiesced to any demand he made. He wanted to hear it when she sighed or moaned in his arms. Connor knew he was obsessed with this need now. Would her curiosity drive her to give in? Would she ask questions he did not want to answer, leaving him without honor if he refused?

"Connor," she said on a whisper.

His body hardened on hearing it. Like a sigh, her voice turned it into something sensual, something sexual. He tried to convince himself to ignore its call, but his body had other ideas.

"Yes?" He stepped closer, opening her legs and standing between them. He was close enough now that she had to lean back to look at him and that exposed her lovely neck and the slope of her breasts to his gaze. She did not stop him from touching her or from being there. "Ask your questions."

"Was Ailsa your nurse?"

A safe inquiry, in his estimation, and easy enough to answer. "Aye. She'd given birth to a bairn a few months before I was born, one that died, and was brought to the keep as my nurse." He could see her mind working, thinking on his words and formulating new questions for him.

"Connor?" There was still a hesitation in her voice saying it, making it sound like two words—conn and nor.

"Aye, Jocelyn?" He ran his hands inside the length of her thighs, over her gown, gently, the lightest touch he could manage. Stopping at the junction of them, he did not touch her intimately. Not yet.

"The babe that died. Was it also your father's?" Her breathing told him that she was responding to his touch.

"Aye."

He decided on the one-word response to make her work for the information she wanted. And to see how long they could draw out their pleasure. She had not objected to his touch or to the obvious game he played, so he would move ahead. Once he'd heard his name coming from her mouth, he knew he wanted to hear it again and again. He slid his hands back down to her knees and tugged the edge of her skirts up until he could feel her bare skin against his.

"'Tis not fair, laird," she argued. He withdrew his hand then and waited. He'd guessed correctly that she enjoyed the game as he did. "Connor," she said acquiescing once more. "How did Ailsa become your father's leman?"

"In the usual ways. A lovely woman catches the eye of the laird. Then a touch follows," he said, lifting her skirts again and sliding his hand along her thighs to touch the place that would be warm and wet already. It was. His hand lingered there, touching and teasing her to arousal.

"A kiss," he whispered, leaning over to touch his mouth to the curve of her neck. Then he used his teeth to graze against the sensitive spot just below her ear. She arched against his hand when he bit lightly and then licked and soothed it with his tongue.

"A tupping," he mentioned, lifting her back to the center of his bed and climbing in over her. He lifted the plaid he wore and moved closer and lowered himself against her. When she opened her thighs and reached down to guide him into her body, he kissed her mouth again, deeply tasting her sweetness. He pulled back and traced the outline of her lips with his tongue and he eased inside her tightness.

"A claiming," he explained as he plunged in as deep as he could and then stopped. Watching her as she arched against him, he moved within her tightness, easing out and pushing back in.

"And another," he repeated fiercely, as he took her to the very rim of release and paused. Jocelyn clutched at him, trying to pull him inside once more so that she could, they could, reach that special place they sought.

"Connor," she offered, begging him with only the sound of his name.

"And pleasure," he whispered to her. Then he leaned back and slid his hands under her soft bottom, lifting her hips off the bed and closer to him. Then he filled her completely and claimed her body with his until his seed flowed. She melted in his embrace, her core contracting around him, milking him of every drop he had, sending her moaning and slipping over into the passion he'd promised. He waited for her body to finish reaching its pleasure and then he remained inside her until he softened and withdrew. He gathered her in his arms and held her until she roused.

"This was your plan all along then?" she asked as she rolled to her side.

He moved behind her, not pulling his plaid or her skirts between them and tucking himself against her naked bottom. If he were lucky… "My plan?"

"To draw your wife to your bed and seduce her in the light of day? Does everyone know?" There was a playful tone in her voice, very different from recent days and very unlike the one of quiet desperation in their recent couplings.

"I think there was one stableboy and one of the laundry maids who did not hear of my instructions," he said. He smoothed her hair from her face and kissed her neck where he could reach it.

"Connor! You jest, do you not?" She started to move away, but he held her tightly.

"I do jest. My only plan was to rouse you from your chambers. As I said, Murdoch was instructed to ask for your help with the preparations."

"So, then, he does not truly want my help?"

"Murdoch has been whining like a bairn to me about how much he needs your help. Think not that this was an empty gesture."

"And this?"

"This was simply taking advantage of the surprise of finding you on the stairs to my bedchamber. And of seeing a bit of lightness in your eyes again," he confessed. "I have been concerned about your condition." The words did not hurt as he said them. Making such a statement should have caused his heart to tear and his blood to flow, but the admission felt…good.

Jocelyn said nothing. She could not. Hearing such words from him gave her pause. When he asked about her, he always asked in a general way. Never was there a sense of personal interest. This was a change, though, and as emotionally drained as she was from the grief over her mother's passing, she did not want to attach too much importance to it.

For now it felt good to lie here in his bed, in his arms. He had shared something about his family and therefore himself with her. Shared under the guise of a game of pleasure, but shared nonetheless.

The weariness she spoke of to Murdoch and Rurik began to creep over her and her eyes began to feel heavy. Satisfied and comfortable, Jocelyn felt sleep closing in on her. Until the yell that shook the shutters.

"Conn!" Rurik shouted from the stairwell.

Connor startled behind her, but instead of leaving, he moved closer and slid his hand under her gown and around her waist. Cupping her breast, he pressed his manhood against her bottom and she felt it grow longer and harder beneath her.

"If I do not answer, he will go away," he whispered as his fingers teased the tip of her breast.

Arousal replaced sleepiness and she found that her body readied for him quickly. "Are you certain? I would not like to begin something we cannot finish."

He pulled away then and walked to the door, opening it and listening there. He shook his head. "He's gone already, looking for me elsewhere."

She watched him walk, his plaid and shirt still on but tented by the hardness between his legs. Then he stopped and circled to the bottom of the bed. Leaning up on her elbows, she realized she lay with her gown shoved up above her waist and her legs and everything else exposed to him.

He climbed up and took her ankles in his hands and tugged slowly until she found herself sliding down the length of the bed. "'Tis time to finish what we started, Jocelyn."

He did not wait on her answer, but lifted her legs over each shoulder and leaned down until his mouth touched her…there. It was only moments before she lost all thoughts or concerns in favor of the wild rushes of passion and heat that moved through her now. From his mouth and tongue, waves of heat pulsed through her and she grabbed his head to keep him there. Doing that. To her.

Just as she felt the scream grow within her, he moved between her legs, thrust himself in to fill her there and captured her mouth with his. The musky taste of her own essence on his lips, the fullness of him within her, the heat and the growing tension all forced her to fall again. She felt him move at her core and felt the muscles there contract and tighten around him. He threw his head back and called out.

"Rurik!"

"What?" Jocelyn, shocked by the unexpected name, pushed up to look at him and saw that Connor stared at the door.

The open door.

The open door where Rurik stood gaping at them.

"Sweet Freya's tits!" Rurik called out before grabbing the door and pulling it shut.

Connor withdrew and pulled his shirt and plaid down. "I will kill him this time," he said as he climbed off the bed and strode to the door. Then he stopped and turned to her. "I am so sorry, Jocelyn. I truly thought him gone."

All she could do at that moment was laugh. The passion evaporated as the humor in this situation struck her. She could never look the man in the face again. God only knew what Rurik had seen, which part or parts of her were exposed when he watched or even what he'd watched. Had he witnessed Connor kissing her in that private place? Had he seen Connor filling her or heard her moaning as she knew shc did when reaching fulfillment?

Jocelyn covered her face with her hands as the scene on display before the man passed through her thoughts. She felt her husband's hand on her shoulder and dropped hers, wiping the tears that ran down her cheeks.

"I am sorry, Jocelyn,"

"You will have to kill him," she choked out.

It took a moment before he realized that she was laughing so hard that it caused the tears, but when he did, he joined her in it. His face brightened so when he laughed that he looked like a different person. She saw it so infrequently that the change in him startled her. His dark eyes turned a dazzling bronze and the sharp angles seemed to soften.

If it could only stay this way between them.

Connor drew back and helped her to sit up on the bed. "I know you spoke of being weary earlier. Rest here a while. No one will disturb you."

"I should go. Murdoch asked me to choose some fabric for new tablecloths."

He placed his hand on hers. "Jocelyn, give yourself the time you need to recover from your grief. Murdoch can wait a wee bit while you rest." He walked to the table and picked up the book and parchments he'd taken from the storage chest. "I must get these to Hamish and kill Rurik on the way. I will look for you at the evening meal."

He kissed her lightly on the mouth and then walked to the door, lifting the latch and pulling it open. Then he was gone. After a moment of worry for Rurik for she had seen her husband enraged and it was not a good thing to be the target for it, she decided to accept his invitation to rest here.

Jocelyn awoke sometime later and went in search of Murdoch. She found him directing several servants, new to the keep, in the cleaning of the chamber that would be Rhona's on the morrow. Connor's words echoed in her mind.

A lovely woman catches the eye of the laird.

She looked back up the stairs leading to the laird's chambers and thought about it. "Murdoch," she said, gaining his attention.

"Aye, my lady?" He stepped over to her.

"Is the laird's kinswoman a lovely woman?"

"Oh, aye, my lady. Rhona is lovely and sweet-tempered and—"

Jocelyn shook her head and held out her hand to stop him from more accolades about the woman she would soon meet. Amazed at what she was going to do next, for she could not explain it, in truth she did not want to examine her reasons for doing it, so she simply carried it out.

"Find another room for my husband's kinswoman, Murdoch. This one will not be suitable after all."

She did not wait for questions or protests from the steward. She made her wishes known and left, walking off to find Cora.

The next day, when Connor's aunt and kinswoman arrived, Jocelyn knew she'd made the correct decision after all.

When the travelers arrived, Jocelyn and Connor were

there, along with most of the elders, servants and some of the villagers, to meet them. A stunningly beautiful woman climbed down from her horse and walked, nay sauntered, past Jocelyn and right up to her husband. She heard him say the woman's name and then open his arms to her.

Rhona appeared to be about four or five years older than she was herself, but she had the figure and face of one younger. Curling blond hair flowed down the woman's back, pulled back loosely with a scarf that matched her gown. A beautiful gown it was and in a style she'd never seen before, but one that showed off Rhona's womanly attributes to all. As if that was not enough to put Jocelyn's plain appearance and garb to shame, Rhona spoke to Connor in a lilting, yet sultry voice. Low enough that she could not hear their words, loud enough to catch the tone and vibrancy in it.

"Jocelyn?" Rousing herself from the bout of instant dislike she was suffering, Jocelyn looked over to see her husband motioning to her. Pressing her damp palms against her gown, her plain gown, she walked to him and stood at his side.

"This is my kinswoman, Rhona. She was related to my mother by marriage. Rhona, this is my wife Jocelyn."

"Jocelyn? What a beautiful name! My thanks for inviting me to meet you." Then she threw her arms around Jocelyn and hugged her. "Have you been able to accomplish anything with these brutes who live here? Most likely not, but with Aunt Jean's," Rhona dragged her over to Dougal's wife who nodded at her, "and my help, you will make this keep the suitable home it should be."

She guessed that her first assessment, based on the woman's appearance, was wrong. Rhona whisked her along into the keep, never pausing to take a breath, asking questions and answering them herself. When Jocelyn glanced back over her shoulder, she noticed the sheepish look on her husband's face, as though he'd loosed the wolves on her.

She heard some comment from Dougal about going hunting and all the men gathered there laughed. Within minutes, Jocelyn found herself in the middle of a confrontation between Rhona and Murdoch that made her dizzy from turning back and forth between the combatants. Rhona must have been the victor, for the steward threw his hands up in the air and cursed before he left. Murdoch's memory of a sweet-tempered woman must have been softened by her time away, for he could not be thinking it now.

Although Rhona complained over the state of the keep, and most especially the deplorable condition of the solar, Jocelyn found the two women and their various maids and companions ensconced there within a very short time. She caught a glimpse of Murdoch as he hurried to and fro outside the room, calling out orders and cursing more than she'd ever heard him do so.

In truth, she felt a failure. If these women were what Connor was used to, she would always disappoint him. Although Rhona seemed to do most of the talking and ordering around, Jean did hers with a glance or with a gesture. Jocelyn had no experience guiding a household this large. And now, watching these two take control with ease, she knew she never would.

Chapter Fifteen

Probably like most other men, he found it was easier to stand aside than to oppose his aunt and her minion when they joined forces. Over and over, Connor reminded himself that inviting them here was a good idea. And tempted though he was to beat Duncan to a pulp for being the one to suggest it, Connor could admit that the changes in the keep, especially the food and the ones involving his comfort, were good ones.

To this point.

His plan, one he'd not shared with anyone, was to allow them to improve the keep and set in motion the ways to keep it clean and well-supplied and comfortable, and then to send them back when Dougal left. Dougal did not yet know that he would be leaving in a matter of weeks for the southern village, at his laird's orders.

Jocelyn did not say much, but he'd heard she won a few battles of her own. He'd not spoken to her since his aunt's arrival two days before and expected that once she got her bearings, he would hear about her displeasure in this. Although he visited her each night, she was so deeply asleep upon his arrival in her bedchambers, that he did not wake her. The dark smudges still discolored the skin beneath her eyes and he knew she needed to rest.

Now it was she who left the table immediately after breaking her fast, for the morning was the time she visited the village. Although Murdoch reported that Rhona thought such an activity was unnecessary and beneath her, Jocelyn argued that as wife of the laird the villagers were her concern.

He smiled as he walked back from the stables. He knew that there was a well of strength within his wife, one that simply needed to be encouraged. And, with the changes coming to his clan and to his life, he hoped that this time with Aunt Jean and Rhona would help her to see her true abilities and begin to use them.

When he'd begun looking for a bride, he thought of finding one from another of the larger, more important clans so that his prospective wife could take her place as a noblewoman with ease. But, that was easier said than accomplished. His reputation limited his choices and his life as a ruthless mercenary, hiring on with whatever noble or clan needed his services after Kenna's death, had not made him such an attractive marriage prize.

With Duncan's aid, he'd discreetly begun investigating the smaller clans and when young Athdar stopped here on his way home, drunk and full of himself and a young man's pride, it had been easy to manipulate the boy into the insult. And into the fight that saw him taken prisoner and turned into the bargaining tool Connor needed to open negotiations with the MacCallum.

Connor got the wife he needed, one intelligent enough to be the spouse of a powerful laird, but different enough from Kenna that he would not be forever reminded of her. Oh, there was much she needed to learn, but now that he realized he needed her to take her place as wife, he also knew she would.

As though thinking of Jocelyn conjured her up before his eyes, she walked through the gate from the village. She stopped when one of the men called out to her and he watched as she answered some question of his. Now, Guthrie left the stables by the door near where she stood and called to her. It took several minutes before her steps brought her closer to him and he'd spent it watching the way she moved, the manner in which she spoke to the people and even noticing that the sadness had not left her yet.

'Twas then that he realized his thinking on her place in his life had changed over the last week or so. Ailsa's words about his anger had caused him to think on his actions and attitudes toward Jocelyn. No matter what happened they were joined in marriage, so what sense did it make to keep her from the roles he now needed her to fulfill?

Duncan's idea to bring his aunt here was the catalyst for the changes he needed to make—both in his dealings with his wife and how his home was managed. Without even realizing it, he accepted the shift in thinking and began to encourage her and those in Lairig Dubh to think of her as the lady of the clan.

In spite of this change in the way he felt about accepting her as his wife and her assuming that place here, he was also just as sure that it would end there. He could have the wife he needed, and the wife he was coming to want, without risking more than that. Giving in here would guarantee that he could limit the potential for another debacle. And capitulating here would grant him many benefits.

Jocelyn approached now and she lifted her hand to shade her eyes from the glaring rays of the early afternoon sun that had decided to shine rather strongly that day. She carried a basket in her other hand which he held out his hand to take.

"Laird," she said in greeting.

"Lady," he replied, letting his irritation show in his voice. It worked.

"Connor," she said this time.

"Jocelyn," he answered smiling at her as he did. "Are you returning to the keep?"

"I must," she said with a sigh.

He could not help himself, he laughed out loud at her acceptance of the inevitability of facing Jean and Rhona again. "'Tis that bad then?"

"Nay, lair—Connor," she answered. Another sigh and then she offered the truth. "Aye, 'tis that bad."

"Could I tempt you with a respite?"

"Rhona and Cora are working on a new gown for me in my chambers and Murdoch has a man building you a set of shelves in your chambers. I fear there is no place for a *respite*."

From the way she emphasized the word, he knew she thought he was trying to take her to bed. Actually, though that notion was never far from his thoughts, he wanted to talk with her now.

"Come, let me show you a place to hide when you do not want to be found."

He held out his hand to her and she took it, walking at his side as he took her around the keep, to the stairs that led through one of the guardhouses to the battlements. He adjusted his pace so that she did not become winded and once they turned the corner and walked into the shadows thrown by the keep, he guided her to his favorite spot.

"When standing here, no one from the keep or the guardhouses can see you." He placed her basket on the stone walkway and turned her to look to the right and then to the left so she could see that he was correct.

"That does not sound safe." She looked past him and shook her head.

"Ah, but the guards pass here at least every quarter hour, unless ordered away by the laird or his commander. 'Tis said that the castle's builder designed it so that he might arrange trysts with the wife of the laird at the time. They were lovers."

She shivered then, for it was colder here in the shadows than it had been in the yard below. "A romantic but dishonorable tale, Connor." Did she realize she stepped closer to him as she spoke?

"You think so?" he asked. "Most women find it touching and somehow exciting." She leaned against him and he wrapped his arms around her.

"Aye, if 'twas but two lovers meeting, it might be."

"And if it were the laird and his lady wife?"

"Ah," she said, leaning back to look him straight in the eyes, "I kenned that was your intention all along."

He laughed then. "Nay, although some parts of me are always ready for such an event." He rocked his pelvis against her and let her feel his hardness. "I did think to show you my refuge on the walls, in case you need to seek some time away from those who harass you."

"And whom might that be, husband?"

"We both ken the answer." He nuzzled the top of her head as she leaned it on his chest now. Standing here felt so right. Holding her did as well. Why had he ever thought otherwise?

"Your aunt is a bit trying on my patience, Connor. And Rhona tries to be helpful, but everything must be done her way."

"And they have only been here for two days. Imagine how you will feel when winter arrives."

"I thought Dougal left sooner than that?" she asked, mimicking his own thoughts exactly.

"I will see what I can do to hasten his departure." He waited a moment for the subject to settle and then started on the real topic he wished to discuss with her. "I brought you here under false pretenses, Jocelyn."

"So, you have decided to try the trysting then?"

"Nay, I mean here, to Lairig Dubh."

"How so? Am I not your wife?" Her voice shook now revealing her unease to him.

"You are my wife, but I did not plan on sharing all that the position entails with you. I thought to keep you pushed aside while I carried out my duties as laird." Jocelyn stilled in his arms and he worried that he was giving her the wrong message. "I told you that you had no responsibilities here, that you were to stay out of the way and not be involved in decisions in running the keep. But, I think that the clan deserves more and you do as well."

"I am content…" she said, but there was no conviction in her voice.

"Are you truly? I think not. I think you would like to tell Murdoch what to do. I think you would like to order the others around as Jean does."

"I confess that there is some appeal in that, Connor. But," she stepped from his embrace and crossed her arms over her chest, "I fear I have not the experience or training to do it well."

"I confess that I chose you in spite of that."

"In spite of my failings?" Her emotions were written on her face at times like this. She worried that she was not worthy. That she would not be able to fill the role.

"I was told that you have been carrying out your mother's duties since she was taken ill some months ago. I heard how you managed to keep everyone fed and clothed and sheltered, sometimes making their garments yourself and giving your food to those in need. Was this incorrect?"

The heat of a blush filled her face now, but this was no false modesty. She was embarrassed that he knew the full extent of their poverty and spoke of it. Her stomach clenched as she realized that he understood the depths to which her family had fallen and that her father was unable to protect and take care of his clan. Better to move on from this. "Nay, laird."

He lifted her chin that had sunk down almost to her chest with his finger. Tilting his head down until their gazes met, he smiled that enticing smile that she'd noticed more often these last days. "The other thing you have done is to save your clan by accepting an offer of marriage from the Beast of the Highlands. And you have survived much longer than most thought you would."

"Aye, I have done that," she said. Why was he teasing her like this? Did he really want her to assert herself after telling her upon her arrival here that she did not matter? Dare she take him up on his offer and try to be the wife he needed and might even be wanting now?

Jocelyn realized that even now things were different between them. He had taken her hand in the middle of the bailey and walked with her here. He had explained his actions to her—something he had not done before. He sought her out during his duties to speak to her, indeed, to ask for her help.

"So," he said. "Are you willing to step into this place at my side? To endure what you must from those two to learn your duties?"

Her husband offered her much with those words—his support, her rightful place, a chance to learn so much and do so much that she never would have in her own small clan. Was she ready?

Her mother had always said that a wife's task is to step into her husband's world and make herself a place there. That there would be good (with a glance at her) and bad (a glance then toward her usually drunken father), but a wife made her own place.

"You may not like what you find, laird."

"Ah, lady. Word did spread that the MacCallum's daughter had the very devil's temper when upset. I wonder if that is true."

Jocelyn laughed then. She did have a temper, but lately she'd been either too fearful or too out-of-place or too sad to feel the need to use it. "I have been known to shout from time to time."

"Truly? Well, mayhap we will hear that in the halls and yards of Lairig Dubh soon?"

"Mayhap."

At the same moment, both of their names were called out—his in the yard, hers from the keep. Their talk was done and it was time to be about their duties. Their duties. She smiled.

"I would make the suggestion that you use the same subterfuge on my aunt and her minion that I do."

"Your aunt and her minion? Oh, Connor!" She laughed. "And what strategy do you use other than avoidance?"

"You have noticed that one, eh?" He winked then and the sheer surprise and lightheartedness nearly took her breath away. "No, not that. Unfortunately you must work with them." He held out his hand to her and once she offered hers, he leaned down and picked up her basket. "Let them believe they are in charge, but speak to the cook and to Murdoch and make your own arrangements with them."

They walked back to the steps and down into the guardhouse. A few more paces and they would part. But this time it would be different. This time she had a place here, a place that he invited her take, the rightful place of the laird's wife. It seemed to her, as they left the shadows of the stone building, that the sun shined a bit brighter.

"Jocelyn!" Rhona called out from the door of the keep. "I have been searching for you everywhere. I expected your return from the village, though why you must spend so much time there I do not know, almost an hour ago."

"Form your strategy now, lady. You are facing a formidable adversary."

"I have been facing one since my arrival here, laird."

Uncertain of how he would take the message, she waited. His boisterous laughter echoed out over the yard and drew the attention of those working there. Rhona hurried to where they stood.

"Cora has the gown ready for you to try, Jocelyn. We have little time now so please hurry."

"Little time for what, Rhona?" Connor asked.

"We are planning a true meal this evening. One that befits the..." Rhona stammered then. "One that befits a clan such as ours. One that requires a finer gown for the wife of the...laird than the ones she wears now."

"Go then, lady, and have your fitting. I will see you both at the meal." He waited until Rhona turned away before winking at her again. Dismissed again, but this time so differently. She did not mind taking leave in such a manner.

"Jocelyn? Cora is in my chambers with the dress. I will join you in just a few moments. I must speak to the laird about another matter."

Now grateful for the escape offered her and not Connor, Jocelyn nodded and walked quickly away. 'Twas Rhona's habit to add something else as someone walked away, so she hurried.

"And call for a bath, Jocelyn. God knows it will take time to get one in your chamber and we must remove the odor of manure from you before our feast."

Jocelyn did not turn around or stop. She handed her basket to a servant in the corridor and asked her to deliver it to her bedchambers. The fruit picked by Brodie and his friends was a special gift to her and she wanted it for later.

She reported to Cora and endured the fitting, all the while thinking of the changes she wanted to make. Not big ones, for most of what Jean and Rhona had accomplished these last few days was exactly what she would have done.

Looking around as she held her arms this way and that, Jocelyn noticed the chests on the worktable that Rhona had moved in here. Small glass jars and bottles, a few metal flasks, small sacks, and other things filled them.

"What are those, Cora?"

"I am not certain, lady. 'Tis said that the laird's cousin brews her own tea and makes concoctions with her herbs."

"You have the right of it, girl."

Rhona entered and walked around Jocelyn, examining the fit of the gown. 'Twas one of hers, generously offered so that Jocelyn would have something suitable for this meal. And to use as a pattern for making others. Reaching up, she pulled the gown tighter across her breasts. Jocelyn inhaled as she felt the tenderness there.

"Your pardon, Jocelyn. Is that too tight?"

Rhona's prodigious bosom was much more than her own, so the gown had been altered most there. This seemed to hurt when it had not before. Jocelyn reached up to adjust it herself and felt the same sensitivity there still.

"Are your courses due?" Rhona asked as she took the pins out and moved them slightly to give more room.

"Aye. They should have started, but Ailsa said that with all that has happened these past weeks, 'twould not be amiss if they were late or altered in some way."

"She said that, did she?" Rhona asked. "Well, she would know of these things."

Rhona had a noblewoman's dislike for peasants, servants and women who slept with their lords. She regaled Jocelyn with tales of court and the disdain she felt for women who served as lemans was clear. Not that in most situations there was anything for a servant or peasant woman to do but accept her lord's attentions. Still that topic was one of few that brought out a meanness in her voice that was heard at no other time.

"Cora, I will finish this. See to your lady's bath and put these herbs and oils in the water." Rhona pointed to a small bottle and a linen packet next to it. "Make certain the water is hot enough that the oil mixes in and does not float on top."

The girl left, as ordered, and Rhona helped Jocelyn out of the gown. Since she could sew a finer stitch and faster than Rhona, she took the gown and threaded a needle to do it. Rhona took two small bowls from one of the chests on the table and searched for something else. Finding a small sack, she opened it and sprinkled some leaves into one bowl, and from another sack, she did the same in the other bowl.

Fascinated, Jocelyn watched as she retrieved the pot of water that simmered in the hearth and poured a small amount over the leaves. Then she opened a jar and poured what looked like honey into both. A wonderful aroma filled the room as the leaves steeped and gave off their scents.

"My husband, God rest his soul, was much older than I and afflicted through most of his life with various ailments. He had a healer who worked with herbs and plants and whose concoctions were able to soothe some of his ills and pains."

She stirred the bowls and then scooped out most of the leaves in each one. Rhona carried them to her. "These are my two favorite teas. I find them very soothing when my woman's time is upon me. Mayhap they will help you?"

"Which one should I try?" Both smelled wonderful, though one was a fruitier scent and the other one more herbal.

"Either. I find this one is more soothing for the days prior to my courses," she said, holding out the herbal-smelling one.

Jocelyn accepted it and took a sip. The warm brew slid over her tongue with ease. The taste of the herb along with the honey was both soothing and appealing. She took another sip and then another. Rhona sipped the other and soon they worked in companionable quiet—she sewed the bodice and Rhona made adjustments to the hem. By the time her bowl was empty, the gown was ready.

Rhona shooed her away to her chambers to bathe. Once there, the sound of her stomach rumbling reminded her that she had not eaten. With so much time before the evening meal, she decided that some of the fruit from the boys would be perfect. In a decadence she'd not enjoyed before, she sat soaking in a hot, soothing bath, and ate the pears and apple.

He waited where he'd been told to do so—at the bottom of the stairway to Jocelyn's tower. Well, in truth, it was simply the south tower, but he'd come to think of it as hers. Rhona's instructions were precise—meet Jocelyn and escort her to the table.

Oh, and be clean and dressed as the prospective earl of Douran should be. He'd argued the point and had won some concessions, but not all. Since no one but the clan elders knew of the coming title, it was not time to make it so boldly public. Rhona would not admit how she kenned it, but agreed to keep silent on the matter for now.

So, here he stood, in a clean long shirt, a newly woven length of tartan in place around him and his father's pin and badge in place on his shoulder, waiting for his wife to descend. He heard some noises up the stairwell and stood a bit straighter. Cora walked first, in front of her, so he did not get a clear glance at her until the girl moved away.

Descend was the correct word, for she appeared to float down the steps toward him. Her hair, usually loosely pulled back, was wrapped and rolled and then covered in some arrangement that gave a new look to her face. The gold trim of the cap and netting seemed to embellish the golden tones he'd not noticed before in her skin. Without her hair hanging down, the curves of her chin and neck looked graceful.

The biggest change was to her eyes. Framed by a few wispy locks that did not stay covered, her eyes looked wider and a deeper, more emerald green than before. Her lips were fuller and her cheeks carried a rosy color.

Was it her or him who had changed? Surely, a new gown and a different style to her hair had not wrought such changes? Rhona's choice in garb definitely contributed for the gown covered nearly every inch of his wife's skin but displayed every womanly curve she had. She came to a stop on the second step so that their eyes were level. He swallowed several times and could get no words to come out.

"Jocelyn, you look…" he began. Not beautiful in the way Kenna had been, Jocelyn's attraction was more earthy, more sensual. Then he glanced at her expression and saw the real Jocelyn there. "You look uncomfortable."

Chapter Sixteen

He knew the words were not what she expected for she turned her gaze away and then back, but he did glimpse what he thought was a glimmer of a smile trying to lie on her lips.

"I am that." She looked down at the gown she wore and touched her hair and nodded. "I feel as though I am someone else completely."

Connor reached out for her hand and drew her closer. As she stepped to his side, he took notice of some enticing scent she wore, or had bathed in, and inhaled it deeply. "You may be uncomfortable, but you look lovely, Lady MacLerie."

"My thanks for the compliment," she said softly as they began walking toward the great hall and those gathered there. When she saw how large the gathering was, she stopped walking.

"Come, keep walking and smile," he said, pulling her along. He knew the reason for this feast even if she did not. It could not have been done without his permission, regardless of Rhona and Jean's belief in their authority and abilities. "I know that our marriage did not start off well, with me holding your brother hostage and you beating up my man on the journey here."

She laughed, a nervous one, as she kept looking from him to the dozens and dozens of people present. "My aunt has berated me several times over, and drawn my uncle into the fray as well, that you did not receive an adequate welcome from our clan. She demanded that I correct the oversight and hold a feast marking our joining."

They were nearly to the head table where the elders and Duncan and Aunt Jean and Rhona sat waiting, but she still looked as though she might keel over. The atmosphere was made more tense by the silence, the absolute silence, that had engulfed the room at the sight of her. He could almost hear their thoughts—the ugly nestling now the stunning swan.

"I thought that after our discussion earlier today this was perfectly timed and well-warranted to mark our new agreement as well." He continued to move along, hoping they would reach the table before he ran out of things to say to distract her from the nervousness he felt in her. What finally made her relax were Rurik's words as they passed him at one of the side tables.

"Ye clean up weel, Jocelyn," he whispered just loud enough so she could hear as they walked by. Others nearby chuckled at his declaration, but the expression on her face said that Jocelyn appreciated it immensely. They reached the table and everyone stood until they sat. He did not release her hand but waited for Duncan's words.

"Laird. Lady," Duncan said as he raised his cup in salute. "'Tis a tradition to welcome a new bride into the MacLerie clan with the words of the history of our family.

However, our bard has gone missing and no one can remember the words."

Those in the hall laughed loudly for they had not had a bard for a generation and everyone here knew their history.

"So, 'twould appear that it is left to me to offer best wishes to the bride and groom on their *recent* marriage." Duncan called out loudly, "A MacLerie! A MacLerie!"

The hall reverberated with the cry as one and all joined in. "A MacLerie! A MacLerie!"

Duncan and all sat down and Connor stood now. He'd thought all day of what to say to welcome her and could not come up with words. So, he kept his salute to the point. "To the lady!"

Once more everyone shouted out in reply and he held the cup between them out to her. She drank deeply from it, then he drank from the same spot, now warmed by her lips. He began to sit when the cry rang out, its source always recognizable.

"To the wedding night!" Rurik called out.

He laughed and sat down as the cheer spread through the whole of the hall. It brought a blush to Jocelyn's face, which made her appear even more lovely.

"In truth," he said to only her, "'Twas the promise of a second wedding night that induced me to give permission for this. You slept through our first, if I recall correctly."

"Then it is your responsibility to make certain that does not happen on this one, laird."

"When I saw you walk down the steps, I confess my first thoughts were about peeling those layers and coverings off you and feeling your naked body beneath mine."

"Connor!" she whispered fiercely as she grabbed his leg

under the table. Touching him was the wrong thing to do. "You must stop for someone might hear you."

He took hold of her hand and moved it up until her palm rested on his hardness. "And you may peel off my layers until you get to this, lady."

Although he guided her hand there, she did not move it away when he let go. Indeed, he felt her slide her fingers around it and under it, holding his sac for a moment. Then he noticed the quiet and the gazes of those all around on them. They were waiting for him to begin the meal so that they could eat. To do that he needed both hands and one of them still lingered near hers under the cloth that covered the table.

Caught by his own game, he nodded to the servants who stood behind them ready to serve the meal. Platters of venison and beef, mutton and pork were placed in front of them. Others of fish and pigeons and several bowls of fruit sauces and other condiments to be used on them filled the table. Then loaves of bread, still hot and steaming, and crocks of butter filled in open space on the table. Dishes of cooked vegetables and apples and pears were added until there was not a place for any more before them.

After taking some of each of the meats and game and fish and placing them on the trencher between him and Jocelyn, he turned to thank Rhona for her part in this. Before he could, she addressed him.

"I did not think it possible, but I suspect you are falling in love with her, cousin." She'd kept her voice pleasant so it did not draw any untoward attention, but he heard the hostility in it nonetheless. "Have you been able to forget Kenna, then?"

"Not that it is your concern, Rhona, however, do not mistake lust for love," he retorted.

The fixed smile on her face melted away and he glimpsed something else for just a moment. It moved across her features so quickly he nearly missed it. Grief? Sympathy? Relief? He could not tell. Then it was gone and she met his gaze.

"Your pardon, Connor. I meant no disrespect by it, to you or your wife."

He turned back to Jocelyn but she was speaking with Dougal and Jean on her other side. Both of her hands, he took note, were above the table now. Although she still sat stiffly, he saw that she was trying some of the food. He did not recall the cook ever presenting such a wide array of foods before and was pleased by it. He did not require such fancy fare often, but 'twas good to know that the man was capable of producing it when needed.

Connor dipped a spoon into the pear sauce and scooped some over the slices of pork on the trencher. He was thinking of the last time he'd had this particular sauce when Jocelyn jostled him. He looked at her and saw her mouth the word *soon*.

She'd been thinking the same thing as he.

Connor laughed and offered a prayer up. Even if it could never be the same between him and Jocelyn as it had been for him and Kenna, even if this union had gotten off to a shaky start, and even if he could offer her only his respect and name and not his heart, he thanked the Almighty that she enjoyed the passion he could offer her.

He'd been foolish to think he could bring her here and keep her out of his life. He'd been shortsighted enough to think that she would simply be the woman to give him heirs and not have her want to enjoy some of the benefits of being the wife of the MacLerie. He'd been wrong about how to handle her and was glad now to realize his error.

Some part of him must have known that this would happen. Something inside had told him it was time to move on in his life, to make the changes necessary and to find a wife. Now, looking around at the people in the hall, his clan, he knew this was the right thing to do. As was asking Jocelyn to step fully into her role.

How much things had changed in just a few weeks for them. With his aunt and cousin's help, Jocelyn would learn her duties. By the time the title and charter were granted by the king, she would be ready to be a countess, at his side. And soon, they would be blessed with children. He had no doubt.

"Connor? I would like to seek my chambers now," she whispered, touching his arm. Her face was pale and her hand was damp with sweat.

"Are you well?" Connor motioned to Cora to come to the table.

"I cannot explain it, but something is not right."

At Cora's approach, Rhona leaned over. "Would you like me to come with you, Jocelyn? You do not look well."

She did not wait for his reply or his wife's, but stood and helped Jocelyn stand. With a word to Cora who went running toward the kitchens, she led Jocelyn from the hall.

He wondered if he should do something, but Rhona was not only a capable woman, she was an accomplished herbalist. If anyone could help Jocelyn, it would be her. A short while later, Cora carried some linens and led one of the cook's men who brought a large pot from the kitchens.

He tried to finish his food, but pushed it from one side of the trencher to the other. Convincing himself that all was well was not working and when Cora came back into the hall a short time later and summoned Ailsa from where she sat with Margaret and Hamish, he decided he should check on Jocelyn himself.

He nearly ran Ailsa down on the stairs; the old woman was not moving fast enough for him. Then he reached the doorway to Jocelyn's chambers and odor hit him. Someone was heaving, and heaving badly. When Ailsa caught up with him and entered, it took but a moment and he was pushed back out of the room and the door slammed in his face. From even the muffled sounds on the other side of the door, he was glad of it.

"Bring word of her condition," he shouted out at the door. When he got no response, he shouted louder. "Bring word..."

Cora opened the door a bit and nodded. The door slammed again as the sounds of terrible retching escaped from within. The recently eaten food in his stomach reacted to the sounds of distress and turned a bit, making him wonder if he was the next one to feel some ill effects.

Deciding to distance himself, he ran down the stairs and back into the hall where many still ate. Some wine was what he needed to calm his upset stomach. Duncan was still seated there, so Connor sat with him and called for wine.

He was still sitting there hours later when news finally came about Jocelyn's condition.

Death could not be as painful as this, she thought as she tried for the fourth time to force her eyes open. She succeeded but was met with such dizziness when she did that Jocelyn decided being awake was highly overrated. When the whispering around her grew more frequent, she used all of her strength to move her head and open her eyes.

"Lady," Ailsa said, "try to lie still for a bit longer." She felt the woman pat her hand reassuringly and decided to pay heed to her advice.

Sometime later, she tried again and this time the room did not swirl around her. When she tried to speak, the burning in her throat kept her from doing so. Ailsa leaned over, helped her to raise her head a bit and tilted a cup to her lips. Not water but some other brew that soothed the terrible burn as it slipped into her belly. Two more sips and then felt her throat moistened enough to try to speak.

"Will I live?" she whispered when she could.

"Aye, lady. It seems that you ate something that did not agree with you."

"Is anyone else sickened? Do you know what it was?" Jocelyn managed to turn her head a bit and saw that Ailsa, Cora and Rhona were standing by her bed.

"No one that we ken," Cora answered.

"Jocelyn, what did you eat before the evening meal? Was there anything else?" Rhona asked.

Thinking back over her day, she remembered having porridge as was her custom to break her fast this morn and then eating nothing else until… "Pears and an apple. From Brodie and his friends."

Cora looked around the room and pointed to the basket, still filled with more of the boys' gift to her. "There they are."

Rhona took one from the basket when Cora brought it to her and squeezed it. Then she sniffed it and held it out to Ailsa.

"Is it bad?"

"'Twould not seem so, lady. But mayhap the ones ye ate were?"

"Ailsa, please do not say anything to Brodie. He will be upset if he thinks his gift to me caused this."

She struggled to sit up, but had not the strength to. Three heads shook at her, telling her it was not a good idea to do so now.

"Rest now, Jocelyn. I gave you something to stop the retching and the other. It should help you sleep for the night." Rhona did not need to tell her about the upheaval of her bowels, Jocelyn could still feel the effects.

But when she touched her belly, the pain came from another area. "Aye," Rhona confirmed with a sad smile, "your courses have begun as well. The strength of the distress in your stomach and bowels may have brought it on."

Jocelyn did not say anything. All of them knew the disappointment that would follow when news of this reached her husband. Although their relationship seemed to have improved, Jocelyn feared that this would upset it.

"Lady, all will be well." 'Twas young Cora who spoke and Jocelyn tried to smile at her words of comfort. But, at this moment, as the fact that she'd failed once more to give the laird what he valued more than anything hit her, all she could do was nod. And turn her face away so they did not see her despair.

She did close her eyes then and sought the sleep that Rhona promised. Her body ached from top to bottom and especially in between and she hoped that most of that would pass during the night. Though the women were still there, they were quiet in their movements and she felt sleep come up to claim her. Just as she fell into its grasp, she remembered their banter at dinner and the night of pleasure promised by her husband.

So much for their second wedding night.

* * *

The tables had long been cleared and those few dozen who still slept in the hall were long at their rest when Rhona shook him awake. Wine followed wine until Duncan collapsed next to him, but Connor waited. Now, as she approached quietly, he stood to receive word of Jocelyn.

"Is she…" He stopped, not knowing which way to ask the question. His hands fisted at his side as he awaited word of her condition or fate. He had never seen someone taken so ill so quickly as she had this night.

"She is resting now, Connor. We think it may have been the fruit from the village boys, either too new or wormy."

"That would explain why no one else sickened after the meal."

"Aye, it would," she said. "Cora is with her and will stay until morn."

"Rhona?" he said, turning to her. "My thanks for your help. Not just this but everything you have done so far. I appreciate that you came with so little notice and that you are helping her."

She stepped closer, so close he could smell the scent she used in her bathwater. She reached out and laid her hand on his chest. "I do not begrudge you happiness, Connor. I only wish that you find the joy you deserve after such pain and suffering."

Uncomfortable with such closeness, he moved a pace back, but she followed, taking his hand in hers and stroking it as she spoke. "Kenna was my kin and I know you loved her, but she was not the one. I will pray nightly that you find what you truly need."

He took his hand from hers and squeezed it. "My thanks for your concern, Rhona."

She stared at him and smiled. "I will seek my chambers now, for I want to check on Jocelyn at first light."

"On the morrow then."

He watched her walk away, back toward Jocelyn's tower where her room was located. She'd taken only a few steps from him when she turned back to face him.

"She wanted you to know that her courses began tonight."

'Twas Connor's turn to look away now, as she told him this news. Disappointment raced through him and he nodded to her. Rhona left without another word, gliding into the shadows at the edges of the hall.

Another month of failure.

Another cycle of the moon and no child in her womb.

Ailsa had tried to warn him about this. With such an upheaval with her mother's death, Ailsa said it might affect her this way. She'd told him about other symptoms to watch for, but somehow hearing it then and knowing it now were very different.

A pang of guilt twisted in his gut. He should be worrying more about the woman in the bed above him than about something that only the Almighty could grant. Jocelyn had suffered much in these last weeks and now this.

She but needed time to recover and then he would be surprised if their efforts were not successful. A few months of health and practice and she would be fruitful. A sickly or frail wife would not bear him children.

Nor, as he began to fear in the next weeks, would a dead one.

Chapter Seventeen

Her strength returned quickly after the incident and soon she felt as though she was growing in her abilities to oversee the duties of the wife of the laird. Murdoch now answered to her and, although she consulted with Aunt Jean and Rhona, she now controlled those who lived in the keep or worked there. By the end of September, most of the fields were harvested and preparations for the winter were continuing at a pace Murdoch assured her was ahead of their usual one.

Connor agreed that Dougal and the others would return to their own home in their southern village for the winter and she was urging Jean and Rhona to accompany them. It was the one topic of discussion that turned Rhona irritable, but that petulance led to Jocelyn discovering two important things, one about her husband's kinswoman and one about herself.

First, Rhona did not like Rurik, in fact, the feelings she expressed toward him bordered on thinly disguised loathing. Jocelyn thought she'd imagined it at first, then when she caught the glances between the two of them on various occasions, she knew it to be true. When she tried to discern the reason for it, Rhona became as charming and evasive as she could and tried to distract Jocelyn from her quest to find the truth.

But Jocelyn took note that she was the only woman, the only one, in the keep or village who was not affected by his presence or attention. The younger women who moved into the keep to carry out their duties as serving maids or laundry maids or weavers would stop their activities when he entered the hall and simply stare at him. If he spoke to them directly, they were useless for the rest of the day.

In spite of his apparent faithfulness of a sort to Nara, he drew women to him like flies to the sweet. Jocelyn realized at some point that he simply liked women and it showed through in his behavior and approach. She'd overheard Connor complaining that unless he was fighting or f—well, tupping, he was not content and she knew it to be true. Hence, the ambushes of Connor when he was not paying attention and the nights in the village.

Jocelyn truly liked Rurik for his loyalty to the laird, his treatment of her—blunt but always concerned—and that he answered her call when she needed him. Sometimes, she thought that it was her own attitude toward Rurik that made Rhona dislike him more intensely.

The thing she discovered about herself came out by accident when discussing her choice of fabrics for a new gown she and Rhona were planning.

"Jocelyn, you should look at these pieces over here. The blue would be very attractive against your skin."

She picked up the fabric that Rhona pointed to and felt it. Too heavy and too ornate for her tastes which were exactly the opposite of Rhona's. Jocelyn lifted another roll of a dark brown and decided that it was the one. With a tunic of the lighter brown, she explained that it would be warm and serviceable. Rhona laughed as she sat back down and took up her stitching.

"You need to cultivate better taste, Jocelyn. In fabrics, in wine, in food. The king's court, even without the king, is a place of refinement and culture."

Rhona had shared many stories about her visits to the court of King David, and about the king's lieutenant and guardian of the kingdom, Robert Steward. Sometime during the last year, Rhona had traveled to Edinburgh and spent time at court.

"Since I do not expect to visit such a place, or live there as you have, I think my tastes in those matters will suffice."

"As countess of Douran, I think you will make many trips to court, Jocelyn. 'Tis best if you learn what is expected of you now."

She pulled the embroidery needle too hard as she heard those words and tore the thread she was placing in the tapestry. Aunt Jean gasped as did Cora and a few of the servants tending them. "Rhona!" Connor's aunt exclaimed. "'Tis not your place to speak of such things."

"Surely Jocelyn knows of it. Do you not?" Rhona tied off a knot on the stitch she'd just finished and bit the thread with her teeth. "That is why we were summoned here, to prepare her for her role as countess. To be the wife Connor will need."

Countess? Douran? She knew nothing of such things. But apparently from the looks exchanged between Connor's kin, both Rhona and Jean knew it to be true. "I did not know." Shaking her head, she asked, "Why would the laird keep such a thing from me?"

"Jocelyn," Aunt Jean began, "Speak to your husband. He will tell you about it."

"Come now, Jocelyn. Do not hold this slight against him, after all, he may have given Kenna his love, but he is making you his countess. At least your title may last longer than his love for her did."

With a sharp hiss, Aunt Jean stopped any further discussion of Connor and Kenna. Rhona's eyes widened and gave the appearance of an innocent mistake, but Jocelyn could not believe she did not know the effect of her words.

So, many knew of his love for his first wife? She was a paragon of womanly virtues and accomplishments. She'd been even more beautiful than Rhona, who did not hesitate to reveal such details when they were alone, loved by one and all in the MacLerie clan, especially the present laird. She'd been perfect.

And Connor had loved her. In spite of her one failure, not giving him an heir, he'd loved her. Then, as those things sometimes did, his love turned to hate and he'd pushed her down the stairs. Rhona hinted during one conversation that Kenna's inability to give Connor a son was a punishment from the Almighty.

She heard Aunt Jean's furious whispers to Rhona, but could not make out the words. Her hands shook as she stood and handed the piece of cloth and the colored threads to Cora at her side. She would speak to him. She would speak to him now.

Ordering Cora to stay in the solar, Jocelyn entered the hall and called to Murdoch. Discovering that the laird was in his chambers, she ran to that tower and climbed the stairs. He was alone in the inner room and she stood in the doorway, waiting for him to notice her.

"Jocelyn, come in. I cannot stay, but you are…" He stopped speaking when he caught sight of her expression. He'd seen anger there before, as well as frustration, pleasure, lust, affection, sadness, but this was something different.

Fury.

If she had been a pot of water over the fire, steam would be bursting from its lid. She stood with her hands fisted on her hips and her eyes glaring at him. He knew he was the target of her ire, but could not think of what he'd done recently to cause it.

"What is the matter?" He would have walked to her, but she looked quite capable of bodily harm in this moment.

"Again?" she called out to him. "Again you keep something from me?"

The volume and tone of her voice was something he'd not heard before from her. Something she'd been lacking in, apparently until now. She needed to exercise her backbone, to learn that righteous anger was something not to be feared. That they could disagree, argue, even yell at each other, and not be afraid of it.

"What is it you think I am keeping from you now, Jocelyn?" He faced her and mimicked her stance with his own, keeping enough distance so as not to intimidate her from her anger.

"A countess? I am to be a countess and you did not think I should know?" she shouted.

"I would have told you when the time was right."

"When would that be, husband? When the king arrives from England with the proclamation in his hands?" She was still shouting.

"When I decided you should know."

Her face turned a brighter red then and she leaned back

her head and let out a scream. She was panting when she faced him. He waited for her to catch her breath before speaking.

"Did that feel good?" he asked, smiling now.

"What are you speaking of? Being the only one not to know something as momentous and important as my husband being made an earl?"

"Nay," he said, now walking toward her. "Being angry and letting it out. Yelling at me when you feel it."

She let out her breath on an exasperated sigh and she glared at him. "You have been taking my counsel, allowing me to be present at the gathering of the elders and permitting me even to speak there. Why did you not tell me this when others know? Simply to prick me into anger?" Jocelyn shook her head.

"I have heard rumors of the laird's daughter who never hid her temper from anyone. I wanted to see if the rumors were true." She screamed through clenched teeth then. "Jocelyn, nay! I have been pricking at your temper for days. The title from the king has nothing to do with that."

Confusion filled her face now, replacing the anger she'd spilled out. "So, 'tis true then. You're to be an earl?"

"Aye. But few know it and I did not want it announced yet."

"Why not?"

"Matters involving the king can be easily upset. I could hardly want the information made known and then have the king's ministers withdraw it. 'Twould not be a good thing if I am trying to maintain my reputation as the Beast of the Highlands."

He held out his hand to her now and she took it. "And I feared putting too much on your shoulders so soon. I think you are settling into your duties here, but I thought you might be overwhelmed facing the prospects of being a countess and not just the laird's wife."

"I am overwhelmed. 'Tis such an honor for you. I only worry that I will fail you in this."

My only worry is that I fail you in this.

She could not know that her words echoed Kenna's exactly, but the pain pierced him as it did whenever he remembered bits of their conversations. Kenna's only failure had been her love for him, for it led to her destruction and nearly his. And now, three years later, after purposely seeking a wife so different from Kenna so as to not repeat the failures of the past, here stood another wife worrying over the same weakness.

The only difference was that he did not love this wife. In keeping his distance, he protected her. By not having his perception clouded by that deep emotion, he could guide her through the difficulties they encountered. He felt affection for her, he certainly wanted her, and he was coming to respect her judgment and her abilities. But staying away from love would keep them from repeating the mistakes of his past.

"You will not fail me, Jocelyn. I will not let you. But you must not fear these challenges facing you, facing us. Surely one who has chased the Beast back to his lair and faced him there is braver than she thinks?"

Jocelyn saw the merriment in his gaze and realized that she did not fear him. She had barged into his chambers, shouting at him—*shouting* at him!—and he seemed pleased by it.

"I have to return to Murdoch and Hamish now, but is there anything else you need to know before I go?"

He was offering? He meant only about this one issue, she was certain. "When will this happen?"

"No sooner than spring according to the letters recently arrived. The cost has yet to be agreed upon."

"What will you do as earl more than you do as laird?"

"I will be at the king's, or rather, the king's lieutenant's call. I will uphold the king's laws in this area as his trustee and must attend court when called."

"And I?"

"You will accompany me to court when invited or rule in my name here if you do not attend. I brought my aunt and Rhona here to help you to learn your responsibilities. Let them guide you so you will be ready."

Could she really do that? He must believe it or he would not seem so at ease with the thought of it.

"Now, I must return to the village. I do ask that you not discuss this with anyone. Until I give word that it is accomplished."

"I will not," she assured him. Hoping that Rhona had only spoken of it by accident, she nodded.

He stepped closer to her and kissed her on the mouth, surprising her. "Did you know that your eyes sparkle when you are angry? They flash and your skin flushes as it does when you reach your peak at my hands." Her nipples tightened at his words. "And the way you yelled…it reminds me of the way you scream when…"

He completed his words in a whisper into her ear, speaking so closely that the heat of his breath tickled her. She shivered as he teased her now, with only words. "You said you were leaving," she reminded him.

"I am," he said, tasting her lips again.

Encouraged by his acceptance of bold behavior by her,

she reached down and cupped him. 'Twas his turn to gasp as she slid her fingers under and around him.

"I am! But I will seek out my mate later...in my lair when none can interrupt us," he said, pulling away from her and toward the doorway.

Then he leaned his head back and roared as though he was the beast he claimed to be. She clapped her hands over her ears and laughed at him. He grabbed the door and pulled it closed with a crash as he left.

She laughed then, first with the giddiness of the news he'd given her and then with the realization that he thought her capable of being his countess. And ruling in his name when he was absent. Could she really do that?

For now, she needed to return to the solar and choose fabric for gowns suitable for the wife of the Earl of Douran. And warn Rhona not to speak of it in front of others.

Jocelyn pulled open the door, which now stuck due to the force her husband had used closing it, and walked to the stairs. She just reached the first landing down when her feet were knocked from under her and she tumbled into the wall. Reaching out to slow her fall, Jocelyn banged her arm against a corner and then her face. The next thing she remembered was landing hard on her bottom a few steps down from the landing.

Reaching for her face, she felt the bruised area and checked for bleeding. Her hair, loosened in the fall, hung around her face. Her arm hurt the worst from hitting first on the corner of the stone wall. Jocelyn tried to move it and nearly screamed as pain shot through it.

She sat for a few more minutes before trying to stand. As far as she could determine, the injuries were minor, in spite of the amount of pain she was feeling. Using her other hand, she guided herself carefully down to the main floor and entered the hall. A bit dizzy after all, she leaned against the wall to wait for her head to clear.

"Lady!"

Murdoch shouted from across the large chamber. Her head throbbed but the sound of his shout caused even more pain. She clutched at her head and tried to stay on her feet.

The whispering began almost immediately. Not sure if it was real or the result of hitting her head, she heard the accusations as Murdoch called for Cora to attend her.

"Did ye hear him yelling up there?"

"She went to take him to task for not telling her…"

"Look at her face! Dear God, he hit her…"

"He was angry…"

They thought Connor had done this to her? How could that be? He'd left before she had and…Jocelyn glanced at those nearest and saw the pity in their gazes. They thought the worst of him.

"Lady? Should I send for Ailsa?" Cora asked, her voice cutting through the mumbled whispers.

"Nay, Cora. I but slipped down a few steps. Some cold cloths should take care of this," she said, trying to minimize what had happened. Then she swayed on her feet and fell against the wall.

"Get that bench," Murdoch called out to someone across the way. "Get some cold water. Move aside." She felt his strong arm around her waist and let him guide her to the bench.

"Is Rhona here?" she asked. Closing her eyes seemed to relieve some of the light-headedness, so she did.

"Nay, lady," Cora answered. "She just left for a walk." Then a cold, wet cloth was placed on her cheek. "Should I send for the laird?"

The quiet around her spread. They waited on her answer.

"Nay. There is no reason to disturb him only to bring my clumsiness to his attention. Murdoch," she said turning to where he stood, "if you would help me to my chambers, all will be well in a short time."

A short time later, with cold compresses on her face and her arm, she tried to figure out how she had fallen. She was no stranger to climbing steep stone steps and had never had any such accident before. Hopefully, this was the last one for she knew that somehow those servants in the hall blamed Connor for her bruises.

The blame instead escalated in the next days and weeks for her clumsiness increased and at least two more *accidents* befell her before Connor did take notice. Unable to explain how tainted meat ended up on her trencher during one meal or how a horse he'd been tending in the stables became terrified and nearly ran Jocelyn down in the yard, he began to examine the incidents to see if there were any links.

Still believing her accounts of each one, he was almost convinced not to look closer and blame it on her nervousness, about her duties, about the title she would bear soon or about simply being his wife. The day when stone on the ledge of the battlements where they met a few times, trysting she would call it, and where she liked to lean over to watch the yard below gave way and she nearly fell to the ground was the turning point.

Someone was trying to kill Jocelyn.

Worse, someone was trying to kill her and make certain the blame fell on him.

One wife falling down the stairs to her death could be explained—an accident, a struggle. No one, not even the king's men would look too closely at that when all witnesses could give no definite testimony against him. A second wife dying in the same manner did not bode well for him.

So, now the question was—who was the real target? He or Jocelyn?

"Connor!" she cried out as she turned to find him in her path. "Have you no other duties than to escort me to the village this morn?"

"Are you telling me that you do not enjoy my company, lady?"

She sighed and laughed, her eyes filled with some merriment. "I tend to not get anything accomplished when you follow me, laird. Things go awry and we end up…"

"Naked?" he offered, taking the basket from her hands and holding out his arm to her. "With lots of writhing and moaning?"

"You are trying to provoke me, Connor. 'Tis just that I need to visit two cottages this morn and you tend to get in the way." She glanced at him then. "Not that I do not enjoy the writhing and moaning with you."

She was being kind, he knew that, but being in her way or not, he would dog her heels for a bit longer this morn. The last accident happened five days before and the others were similarly spaced apart. If something was going to happen soon, he would be there, as witness or to intervene and protect her.

He'd called both Duncan and Rurik together and asked them to keep an eye open for any suspicious occurrences in the keep or village and especially around Jocelyn.

Without a coherent explanation, Connor knew he sounded like a lovesick puppy, but his men listened and accepted their charge. He could not, in spite of his own best efforts, be at her side every moment of the day. The nights he could claim as his, but the days and her busy schedule tested his limits.

If he could have involved one of the women, if he could ask Rhona to keep watch, it would have been much easier. But, he only knew that the fewer drawn in the better…and safer for her.

His plans were thrown asunder when Duncan arrived with his horse and a reminder that they were hunting this day. Hesitant to leave her alone, he began to refuse until Jocelyn promised to stay within the village until he returned for her.

The morning was misty and cold and not a particular good one for hunting, but they needed more game and deer to put by for the coming winter and any man with hunting skills joined in. They were just about to return to Broch Dubh when disaster struck.

Connor was standing by his horse waiting for the latest of their quarry target to be roped and tied to the wagon when a boar darted from a thick copse of trees near him. Without warning and him without a weapon, the animal stopped and sniffed the air. With a wave of his hand, Connor managed to bring everyone to a standstill and motion to Rurik who held a spear. As Rurik sighted the beast, the boar kicked at the dirt with its front hooves and charged at Connor.

Too slow in getting out of the way, he felt the tusks gore his leg as Rurik threw the spear. Falling to the ground, he watched as blood poured from the wound, turning the dirt below him into a thick pool of mud. Duncan reached his side just as Rurik pulled the boar free and stabbed it to make certain it was dead. Connor felt himself losing consciousness, but knew he must tell someone about the attempts on Jocelyn's life.

"Duncan," he said, grabbing his cousin's arm. "Jocelyn is not safe. Someone is… Someone is…trying to harm her."

"Rurik, give me a piece of plaid. Connor, lay back and let me get this bleeding stopped," Duncan ordered. Tying the length of wool around his thigh, his cousin wrapped it tightly and knotted it even tighter. "Who is trying to harm her?"

"I know not, but she is in danger," He fell back on the ground and found it difficult to breathe. "My chambers. Bring her to my chambers. No one else."

"What is he saying about Jocelyn?" Rurik asked, his voice fading as though he was walking away.

The forest became a murky pit to him, screeching birds flew overhead and Connor could not see or hear well now. "Rurik, protect her with your life." He reached out and grabbed for the Viking. "With your life."

Rurik took hold of his hand and whispered an oath. "With my life, Connor."

Knowing that Rurik would now die before allowing harm to befall Jocelyn, Connor let go and the world around him went dark.

Chapter Eighteen

The clatter of a riding party going through the village drew her attention for a moment, but then she went back to holding the bairn while his mother prepared their meal. Menial work unfit for the wife of the laird, Rhona called it, but Jocelyn found it soothing and fulfilling. Sitting in the solar, talking about the frivolous events that happened at court or being idle did not feel right to her. So, now that she was growing in control of the way things worked in Lairig Dubh, she spent her mornings here, helping as she could. Jocelyn was handing the bairn back when the door of the croft was torn from its frame and thrown aside.

Were they under attack? In danger? She placed herself between the door and the new mother and babe and looked for a weapon to use to protect them. But it was Rurik who strode into the small dwelling and called her name.

"Jocelyn. Come now, lass," he ordered in a quiet voice that disturbed her more than when he yelled his battle cry.

"What is it, Rurik?" she asked, nodding to the woman and walking to him.

He gave no explanation, but grabbed her wrist and

pulled her out of the cottage. Once there, she was surrounded by soldiers. Something was terribly wrong. Before she could ask again, Rurik mounted his horse, leaned down and lifted her bodily onto his lap. With a nod of his head, the soldiers grouped around him and he called out orders to ride.

"Rurik, I cannot breathe," she said, trying to pry his hands loose from around her. His grasp loosened a scant bit but she could take a breath now. "Rurik, tell me what's wrong."

"Keep yer voice down, Jocelyn. Connor's been hurt in the hunt and is being taken to the keep ahead of us."

"Hurt? Is he…?" She could not say the word she was thinking.

"Nay, not when I left him to get ye. He thinks yer in some kind of danger and wants ye protected."

"What happened?" she asked.

He squeezed her and she stopped talking. They rode in through the gate at full gallop and stopped at the steps of the keep. People stood watching as Rurik slid from his horse and lifted her off. With him as a shield before her, he took her hand and pulled her closely behind up the steps, into the keep and toward the north tower. They did not stop or slow even when Rhona called out to them as they passed her in the hall and Jocelyn tried to speak to her. Rurik simply warned her off with a look and their pace continued up the stairway and into the small chamber at the top.

She walked into his back, not realizing he'd stopped then. Peeking around him, she saw the crowd that surrounded her husband's bed. Tugging loose, she pushed Rurik aside and rushed in. Connor's skin was white and his breathing labored as she drew closer.

"Rurik, get her away," Connor rasped out.

"Connor?" Jocelyn began to climb up on the bed to get closer to him. Rurik's arm closed around her waist and she found herself dangling in his grasp. He strode from the bedside to the corner of the room and held her there.

"Rurik, put me down. Someone must tend to him." All the struggling she could manage was not even making the slightest bit of success in freeing her. "Please, Rurik, I will stay here."

"Ailsa is on her way," Duncan said. He leaned over Connor and listened to some whispered orders. "Rurik, he wants no one else in here but she and Jocelyn."

Her captor nodded and met her gaze. "Stay here, Jocelyn. Do not make me hold ye." She nodded her assent and he placed her back on her feet. Tugging her gown back into place, she called out to Connor.

"Please, Connor, let me help you."

He did not move then. Rurik and Duncan talked in tones too low for her to hear and then ordered everyone else out. Once they were gone, Duncan spoke. "He is unconscious, Jocelyn. Probably from losing so much blood. He will need to be cauterized when Ailsa gets here," he explained.

"I am here, Duncan. Lady," she said, as the guard outside the chambers allowed her entrance. "What happened?"

Duncan gave a succinct explanation of the injury and how it happened and Ailsa lifted Connor's plaid to examine the wound. Trying to see around Rurik was impossible, so Jocelyn finally ducked under his arms and ran to Ailsa's side. The gaping wound took her breath away.

"Ye will need to get Niall from the smithy. Tell him to bring his tools."

"The laird said no one but you and Jocelyn," Duncan repeated the orders he'd been given.

"The lady and I cannot manage this type of wound without help. The laird trusts Niall. Bring him quickly," she said.

"Duncan," Jocelyn begged. "Please do as she says. Look."

The plaid he wore and the bed linens beneath him were soaked with blood, and it was not stopping. The woolen strap was not enough to stanch the flow. Stitches would not be enough. Only the terrible burning of a hot instrument could seal his veins and save his life.

Duncan thought about it for a few seconds before giving new orders. Niall was summoned, Jocelyn was freed to be at Connor's side and she and Ailsa prepared what would be necessary. When Duncan suggested that Rhona's herbal concoctions might be helpful, Rurik stopped him with one look. She'd found Rhona to be very helpful and knew that many in the keep sought out her brews and concoctions for small ailments and woes. But, as she suspected, something was most definitely wrong between Rurik and her husband's kinswoman.

Soon, too soon and not soon enough, Niall arrived and he and Ailsa examined the bloody gash in Connor's leg. They planned out what they would do and assigned each person a task in it. Two more soldiers were summoned to the room, huge men like Rurik, and Jocelyn knew they would hold Connor down while his leg was cauterized. With everyone in place, Ailsa untied the strap and, while Niall pressed above the wound, cleaned out the dirt and as much blood as she could.

Jocelyn looked away and stared at Connor's face while the iron rods were heated in the fire of the hearth. What kind of trick was fate playing on them now? Just as she was beginning to fall in love with her husband, he might be taken from her.

She felt the blood drain from her own face as she realized what she had just admitted to herself. These last weeks, finally having the chance to be with him and to see him at his best after seeing him at his worst, she knew she had given him her heart. She knew he did not love her, but he did care for her. Affection was not love, but with time, it might become love.

Now, their chance might be slipping away.

"Lass, ye will no' faint, will ye?" Rurik asked. "Look, Ailsa, she's lost all her color."

"Do not worry about me, Ailsa. Do what you must."

Duncan took hold of Connor's left arm and placed his back to Jocelyn's. With him sitting as such, she could not watch what they were about to do. Grateful, she leaned over and began to whisper words of comfort to him. One of the soldiers climbed on the other side of Connor, took hold of his other arm and pressed a knee on his chest to secure him. The second soldier did the same thing to Connor's uninjured leg. Rurik took hold of his torn leg from the knee down and placed it as Niall directed. Then there was a pause and then it began.

In spite of the strength of those holding him down, Connor bucked and reared against their hold...and against the fire they applied to his thigh. The sickening smell of burning flesh wafted through the room as Niall plied his craft.

Just when Jocelyn lost her confidence that she would not faint, it was done. Connor had passed out some minutes before, but she continued to whisper to him until they stopped. Then, unable to speak, she clutched his hand, slid down to her knees and cried. The room grew quiet and she looked up to see that she was alone with him.

Ailsa, Duncan and Rurik gathered at the doorway, whispering among themselves, glancing over at her only once. After a few minutes, the men left and Ailsa carried a tray with several small jars and a basin and cloths on it toward her.

"Lady's mantle to soothe the burn," she said, placing the tray on the table next to the bed. "It should be rubbed into the wound three times a day. Hopefully it will draw out any infection."

Wiping her tears, she nodded. "What must we do?"

"The bleeding is stopped, but that is not the greatest danger now. The fever may begin at any time."

Fever. If not the bleeding, the fever might still kill him.

"Ye should get some rest now, lady, for he will need ye soon enough."

"I could not rest now, Ailsa. Mayhap I will send for my embroidery." She walked to the door and found Duncan and Rurik both standing there, blocking her path if she was trying to leave. They promised to send for her things and then pulled the door shut. Walking back to the bed, she examined the other jars and bowls on the tray. "What have you there?" she asked about the medicaments. "Are they from Rhona?"

"Nay, lady. I have my own ointments and such."

"Well, I hope they help him."

He slept then, for a few hours, not in complete silence, but with fits of shifting and tossing. The fever began by sunset and worsened through the night. Ailsa was there at her side as first he shivered with cold and then sweated with the heat of it. They bathed him with cool cloths and water and they tried to drip small amounts of a tea made from feverfew into his mouth. With his thrashing to and fro, most of it ended up on the pillow or the bed linens or them, but a bit trickled down his throat.

It continued through the next day and into the night. Ailsa and she each took a time of caring for him and then resting, although it was difficult to rest with him in such dire condition. Duncan allowed Cora to clean the room and help them for a short time, but he stood in the room and watched every move the girl made as though he suspected her of some treachery. His surveillance made Cora so nervous that she dropped a tray of soup and ran crying from the room.

In the middle of the second night while his fever still raged, he suddenly quieted and it woke Jocelyn from the nap she took in the chair. She'd had Rurik move it closer to the bed, so she could see his face while sitting in it. Ailsa had gone to rest in the chamber below this one for a few hours and so they were alone.

After a moment or two, she realized that his eyes were open and staring at her. "Connor?" she asked softly. "Are you awake?" Before she could move, he nodded and spoke to her.

"Kenna, love. I am glad to see you."

She shook her head and slid from the chair to stand next to him. "Connor, I am not…"

"I had the worst nightmare, sweet. I dreamed you were dead and gone from me. I dreamed that you fell to your death. Oh, Kenna, I dreamed that you…" Tears streamed from his fever-glazed eyes and she knew he was caught in the depths of it.

"Shh now, Connor. Rest," she whispered, taking hold of the hand he held out to her. "All is well."

But he didn't quiet, at least not completely, for he continued to speak to her as though she were Kenna. Just when she thought him done, he would talk about something else they had done or seen in their lives together. His words told her more than she ever could have asked about his first marriage and the depth of love he'd felt for his wife. Jocelyn did not know she cried until he reached up and touched her cheek.

"Dinna greet, love. I will not let any harm befall you."

His eyes closed then and he did not speak. With the edge of her shawl, she rubbed her own eyes clear of tears and checked his breathing. Then she felt his face. Still hot. Still fevered.

She did not understand. How could a man who loved a woman so deeply be accused of her murder? She knew that most here accepted it as fact. She sat down to watch him again and the next interruption did not wake her, it shocked her from her sleep.

"Kenna!" he cried out so loudly that Rurik came bursting in the door.

She startled and nearly fell out of the chair this time as she jumped up to get to his side. He was wild now, yelling Kenna's name and screaming to his dead wife as though he could see her. Rurik came in and shut the door behind him.

"Should I hold him down, Jocelyn?" he asked, all the while watching Connor thrash on the bed.

"I think not. So long as he does not harm himself, I think we should let him be."

"Would you like me to stay?" He made the offer, but she could see in his expression that he was hoping she would decline it.

"I will call you if I need anything. Ailsa promised to return in a few hours."

He nodded and left the chambers and she turned back

to Connor. She discerned a pattern over the next hour or so as she watched him suffer the delirium of the fever. He would call Kenna's name over and over, sometimes so loud that she imagined the walls vibrated with it. Then he would begin to beg for her forgiveness. Each time, with each repetition, he revealed more of the truths that he held inside, long hidden from the clan and anyone who heard the stories of the Beast.

He had not killed Kenna. Kenna had taken her own life.

Driven to despair by her continuing failure to give him the heir he needed, the child they both wanted so desperately, she took her own life. Believing it was the only way to free him to seek another wife who could bear him children, Kenna sacrificed herself for the man she loved never knowing that it would destroy him as well.

When he found her at the stairway and realized what she planned, he'd begged her to step back. He promised that he would find another way. He tried to grab her, but she stepped away and plunged to her death. She knew Connor was seeing it happen over and over again in the fantasy of the fever. He began screaming then, so loud and in so much pain that she cried with him. When he finally grew quiet, the sound of the door drew her attention and she discovered that Duncan had been standing there all along, listening to his laird's confession.

"He must never know that we heard this, Duncan. He must never know that he broke his word to her."

"Jocelyn…" She could see that tears stained his cheeks.

"Swear to me now that you will not tell him. He has suffered so much trying to protect her. He has been trying to give her soul the peace in death that he could not give her heart while she lived."

He did not respond quickly enough and she ran to him. Grabbing his shirt, she pulled him down to her. "Swear to me now!"

"I will not speak of this," Duncan whispered.

"Ever, Duncan. If anyone knows this, everything he has done is for naught. Her soul will be damned by one and all."

"Never."

She nodded and released him. She stumbled back to Connor's side and blotted his forehead with a cool cloth, hoping to soothe him back to sleep. What she heard next broke her heart over and over, for he became calm and talked to Kenna again, but this time it was about his heart.

By the time his voice weakened into a raspy whisper, she knew that no matter what she brought to him, no matter how she excelled in her duties, no matter how many sons she gave him, she would never have the one thing she knew now she wanted.

His heart. His love.

And when he bid the woman he loved farewell that morning, she knew that he would never love again.

Every inch of him ached. Had he fought with Rurik again and lost? Connor reached up to rub his face and felt the growth of beard there. Puzzled by it, he lifted his head and looked around the room. He was in his bed, but the chamber appeared to have been the site of a battle. Clothing and trays were strewn around on every possible surface. Dried blood marked the floor and bloody rags lay in a pile.

His mouth felt as though filled with dirt and he tried to reach for the goblet he could see on the table next to him. Now, his hand would not do his bidding and flailed uselessly next to him. The only choice he had was to wait for someone to enter the room. A few minutes, or maybe a long time, later, he could not tell, Rurik walked in and began to stir the fire in the hearth.

"Is there any way that you could lift that goblet to my mouth?" he asked. He did not recognize the voice that came from his lips.

"Mighty Thor's Arse! Yer awake!" Rurik yelled out.

Then he covered his mouth and glanced at the chair off to the side of the bed. Jocelyn sat there sleeping. Rurik held his breath as she shifted in the seat and settled back to sleep. Then he waved a finger at Connor as he tread lightly, making sure not to knock into the chair where she slept.

"I didna think ye were going to make it, Conn."

"What happened?" he asked, as Rurik finally brought the cup to him and let him drink. The ale moistened his mouth and wet his throat.

"Do ye no' remember the hunt? The boar that attacked ye?"

He laid his head back down after another mouthful and thought on it. "Aye, it darted from the bushes and..." He paused and looked down at his thigh. The angry scar on his leg, extending from near his knee to nigh his groin, hurt badly.

"Ailsa and Niall..." Rurik began and then he just shivered. "Ye ken?"

Niall the blacksmith's other talent was repairing the damage wrought by the weapons he made. The irony had always been evident to Connor. Niall'd saved many a life by taking off limbs or stanching wounds. Now he'd saved him.

"Connor."

Her soft voice was filled with concern and caring. He

watched as she woke, the evidence of her presence through this illness in her bearing and in the weary expression in her eyes and on her face.

"Jocelyn." He could only speak her name.

"Are you truly awake this time?" She slid from the chair and came to stand at his side.

"Have I been awake before?" He tried to remember. "How long have I slept?"

Rurik and Jocelyn looked at each other as though trying to figure it out. "Three days and nights," Rurik offered.

"The fever finally broke late last evening and you slept peacefully through the night," Jocelyn explained. "Have you need of anything now?"

"Rurik just gave me some ale."

She met his gaze, but hers was unreadable. He finally made his hand move and reached for hers. She entwined their fingers and he pulled her closer. "You have been here through it all?"

"Aye, Connor." Again, inscrutable.

"At first, we were following yer orders to keep her here. Then she would no' leave."

"My orders?" He tried to recall what he'd said, but that day was somewhere in the fog of the fever. Shaking his head, he admitted not remembering. "I cannot bring the words to mind, Rurik."

"Ye said that Jocelyn should stay here wi' ye. Ye said…"

He never completed his answer because Duncan arrived and interrupted. "Connor! Welcome back to the land of the living!"

To his disappointment, Jocelyn dropped his hand and stepped away for Duncan's approach. Duncan took his hand and shook it vigorously and then stood back and examined him from head to toes. He could read the message in his cousin's face—they needed to talk privately. His gaze went back to Jocelyn.

"My thanks for your care, lady." She only nodded at him in reply. From the look of it, she was about to pass out from exhaustion and he felt overwhelmed just by waking up. "You need to rest," he said.

"As do ye, laird."

Duncan and Rurik both jumped back to let Ailsa closer. Apparently, the tyrant had been giving orders while he slept. Ailsa walked over and touched his cheek, then his forehead, and when satisfied by what she felt there, she began probing the wound. Just before he was tempted to yell, she stopped and smiled.

"I think it will heal well."

Everyone in the room let out a sigh he did not realize they held in and he yawned. Not the reply he wanted, but his body had other plans. The yawns were catching because once he started, the others joined him.

"Jocelyn, you should get some rest."

"If you are well, I will," she answered. She turned away but her feet stumbled as she collapsed. Rurik caught her up in his arms.

"I will take her to her chambers and stand guard there."

He thought on it for a few seconds and then stopped him. "This bed is big enough that she will not disturb my rest. Rurik, put her here," Connor pointed to the empty spot next to him.

With minutes, Jocelyn was sound asleep beside him, Ailsa was content that they would both be resting, and Duncan promised to come back in a few hours to talk.

Rurik simply took a place outside his door and stayed there. Sleep overpowered him then, but he relinquished himself to it knowing that she was safely at his side.

Chapter Nineteen

His recovery was too slow. The muscles in his thigh did not heal as quickly as he thought they should and, unless he wanted Rurik to carry him down the stairs on his back, Connor was a prisoner in his chambers. Although everyone came to him with questions, he wanted to be out of these two rooms.

Jocelyn returned to her chambers that night. They'd awakened later that day, hands entwined, and she had climbed from his bed and not returned yet. When he tried to initiate more than the chaste kisses she now gave him, she murmured something about not wanting to hurt his leg and would escape.

And the damned stairs kept him from following her.

When Duncan revealed to Connor what had happened during the fever, he wondered if he had frightened her in some way, for his cousin told him how the entire keep could hear him screaming Kenna's name. If he said more than that, no one told him of it.

Rurik explained how some who heard thought the fever was God's retribution against him for his sins—Rurik tactfully did not mention which sins—and others thought him absolved since he survived it. Rurik shrugged it all off in his way and left to find someone who could give him a good fight until Connor healed enough.

Deciding that he had no evidence other than a gut feeling to prove his suspicions about Jocelyn's safety, he did not share all of it with Duncan. He only asked Duncan to find a truly discreet soldier who would keep watch over Jocelyn until he was well enough to do it.

Thinking on the strange occurrences, he could not see the connection between them, but knew there was one. And something tickled his memory, but stayed just far enough out of his recollection that he could not place it. Until he could, he would watch and wait.

Dougal declared that he would stay in Lairig Dubh until Connor was healed and that meant that both Aunt Jean and Rhona were staying as well. Jocelyn did not indicate that she wanted them gone, so he was glad they were company for her. And a good influence in some regards, since she began to dress in more colors than only the brown and green she'd been favoring.

In spite of his survival, in spite of no sign of further attacks against her, in spite of it all, something was wrong between them. The strange thing was that he knew it was not on his part. A result of the odd dreams he'd had during the fever was that he finally felt ready to let go of his past.

He would never forget Kenna or stop loving her, but the bizarre conversations with her during his illness had in some way allowed him to bid her farewell. The only thing he had to continue was the ruse that he had killed her, but no one would dare ask him about it. Her soul would not be damned for all time as it would be if others knew about her death.

Connor also discovered that, with this peace, there was room in his heart to love again. Unfortunately, the woman whom he loved was not interested. His attempts to talk about his feelings for her were rebuffed each time he tried.

She did not reject his efforts to resume their physical relationship once he finally conquered the stairs. Connor joined the rest of the clan for a meal in the hall and then brought her back with plans to seduce her into his bed. When she agreed to help apply the ointment that eased the tightness and burning in the long scar on his thigh, her hand slipped, whether apurpose or by accident he knew not, and they found their passion for each other was not affected by his injury.

But, something was still awry and he was determined to find out what it was and fix it. He could not allow his wife to be less happy than he was now that he discovered he loved her after all.

"Conn," Rurik called out to him.

Jocelyn sat next to him in Murdoch's workroom reviewing some of the numbers of the harvest. A nod from Rurik was all it took to tell him that the surprise he'd planned was here.

"Jocelyn, would you come into the hall? I think we have visitors."

"I did not hear the guards call, Connor. Are you expecting someone?" Then the woman in her took over. "Should I change my gown?"

But, he knew it was not about vanity for her, it was about not shaming him by her appearance in front of guests. He'd deduced that the first time the messenger from Robert Steward arrived in Lairig Dubh and she'd been caught in a gown she wore to work in the village. He shook his head.

"Nay, just be at my side."

Her eyes narrowed but she agreed and they walked down the corridor to the great hall where, indeed, guests were arriving. She whispered orders to Murdoch to prepare food and drink for their guests and was so busy being the laird's wife that she did not see who they were. When she did finally look at them, she gasped.

"Father? Athdar?" He could see her blinking as though she thought she was seeing ghosts who were not truly there. Then she turned to him and her face held such joy that he felt the burning of tears behind his eyes.

"Jocelyn!" her brother yelled as he crossed the distance between them first and pulled her into his arms. The young MacCallum appeared well-healed since their last encounter.

Her father approached a bit slower and gave his regards to Connor as was befitting his position as laird. But, when Jocelyn pulled back from Athdar's embrace and saw him, he hugged her fiercely. Connor guessed that they never expected to see her alive again once she'd been given to the Beast.

"Connor...Laird MacLerie," she said to him when they released each other. "Have you met my father before?"

Connor stepped up to the MacCallum and refrained from mentioning the tears on the older man's cheeks. "Nay. Our negotiations were always through an intermediary." He held out his hand to his wife's father. "Welcome to Broch Dubh."

Before he realized what they would do, Tavish MacCallum went down on one knee before him. Athdar and the others in their party did the same. Connor pulled the proud old man to his feet. "We are all kin now, MacCallum. There is no need to kneel before me."

"Aye," he answered looking at his daughter, "we are that."

"Have your man meet with Murdoch to review the records and we can talk later about any adjustments needed," Connor said. "But for now, come, refresh yourselves from your journey."

If she continued to look at him as she did now, he knew that the expression in her eyes would be enough for him forever. But, he did not want her gratitude, he wanted her love. She tugged on his arm and he stepped back to let the others go ahead of them to the table, now set with platters of food and pitchers of ale.

"You knew? You knew my father was coming here and did not tell me?" she asked.

"What good is a surprise if one tells of it first?" Connor glanced at the MacCallum group and leaned down to whisper to her. "I think he was surprised to see you alive."

"Connor!"

"'Tis true, I think. They expected you dead by now and continue to watch to see if I will do it in their presence." He paused to enjoy her gaze. "Look! Now!"

She did look away for just a moment and then faced him, laughing. "You bring this on yourself, husband. The fear others feel is something you have manipulated. Besides," she said, sliding her arm under his and leading him slowly to the front of the hall, "my father must have known that you are an honorable man or he would not have permitted our marriage."

Now it was his turn to laugh. "Not permitted, eh? Mayhap getting the foodstuffs, supplies, workers, soldiers, wood, stone, and gold as well as your brother Athdar's life and freedom influenced his decision somewhat?"

She did not answer for they were closer now and his words might be overheard. But he did add a warning.

"Your brother should probably be warned that challenging Rurik again might end with his own death."

"Rurik? He fought Rurik?"

"Who do you think broke his arms?" He watched her face and a flash of guilt passed over it. "Me? You thought I'd done that to your brother?"

She did not answer, but the spreading blush confirmed it. He shouldn't be surprised, everyone thought the worst of him and he never disabused them of the errors. It helped him maintain the facade he had worked hard to get. He guided her to their seats and added one more thing before releasing her.

"He disparaged my name, which was bad enough in Rurik's opinion, but then he insulted Rurik's manhood. And you know how much value Rurik places on that."

"And for good reason," she answered, remembering what she'd seen in the meadow all those weeks ago. The words slipped out and she looked to her husband to see his reaction.

His eyes widened and then he leaned his head back and laughed. Thankfully, he saw the humor in it. She turned to the table and found everyone staring at Connor as though he were a madman. She supposed that they would if all they knew of him was his reputation as the Beast. But she knew there was so much more to him than that.

She sat and listened as Connor asked several questions

of her father and brother. Hesitant though they might be, soon, he had engaged them all in conversation about Lairig Dubh, their fighting strength, improvements to the village and mill and other subjects of interest to men who control lands and men.

He never treated her father with disdain through it all. If he disapproved of a man who lost control of his life and allowed his clan to fall on hard circumstances, his voice gave no sign. When she looked around the table at faces she had not seen in months, she knew she would never have thought this possible.

A few minutes passed as each partook in the bread and cheese and fruit. Then, he took her hand under the table and cleared his throat to gain everyone's attention.

"I have monopolized you for long enough now. We can speak more at our evening meal," he said as he stood. He did not release her hand. "I am certain that Jocelyn has much to talk about with you though. Lady," he said now turning to her, "why do you not show your father and brother to the chambers Murdoch has arranged and then show them Broch Dubh?"

"Murdoch knew?" she asked as her throat tightened with tears.

"Aye. Everyone except that boy in the stables and…"

"One of the laundry maids," she finished his words.

"Aye, that one," he laughed. Then with a quick kiss on her hand, he left the table and walked toward the north tower.

Jocelyn watched him leave before sitting down next to her father. They had much to talk about, she had much to show them. And all because her husband had been thoughtful enough to bring them here.

If this was how he would treat her, she thought she might be able to find some happiness in their life together. Even if he could not give his heart.

He stood in the doorway, watching her once more when she did not know he was there. She sat next to her father now and when their voices lowered and his arm encircled her shoulders, Connor knew they spoke of her mother's passing. He wanted to go to her now and hold her through the grief, but he knew she needed, as did her brother and father, this time with them.

There would be time enough later to hold her. After the surprise was done.

"Here, I have brewed some of the tea you like, Jocelyn." Rhona moved the small bowl closer to her. "Mayhap it will settle your nerves?"

Jocelyn glanced at the tea and then at the section of the tapestry she'd just had to pull out for the third time. 'Twas difficult to sit here and wait, knowing that her father and brother were out there in the yards, training with Connor and his men. In spite of Connor's promise to keep Athdar from Rurik, she wondered if that was possible. Men being men, fighting came to them as naturally as f—tupping.

Although she did enjoy the teas Rhona made, she shook her head. Nay, what she needed was some fresh air, mayhap a walk to refresh her. She seemed to grow tired at this same time each day lately and feared she would fall asleep at the table during the meal.

"My thanks, Rhona, but I think I need to walk." Cora stood as she did, ready to accompany her, but Jocelyn preferred to walk alone, so she shook her head. "Cora, I will not need you until I dress for dinner so you may remain here or do as you please."

"May I join you in your walk?" Rhona asked as Jocelyn stood.

Although she wanted to make a strategic retreat as her husband had warned her she might need at times, Jocelyn nodded and accepted Rhona's request.

Cora waited for Jocelyn and Rhona to leave and followed them to the doors of the keep. If Jocelyn was correct, a certain young man who worked in the stables would be receiving a visitor shortly. Jocelyn guided her companion toward the guardhouse for her destination was the battlements and she did not intend to change that for Rhona's presence. With the winds of autumn blowing, she could walk off this restlessness. Perchance Rhona would tire of the wind and leave her alone after all?

They reached and turned the first corner and stopped in the place where she could look down into the yard and even see as far as the gate. Some of the MacCallum men were returning to the keep and she watched as they pushed each other and carried on some lively chatter as they walked. She pointed out her brother to Rhona.

"Tell me of your family. I have not met them yet, but I would like to know of them when I do."

"There is little to tell you, Rhona. We are not a large clan like the MacLeries. Other than my father and brother and a few cousins, none of our name remain."

Somehow it was easier to talk to the women of the village about her family than it was to speak of them to Connor's kinswoman.

"Is your brother betrothed yet?"

"Athdar? Nay. There was not time or..."

"Family connections?"

Startled by her candor, Jocelyn realized that now that he was related to Connor, even through marriage, Athdar's chances at a better match had improved, too. Another good thing that occurred because of her marriage to Connor.

"Nor connections, as you say."

"Mayhap Connor will find him a bride as he did Kenna's brother. He seems to take an interest in his wife's family and their marriage plans."

Jocelyn turned to meet Rhona's gaze and was surprised to see nothing in it but a seemingly honest appraisal of the situation. "Then mayhap he will aid Athdar when the time is right."

She paused, wondering if Rhona would reveal any more about Connor's past to her. Sometimes, she was the only one who would speak of it, even though Rhona limited herself to general comments about perfunctory matters that were known to everyone, but Jocelyn, of course. Sometimes it bothered her, as a dig at some unseen yet unhealed wound, but at times, Jocelyn accepted the information because it gave her some insight into her husband. Now however, she felt the sting even though she did not see it.

And it made her want to sting back.

"And you, Rhona? Will Connor help you find a suitable match?"

Noticeably she had caught Rhona off her guard, for she stuttered and mumbled her reply at first. Then she cleared her throat. "I am certain, that when the time is right, he will. But, I am in no hurry for now."

The wind increased then, buffeting them and making it difficult to talk for a few minutes. When she had to grab her hair covering, Rhona shook her head.

"I am returning to the solar, Jocelyn. Do you come now or are you staying?"

Part of her wanted to continue their discussion, for Jocelyn felt as though there was much more to Rhona's opinion about marriage and about any in her future. Instead, she decided to stay and enjoy more walking on the walls. She shook her head and smiled.

"Nay, Rhona. I want to walk for a time. Mayhap we can continue our talk of Connor and matches later?"

If Rhona would deign to run instead of walking like a person of royal bearing, Jocelyn was certain it would have been right then. An expression of complete and absolute terror, with a hint of anticipation, filled the woman's gaze and then she turned and walked away quickly.

Ironically, the winds calmed as soon as Rhona left the battlements, allowing Jocelyn to enjoy the warmth of the sun's rays and her view of the yard. Her father and brother along with their men were still gathered there and some walked toward the keep.

It was the tallest of the men who commanded her attention, even from this distance.

Ewan MacRae.

Ewan was here.

As though he had heard her think his name, he tilted his head back and saw her. Then he waved and her heart pounded in her chest until she thought it would burst. He left the men and trotted toward the guardhouse.

He was coming here. She turned and leaned back against the wall, as heat filled her cheeks. She'd not seen him since the day she left to become Connor's wife. What would she say to him? What would he say to her? His gaze met hers as he turned the corner on the battlements and he saw her. She pressed her palms against her gown and waited as he approached.

Had he always been that young? Seeing him now after growing accustomed to Connor, she marveled that she'd never taken note of his youth before. They were the same age, but he seemed younger to her as she watched him now.

He stopped a pace away and they stared at each other across the space. Then, he moved closer and opened his arms and she stepped into his embrace.

"Jocelyn," he whispered as he hugged her. "Are you well, lass?"

She breathed him in, remembering his scent and the feel of his arms around her as he held her now. "Ewan. I have missed you." She took in his strength and let it soothe her.

He leaned back and inspected her. "I am sorry for your mother's passing. Sorry that you could not be there."

Realizing that she stood within his arms, Jocelyn moved away, but he still held her hand as he offered his sympathy on her mother's death. It felt good to speak about her mother with someone who knew her. She'd never spoken to Connor about her, but they had not been on good terms when she'd received the news.

"Are you happy here, Jocelyn? I have worried for you since you left."

She sighed. "I am happy, Ewan. He is not the Beast as everyone believes."

The words no sooner left her mouth than she heard footsteps on the walkway behind her and turned to face the very creature she'd just denied existed. She'd not seen the fury on his face in some weeks and had nearly forgotten what he looked like when his blood boiled. From what she could see, his blood boiled now. He stalked toward them, breathing in as though scenting his prey.

Her heart pounded now for another reason. Not the nervousness of seeing a man from her past. Not from the excitement of her family visiting. No, her heart beat as it did because she was the prey. And her body readied itself to be taken.

He'd gone searching for her, to ask if she wished to invite her brother to stay with them for a longer visit, when he discovered she was not in the solar with Rhona. In spite of Rhona's efforts to draw him away, he sought his wife. She was not in her chambers. Nor in the kitchens with Murdoch. Or in the workroom. Or, according to the guards at the gate, in the village. He finally found Cora as he walked past the stables and she told him of Jocelyn's plan to take a walk.

There were only two places where she walked and one was the village, where he knew she was not. The other was the battlements above the walls. He shielded his eyes from the late afternoon sun and saw her. Talking with a man.

In the arms of another man. As he watched, the man approached her and then took her in his arms. He did not remember deciding to go to her, but his feet were moving him there. They were still wrapped around one another when he reached the walkway and, when they finally did part, the man still held her hand.

Until she saw him.

He smiled as she dropped the man's hand and wiped her palms on her gown as she did when she was nervous. The blush in her cheeks rose and he could almost feel her heart pounding in her chest. The man with her paled at his approach. Good. He should be very wary of encroaching on his woman.

"Connor," she said, stretching his name out the way she did when he pleasured her. She stepped nearer and took up a position between him and the man. Did she think to protect this invader from her lawful husband? "Laird," she said then, using his title and not his name. It did not distract him from his need to claim her.

"This is Ewan MacRae, of Kintale," she introduced the man who had not been in the hall earlier. Connor nodded but did not hold out his hand. The man, nay boy, met his gaze and nodded. Admirably, he tried to step between Jocelyn and him in almost a defensive move. "Ewan has fostered with us, with my father, for some years now."

Ah, the foster son. Connor glanced from one to the other. 'Twas common for the daughter of the household to marry the foster son. Many clans joined in that way, it was one of the reasons sons and even daughters were fostered out to others. Had that been their plan?

"Are you eldest son?" he asked.

"Nay, laird. I have an older brother."

He smiled. A daughter in such an impoverished clan was not good enough for the eldest who would inherit. There must be some old bond of friendship or pledge between their fathers to join them. He knew enough now, they had been lovers, nay, they'd been in love, and now he must show her what it meant to be the mate of the Beast.

"I would speak to you, wife," he said, reaching for her hand and pushing the young whelp out of the way.

The young MacRae moved, as he had to, and then spoke to her. "I will see you at the meal this evening, Jocelyn."

"Lady MacLerie," Connor said staring at the boy.

He cleared his throat and repeated, "Lady MacLerie."

Connor's eyes never left her as she watched him walk away. Then she faced him and met him with a clear gaze. "You wish to speak with me?"

"In private," he said as he took her hand and pulled her along the battlements to the nearest steps.

She said nothing, simply followed where he led. When he realized she was out of breath, he turned and lifted her into his arms and carried her the rest of way to her bedchambers. He cared not who saw him, or what they thought, his only thoughts were of her, of claiming her, of making certain that she knew she was his. Once there, he pushed the door closed with his foot and put her down.

"You should not have done that, Connor," she said as she lifted the edge of her tunic and tugged it off over her head.

"I did not like the look of you in his arms," he admitted, his voice husky with desire for her. "You should not have teased me so." He loosened his belt and let the layers of tartan fall to the floor.

"I meant carry me all that way. You could open your wound again." Now she took off her gown and threw it aside. "I have no wish to repeat those days after your injury."

He smiled. She was concerned for him. Now she stood before him in only her shift and the sight of her nipples through it made his mouth water in anticipation. "What are you doing?"

"I see the look in your eyes and I worked too long on this gown to have it ripped from me."

"And this," he asked as he reached out to her and let the back of his hand glide over the fine linen of her shift. "Should I not rip this?" Those nipples pebbled under his touch now and she arched just enough to let him know she liked his touch.

"Why must you rip anything? I am here. You are here. There is time."

She was trying to explain the irrational reaction within him and it was not working. The sight of her in another man's arms drove him to claim her, to mark her as his so that she belonged to him and no other.

"This is not about time, wife. This is about finding you in another man's arms." Then he did rip her shift in two with little effort on his part.

"Ah…Ewan."

He moved her closer by tugging the two ends of fabric closer so that she was forced to look up to meet his gaze. "This is all you can say to me? I found you in his arms!" he yelled. When she looked away, he grabbed her at her waist and lifted her up until their eyes were level. "In his arms!"

Jocelyn reached over and stroked his cheek like he was some wee kitten and not her angry husband. "He is not my castle builder, husband."

Her words disarmed him. She understood his fear. "He would be dead if I thought he was." He pulled her close and kissed her. "I did not think you capable of such dishonor."

"So this is not about jealousy, then? I took my gown off and you tore my shift for nothing?"

He saw the glimmer of desire in her eyes and smiled. "This is about more than just jealousy." He still held her off the floor, now he wrapped his arms around her and she did the same with her legs, encircling his waist. "This is about more than that…" He covered her mouth with his, dipping his tongue in to taste her. "This is about wanting." He deepened the kiss, taking possession of her mouth until she was breathless against him.

"This is about taking…" He took the few steps needed to lean her against the door and, bracing her with his body and one arm, Connor reached down between them and guided himself into her.

"But mostly this is about claiming." And then he thrust into her, pushing her against the door until he could go no further. Her head fell back against the door and she moaned in pleasure as he took her.

"You are mine, lady. Do…not…forget…it." He moved in her until he felt her inner muscles begin to clench around him. "You…are…mine!" He thrust deep, pinning her to the door with himself and his body.

This time, as she reached her peak, she simply gasped over and over again until her head fell forward on his shoulder and she panted in his ear. "I am yours, laird," she whispered to him.

"Dammit, Jocelyn! My name! Say my name!" He pushed into her again and again, rubbing the sensitive and aroused flesh between her legs until she keened out the sound he wanted to hear.

"Connor!" she said and then he joined her in completion.

He accepted her surrender, but he was not done with her yet. His insulted pride, his jealousy of this young whelp, his worry that she might prefer someone else over him was not assuaged by taking her once. He needed several times and, on the last one, before sounds outside her door indicated the presence of her maid, he marked her as his own with his mouth and teeth.

The love bite on the inside of her thigh was for her gaze only, so she could remember what happened when she tempted the beast within him. The one at the place below her shoulder where the slope of her breast began, just above the edge of her gowns, would be seen by all and be recognized for what it was—a mark of claiming.

And if the one visible to all angered her, he would let her mark him as her own later this night, for surely he was hers.

Chapter Twenty

"I cannot believe you did this," she whispered to him. "I can believe you did it, since you have done it before," she said, feeling very overheated at the thought of what had led to the mark on her breast, "I just cannot believe you placed it where others could see it."

Her beast of a husband had the nerve to simply smile at her and offer her a piece of beef from their trencher. She glared at him, but he rubbed it against her lips until she opened and accepted it.

"Would see it, Jocelyn," he answered. "I placed it where *he* would see it." He held his goblet up to those who sat at the other tables, but she knew his gaze was on Ewan.

"You are insufferable." He took advantage of her mouth being open to plop another piece of meat in it.

"Did you find the other one I left for only your eyes?"

She choked on the meat and he held the goblet to her mouth now so she could drink. When she could speak again, she did not dare ask where the other mark was. No doubt he would tell her, in great detail until they were both breathless again. He'd claimed her so many times in her bed that the mark could be anywhere…*anywhere.*

"'Tis not as though you must worry, Connor. I only thought I loved him, but I *know* I love you."

He stopped at her words and she realized the declaration she'd made to him. 'Twas not one she'd planned to make for it left her too vulnerable. She knew the truth of his heart and it would not include her.

Connor lifted her hand to his mouth, turned it and kissed the inside of her wrist. "Thank you for such words, Jocelyn."

Suddenly it was just the two of them in the room. The sounds, the smells, the presence of all the others faded until she could see only him. His eyes blazed with some intense emotion that turned them into the warmest shades of gold and bronze. Jocelyn felt as though she was melting inside from the heat of his gaze. 'Twas not only passion there, though, something else deeper and more intense made her stomach stir and her breath catch.

And, quickly as the feeling came, it went and she heard Murdoch calling out to her husband. He tore his gaze from hers and nodded permission to the steward. Jocelyn struggled to regain herself, taking a few deep breaths. Rhona spoke to her, but Jocelyn could focus on very little other than her husband at her side.

It was then that she took note of the villagers entering the hall. One carried pipes, one a flute, one a goatskin drum and another a clarsach harp. A place was cleared, a few tables moved to give room around them and benches and stools brought forward for them to use. As they sat and began to tune their instruments, a woman came from the crowd and stood before them.

Jocelyn looked at Connor. "What is this?"

"I thought some music might be just the thing to mark your father's visit here." He laughed and then became serious. "I was once asked if I knew about entertainment other than fighting. I wanted to prove that I do."

The musicians began to play a lively tune and soon everyone there was tapping their feet or clapping their hands to the tempo. By the second tune, more tables were moved aside for dancing and soon the hall was filled with music and singing.

He'd done this for her, even using her words, said in anger to him during her first days here, to explain it. How had he remembered those? She thought that falling in love with him had been a good thing to do, but the next song proved it.

Siusan moved to stand with the players and a drumbeat started, quietly at first and then more insistent. Siusan began clapping to the beat and then the pipes joined low and steady. The flute player added his tune to the mix and then the harp. When Siusan sang the words clear and smooth, Jocelyn could not believe what she heard.

'Twas her mother's favorite song.

Then the beat picked up speed and many of the couples joined in and danced to it. Connor laid his hand on her arm.

"How did you know?" she asked, not even trying to hide her tears.

"I heard you speak of it to the women."

And he remembered. And he planned this.

Loving him was a good thing.

"Would you dance with me?" he asked.

She looked out and saw that her brother danced with one of the girls from the village and her father clapped along to the tune. "Aye."

She must know now how he felt in his heart. Surely, his

actions told her of his love and, from her own accidental admission, she understood.

He stood, held out his hand to her and led her to where the dancing was. Moving in a circle with the other couples, he watched her face as she stepped and stopped, stepped and stopped, and then swirled under his arm. With his arm around her waist, he guided her through the dance and when it ended she looked at him with such love in her eyes that it took his breath away.

That night when they joined, it was not about taking, but about giving. It was not about claiming, but offering. Not about passion, but about love.

When they finished, he did not leave. Connor felt more at peace than he had in years. Wrapping Jocelyn in his embrace, he held her until they both fell asleep.

The screams that woke him in the morning were a surprise. Cora walked in not expecting to find anyone but her lady, so a naked laird startled her. Especially one draped over his equally naked lady.

His lady's reaction was just as shocking for she sat up, examined him with wide eyes and promptly threw up on him.

Their first morning awakening together was memorable, but not how he would like to remember it. Their second morning together, for he was not easily daunted once he made up his mind to do something, did not have the same screaming. He'd taken her to his bed that night and no one, especially not Cora, would ever set foot there without his expressed welcome.

The vomiting was the same and he found Jocelyn heaving, hanging her head over a chamber pot as soon as she opened her eyes.

The third morning found them back in her chambers.

The stomach ailment continued unabated, but only when she first rose in the morning. She admitted to confusion over it, but he had experienced this before. When the fourth day followed the same pattern and she also slipped away for a bit of rest after the midday meal, he knew for certain although he knew she was either ignorant of the facts or avoiding confronting the truth.

Jocelyn was breeding.

Two weeks later, Connor watched as the MacCallums prepared to return home and he watched as Jocelyn battled her sadness at their leaving. 'Twas that sadness that convinced him to allow her to speak to the young MacRae alone. He insisted that it be in plain sight, but that was not because he did not trust her. Indeed, he simply was having a care for her tender condition, one that she had not shared with him in words yet.

The decision to allow it was much easier than waiting for her as she did. Connor stood with his back to her and the MacCallum's foster son and tried to speak on matters of consequence. As though he knew the problem, Jocelyn's father patted his shoulder and nodded.

Ewan kept looking over her shoulder and no one needed to tell her who stood there. After his absurd behavior over their last encounter and to spare him from needless worrying over her affections being misplaced, Jocelyn had asked Connor's permission to talk with Ewan alone before he left with her father. Now, as she stood facing the man she thought she'd loved, few words came to mind.

"You seem content, Lady MacLerie," Ewan stuttered out.

"You can call me Jocelyn, Ewan. He was being insufferable to make you think you cannot." She peeked over her shoulder and watched as Connor turned quickly away. "He cannot hear you."

"You do not fear him now?"

"Nay. I have not feared him for some time." His eyes showed his disbelief. "I admit it took some effort to ignore the scariest parts of him, but I have discovered that there is much to like about him."

"And us?" Ewan asked.

"There is no 'us' now, Ewan. I think that we would have been very happy if we had married, but now, well now, I am his wife and want no other."

She was not certain what reaction she expected, but she was pleased with the one she received. He lifted her hand to his lips and touched it lightly. Smiling at her, with a quick, nervous glance over her shoulder, he bowed.

"I wish you much happiness in your marriage, Jocelyn. Nay, I think you have already found happiness. I will simply say farewell to you."

"I hope that you find happiness, too, Ewan. As I have," she offered. Unable to resist, she leaned in and kissed him on the cheek. "Farewell to you," she whispered.

His hasty retreat revealed her husband's approach from behind and she took a deep breath and turned to face him. This time, it was not the Beast who waited for her. This time it was a man who seemed supremely pleased with himself, one who had won the battle and knew it.

And she did, too.

Connor was about his business a few days later when he passed by the door to Rhona's chambers. It was open and the sound of soft weeping could be heard. He did not recognize the voice, but he was certain it was one of the girls who'd come with his aunt to work here in the keep.

"Hush, now. This will take care of it for you," Rhona said softly.

"Are ye certain, lady?"

"Aye. Take one sip today and then two on the morrow, and three the next, each day one more, until your courses come. Your stomach may be upset by it, but continue until you bleed."

Connor listened to the instructions, but moved away when the door opened and a serving maid came out. He let her walk away, however he stopped her in the corridor near the kitchens.

"Girl," he called out until she turned to him.

"Aye, my lord," she stuttered out. She clutched a small bottle in her hand and tried to tuck it under her apron.

"What were you doing in the lady's chambers?" he asked. "What have you there in your hand?"

The girl lost all color in her face and started trembling. "The lady said I couldna go back wi' her if I am breeding, my lord. My parents need the money, so she gave me this to take care of it." Her hand shook so badly he thought she would drop the concoction.

He took it from her, examined it and then tucked the small vial inside his shirt. "The man who bedded you?"

"He wants me to stay, my lord, but the lady will have none of that. I came wi' her and will leave wi' her, she says."

Connor thought on the predicament for a moment. "I want you to go to the village now. Ask for Margaret's cottage and tell her I said you need to stay there."

"But, my lord, the lady said..."

Waving a hand to stop her, he shook his head. "I am laird here and you will listen to me."

She curtsied to him and ran off without another word. Margaret would keep her there until he could speak to Rhona. Healing with herbs, even easing pain, was one thing, but this concoction was another and he did not approve. Connor was about to seek her out when her words of instructions came back to him.

Each day one more, until your courses come. Your stomach may be upset by it, but continue until you bleed.

If a girl took too much of it would she become very ill, he wondered. Something about this seemed familiar. Too familiar.

Kenna had gone through months and months of trying to have a babe and each month she failed. Those months when she thought she might be, she would have terrible cramping and then bleed. It had happened at least four times. Once, when she thought she might carry, she fell and miscarried the babe in her fifth month.

He needed to speak to Duncan. His cousin had been here through most of that time, not the night Kenna died, but the rest of it. He might remember something more. Knowing Jocelyn was in the village, he was certain she was safe for now.

It took some time, but he was able to find Duncan and his uncle and they spoke at length. Like a quilt, piece by piece they put together the events of three years before and all of it pointed to one person—Rhona. She had arrived shortly after his marriage to Kenna and lived here through it all. His uncle recalled talk of a betrothal between her and Connor, one that her father stopped when a better offer was made.

The men shared with him the rumors of her husband's untimely but not-mourned death. A death that left her free to attend Kenna. Indeed, now he remembered her offer to travel to Lairig Dubh even before his marriage to Kenna. And Rhona was always there, always ready with a kind word, with a concoction for this or that, learned, she said, for her late husband's care.

Connor knew he must get her away from the keep and question her about these matters and he must get her away from Jocelyn. He hated even suspecting Rhona after all the help and support she'd given him in his times of need, but he now believed that she created many of those situations to place herself at his side.

Ready to confront her, he sent Rurik to the village to see to Jocelyn's safety and his return with word that she was not there, turned his blood cold. They rushed to the keep to find her.

"Just another sip, Jocelyn. It will ease the nausea and help you rest."

Rhona's brew had helped her in the past and, as the symptoms in the mornings had worsened with each passing day, Jocelyn sought her out for help. She'd gone to the village this morn, later than her custom due to the sickness and now drawn back early due to the fatigue. She would be worthless to one and all if the symptoms did not abate soon.

The tea went down smoothly and, as she sat in the chair in the solar and waited for it to work, she asked Rhona about the symptoms. "How long do these usually persist?" Concerned over the sickness, she'd shared her suspicions with Rhona only this day.

Rhona began to talk about what she should expect during her pregnancy, but the warmth spreading through her body made it difficult to concentrate on her words. Then she realized that Rhona stood in front of her waving her hand before her eyes. Jocelyn found it impossible to watch so she closed her eyes and let the warmth fill her.

When she opened them, she was walking next to Rhona through the hall. They stopped in front of the steps leading to the middle tower and Rhona guided her toward them. Jocelyn did not intend to go there, indeed, Connor had ordered her and the others to stay away. "Rhona, Connor does not want…"

"Connor asked me to take you there now, Jocelyn. Worry not."

She tried, or at least she thought she tried to refuse, but the warmth pulsed like fire in her veins and she could not resist Rhona's wishes. They climbed to the first landing and then continued on to the second one. She thought to protest again, but thoughts did not seem to stay in her mind. Rhona spoke so soothingly and the next time she remembered herself they were sitting in Kenna's chambers.

"Did you know that he was supposed to marry *me?*" Rhona asked.

"Connor?" Her head swirled and she could not follow the threads of the conversation.

"Aye. His father and mine planned to betroth us when we were but children." Rhona moved around the room, making Jocelyn dizzy when she tried to watch her. "Then my father's fortunes changed and he sold me to a rich, old lecher who thought that a young virgin would cure his ailments."

Rhona was to have married Connor? It did not make sense.

"I've loved Connor since we were children, Jocelyn. I have waited long enough."

Rhona now held a cup to her lips and tilted it up. When she did not open her mouth, Rhona pinched her nose shut until she did and then poured more of the tea in. Jocelyn knew she should not swallow it, but Rhona poured more and more until she could not help it.

"When I heard of his betrothal to Kenna, I knew I must stop it. My husband lingered too long and by the time I arrived here, the marriage was a thing already done."

The room spun round and round and Jocelyn could not sit up. Everything in her screamed out that she was in danger, but her body would not cooperate.

"The worst part was that he loved her. I warned him that she was not right for him, but he did not listen. No matter what I did, he would not agree to put her aside."

This was not right. Jocelyn knew deep inside that she must escape. Her life and the one she carried inside were in danger.

"Do not struggle, Jocelyn. It will not hurt if you let the tea work."

"Rhona, nay," was all she could force out.

"I think it may be too late with you as well. I watched him fall in love with Kenna and I see the same signs now with you," she said, coming closer and holding her head still. "'Tis not that I dislike you. Nay, if I disliked you, you would die a painful, bloody death like my husband did."

"He does not love me, Rhona. He cannot." She tried to explain about Connor, but the words would not form. The only thing she knew was that he did not love her.

"This time," Rhona whispered as she pulled Jocelyn to her feet. "This time, I will be here when he grieves. This time, he will turn to me and we will marry as we should."

They were walking again, out into the chamber that led to the stairs. Rhona stopped and Jocelyn could see the stairs in front of them. She must not go near the stairs. Rhona forced her forward.

"This time, he will not take the blame. There will be no mistaking your death for anything but suicide."

"He does not love me, Rhona."

"It matters not. I waited too long with Kenna and then he made it look like he'd killed her. I will not wait this time."

"Rhona, do not do this."

Connor's voice filled the tower and Jocelyn smiled at the sound of it. She tried to see him, but her sight was growing dark.

"Connor, I am just bringing Jocelyn down from Kenna's room. She insisted on disobeying you and going there."

"Wait there, Rhona," he called out. "I will come up there." He started up the steps, but she yelled for him to come no farther. The sight of Jocelyn swaying on her feet at the top of the stairs made his heart stop.

He glanced behind him and found Duncan three steps below. Rurik was out of sight on the first landing. Connor took one more step and then another until he heard Jocelyn cry out. Rhona dragged her closer and closer to the edge.

"Let her go, Rhona. Let her go and I will see that you leave here unharmed," he offered. He heard Duncan curse under his breath, but he would promise whatever he needed to in order to get Jocelyn to safety.

"After she falls, Connor, you will be free to marry again.

Everyone will know that she took her own life and we can marry as we were supposed to."

She was mad. Absolutely and completely mad. And a wrong word or move on his part would send Jocelyn to her death. Of course, she could already have poisoned her. Sweat broke out on his brow as he realized she could already be dying.

"I know you are starting to love her, Connor, but you will not take the blame this time. Her death will be of her own choosing."

"What did you give her, Rhona? Is it the same potion you gave to her and to Kenna to make them lose the bairns?" He did not know what made the connection in his thoughts, but his suspicion made sense now. Same timing, same symptoms, same person—Rhona.

"You know?"

He could see her demented smile from where he stood, but the admission, so calmly made, chilled him to his soul. Duncan whispered a curse that Connor could hear as she acknowledged in that moment causing the death of at least four of his bairns. Rhona was a dead woman regardless of whatever else happened here.

"Nay, not this time. I gave her only a sleeping potion. I told her if she just follows my instructions, there will be no pain."

"No pain?" he asked.

"When she falls." Rhona lifted Jocelyn's hair away from her face and smiled. "I like her, Connor, I truly do. She has been nicer to me even than Kenna was and I do not wish for her to suffer. I am waiting so that the potion will be working in her and she will not know."

"Rhona, please do not push her." He managed two more

steps closer without her attention being drawn to his movements. "Step away from the edge now," he pleaded.

"I will not need to, Connor. Once I let go, she will take the last step herself. Kenna would have if you had not interfered. So much time lost between us, Connor."

Holy God in Heaven! She'd not only caused the miscarriages, she'd drugged Kenna and led her to her death. And he'd not seen it at all. So focused on his own pain, he'd never even suspected Rhona.

"I am so tired, Rhona. I need to lay down," he heard Jocelyn murmur.

"Just a bit longer, Jocelyn. Then you can take your rest," Rhona said.

"If anything happens to her, you will not live," he promised. "Let me take her and then we will make arrangements for you to leave," he urged again.

This time as he moved a step closer, Rhona moved to stand behind Jocelyn, using her as a shield and, as he could see, placing her in a better position to shove her over the edge when she deemed the time to be right. Now, however the noise from a crowd gathering below began to distract her. She shook her head over and over and Connor could see her control slipping away. If she pushed Jocelyn now, he could never get to her in time. And if she decided to fall with her, there would be no chance of saving either one.

He made it to the landing and stopped. Rhona shifted Jocelyn and he could see that Jocelyn was resting more weight on her captor and less able to stand on her own. Rhona could not hold her up much longer. With a nod as a warning to those below, he held out his hand to Rhona.

"Come now, lass. Leave her there," he cajoled. "I will put her aside and we can be together."

"I told you he loves me not," he heard Jocelyn whisper.

Then he watched in horror as her legs gave out and she tumbled. Rhona tried to keep her hold but as Jocelyn fell over, she could not. Before he could move, Rurik's arrow found its mark in her neck and she died before her next breath. Connor lunged for Jocelyn and caught her at the last possible moment. Duncan raced to his side and together they lifted Jocelyn away from the edge.

She was sound asleep.

He carried her to his chambers and laid her in his bed, leaving Duncan and Rurik to take care of Rhona's body. If what Rhona said was true, Jocelyn was only sleeping. But, could he trust the word of a madwoman who had already killed his first wife?

Chapter Twenty-One

"Do you feel better?"

At the sound of her voice, he opened his eyes. She was awake. However, the green tinge that moved up into her cheeks warned him that she would not be feeling well in a moment. Grabbing the pot, he held her head as she retched. When she stopped, he helped her to lie back.

"Do you feel better?"

"Aye, I do now," she whispered.

"Margaret told me that retching brought more relief than waiting it out and I did not believe her," he said.

"Believe her, Connor, she has it right about this."

He carried the odorous pot to the door and held it out until someone took it. Furious whispering began outside until he pulled the door open wide enough that she could see the group gathered there.

"She is awake, as you can see," Connor announced.

"Good morrow, Jocelyn," Rurik called out to her, waving. "Ye look well for having nearly died."

"How do ye fare?" Margaret asked. Hamish was at her side.

Ailsa simply crossed her arms and glared at Connor. Duncan nodded at her, but said nothing. Cora stood holding the pot that Connor had handed her.

"You have seen her, now go away," Connor said loudly as he slammed the door closed. "Pardon," he said as he turned and realized that the noise had probably bothered her. She was awake and she was smiling. Those had to be good signs.

"How long have I slept?" she asked as she pushed herself up from the pillow and sat.

"The rest of the day and the better part of this one."

Connor sat at her side and took her hand in his. He could see that she had questions about what had happened. Then he remembered her first words to him. "Why did you ask if I felt better?"

"Now that you know that Kenna did not take her own life, you must be relieved. Well, not relieved, but…"

He was torn between denying it and speaking the truth to her about Kenna's death. He'd held the secret for so long, he did not know what to say. "What did she tell you?"

"She told me of drugging Kenna and convincing her that her death would free you. Kenna died believing she was helping you." She paused for a moment as though deciding how much to say about it. "I knew you thought she killed herself for you told me during your fever, Connor. You thought you were speaking to Kenna and kept asking why she would take her own life. But now you know that Rhona caused her death."

"Rhona killed her so that she could marry me," he whispered. "Her death is still on my hands."

"Nay!" she cried. "You were taken in by a madwoman. All of you, all of us," Jocelyn explained. "You did not

know she was the cause of all the problems Kenna had."
She clutched his hand tighter, making him meet her gaze.
"But you knew it this time."

"But I was too slow in making the connections and
nearly lost you, too."

They sat in silence for a moment and his thoughts went
back to the night of Kenna's death. He'd poured over it and
over it since yesterday, but could still not understand how
one woman's dashed hopes could wreak such havoc in so
many lives.

"The babe is safe," she said, the first time she actually
admitted she was pregnant.

"So, you have decided to tell me?"

"I did not know at first, then I feared speaking of it
too early."

"That may have saved you. She did not know soon
enough to try to end this one," he said.

"I try to remember the rest of what she said in
Kenna's chambers and on the stairs, but it is all in a haze.
Tell me what she did. I would rather hear the truth of it
from you."

"She admitted causing the illness that brought on your
cycle the first month." Her eyes filled with tears at that, so
he stopped. Reaching to the table, he poured some of the
watered wine in a cup and offered it to her.

"More importantly than this sad news, what did I tell
you while in the fever's grasp?"

She sipped from the cup and then handed it back to
him. Patting his hand, she put on a weak smile that did
not fool him.

"I understand my place, Connor."

He was confused now. "Your place?"

"You spoke of the love you had for Kenna and how you could never love like that again."

He shook his head. "I said that?"

She was patting his hand again. "Aye, and I understand."

"Obviously you do not." He crossed his arms and glared at her. "I thought you did."

"What do you mean?"

"When I brought your family here, when I arranged the dinner, when I did not kill your first love, I thought my actions were speaking for me."

"You mean that you love me?" she asked. He could see her uncertainty in her face as, once again, she doubted her own worth.

"When I had that fever, I thought I was speaking to Kenna, saying farewell to her. I woke up knowing that I loved you, but when it seemed that you were not interested in it, I did not say so."

"But I told you of my feelings," she began and then she stopped.

"Aye, you did, and I thought I was making my feelings clear to you with my actions."

She thought on all he had done then and realized that the message had been right in front of her for some time. "You did not kill Ewan for me?"

He laughed then and the sound echoed over and around and through her, lightening her spirit and her heart. The daft man should just have said the words. He gathered her in his arms then and kissed her breathless.

"You will be known forever as the woman who tamed the Beast of the Highlands."

"We will need a bard to tell that tale."

"See to it, Lady MacLerie."

"I will, laird."

But one thing led to another and it was some time before either the lady or the laird took up their duties again in Broch Dubh.

Epilogue

The tale is told on long winter nights of a Beast that roamed the Highlands. So fierce was this creature that even the bravest of men feared him. His name was used as a curse when wielded in anger. Prayers were said to keep him at bay.

And, as in many tales told on long winter nights, love was expected to conquer all and the beast would be tamed by a beauty.

However, this beast was captured by a woman considered a beauty by no one and brought to his knees by the sight of that mate giving birth to the long-awaited child of their dreams.

So, at the end of this tale, it was love that conquered all and love that tamed the beast.

On sale 3rd July 2009

LORDS OF NOTORIETY
by Kasey Michaels

THE RUTHLESS LORD RULE
Bewitched and bewildered…

His reputation is notorious. Courageous officer Lord Tristan
Rule has any young lady of the *ton* for the taking, though Miss
Mary Lawrence has specifically caught his attention… But the
ruthless Rule soon finds that Mary has the power to forge his
hard-as-steel heart into something much more malleable!

THE TOPLOFTY LORD THORPE

The Earl's undoing…

Julian Rutherford's greatest admirer is Miss Lucy Gladwin,
an outrageous imp desperate to catch the Earl's eye. In the midst
of a scandal, she finally has Julian all to herself – and Lucy
will stop at nothing to show him they can overcome any trial
through a true meeting of souls…and bodies!

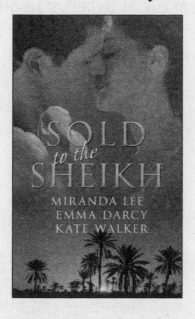

Sparkling ballrooms and wealthy glamour in Regency London

Kidnapped in the small hours,
Miss Helen Walford was rescued by the
infamous rakehell, the Earl of Merton!

Her only defence lay in anonymity. But captured
by her beauty and bravery, the Earl of Merton
knew that he had to find his mysterious lady.
He'd move heaven and earth to track down the
woman he knew to be his destiny.

Available 19th June 2009

www.mirabooks.co.uk

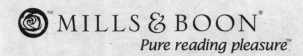

FREE!

2 Books
and a surprise gift!

We would like to take this opportunity to thank you for reading this Mills & Boon® book by offering you the chance to take TWO more specially selected titles from the Historical series absolutely FREE! We're also making this offer to introduce you to the benefits of the Mills & Boon® Book Club™—

- ★ FREE home delivery
- ★ FREE gifts and competitions
- ★ FREE monthly Newsletter
- ★ Exclusive Mills & Boon Book Club offers
- ★ Books available before they're in the shops

Accepting these FREE books and gift places you under no obligation to buy, you may cancel at any time, even after receiving your free shipment. Simply complete your details below and return the entire page to the address below. You don't even need a stamp!

YES! Please send me 2 free Historical books and a surprise gift. I understand that unless you hear from me, I will receive 4 superb new titles every month for just £3.79 each, postage and packing free. I am under no obligation to purchase any books and may cancel my subscription at any time. The free books and gift will be mine to keep in any case.

H9ZEF

Ms/Mrs/Miss/Mr ....Initials ....

BLOCK CAPITALS PLEASE

Surname ....

Address ....

....

....Postcode ....

Send this whole page to:
UK: FREEPOST CN81, Croydon, CR9 3WZ